New York Times bestselling author Melody Anne

HER UNEXPECTED HERO

"Don't you like it that we both have an air of mystery about us, Alyssa? Isn't that what makes this so exciting?"

She felt caught. Did she admit how exhilarating all of this was for her? Or did she stay cool and collected? Was she making a huge mistake by flirting with a man she barely knew?

Her entire world had been flipped upside down, yet lying here beside this stranger seemed to drown out the disappointment, the sadness, the emptiness.

Could she surrender to the desires of her body and continue down this road with him? It wasn't as if they could have sex. They were on a plane filled with people. What would a little harmless flirting really do?

Also available from Melody Anne and Pocket Books

Baby, It's Cold Outside

(with Jennifer Probst, Emma Chase,
Kristen Proby, and Kate Meader)

MELODY ANNE

Her Unexpected Hero

Pocket Books

New York   London   Toronto   Sydney   New Delhi

Pocket Books
A Division of Simon & Schuster, Inc.
1230 Avenue of the Americas
New York, NY 10020

This book is a work of fiction. Any references to historical events, real people, or real places are used fictitiously. Other names, characters, places, and events are products of the author's imagination, and any resemblance to actual events or places or persons, living or dead, is entirely coincidental.

First Pocket Books paperback edition March 2015

POCKET and colophon are registered trademarks of Simon & Schuster, Inc.

For information about special discounts for bulk purchases, please contact Simon & Schuster Special Sales at 1-866-506-1949 or business@simonandschuster.com.

The Simon & Schuster Speakers Bureau can bring authors to your live event. For more information or to book an event, contact the Simon & Schuster Speakers Bureau at 1-866-248-3049 or visit our website at www.simonspeakers.com.

Interior design by Yvonne Chan
Cover design by Eileen Carey
Cover art by Jim Jordan Photography/Getty Images

Manufactured in the United States of America

10 9 8 7 6 5 4 3 2 1

ISBN 978-1-4767-7854-9
ISBN 978-1-4767-7860-0 (ebook)

This book is dedicated to Mike and Krisi Dame.
Sometimes you meet people who truly inspire you,
and this couple has become great friends and their
love of each other inspires me to be a better writer.
Love you both and your beautiful daughters.

ACKNOWLEDGMENTS

I'm so excited to take this new journey with the Pocket Books family. What a joy I've had with this wonderful team of people. I adore my editor, Abby, and feel that I have grown as an author with her guidance. And Lauren is amazing and fun, and makes me feel like a rock star.

Thank you to the many authors who inspire me, help me, guide me, and listen to me. I read their material and am awed. There are so many and I have no doubt I will look over this later and cringe because I left some out, but to name a few, Ruth Cardello, J. S. Scott, the fabulous Jennifer Probst, Lynn Raye Harris, Kathleen Brooks, JL Redington, and Sandra Marton. I love you ladies!

Thank you to my team members of family and friends who do everything for me so I can write, and who ensure that I also take time to have fun. I love you guys so much and can't imagine what my life would be like without you: Kathiey and Krisi Dame, Jeff and Patsy Winchester, Edward Hart, Adam and Mary Ragle, Nicole Sanders, Stephanie Gerard, and Alison. Family and friends are the same to me. If I love you, I love you forever, and that's how I feel about you all! As my fans know, I ADORE my nieces and nephews and honorary nieces and nephews. They inspire me and little snippets I get from them continually run through my books. I love you, Breezy, Jacob, Isaiah, Makayla, Jasmine, Maycie, Kaylee, Ryder, and Reese. I know there are so many more people who help to make my dreams come true, and thank you for that.

The biggest thanks of all go to my fans. Thank you, thank you, thank you for continuing to believe in me and for inspiring me, and for sharing this journey with me. I appreciate and love you!

PROLOGUE

"Help . . ." A gurgling cry whispered faintly on the wind, and three teenagers walking by turned and listened.

"Did you hear that?" Spence asked.

"I think so. It sounded like someone yelling, but I'm not sure," Camden replied.

"Please h-help . . ." This time there was no mistaking the cry. It was faint, but the three boys turned toward the lake.

"Someone's in trouble," Jackson said, and he took off sprinting in the direction of the sound. Spence and Camden were in hot pursuit behind him. They ran the short distance to the shore and spotted a body thrashing around in the water. As they neared the water's edge, they saw the kid's head disappear below the surface.

The three teenage boys stripped down to their underwear in seconds, then dived into the freezing water without hesitation. All of them strong swimmers, they quickly reached the part of the lake where they'd seen the boy and plunged beneath the surface, frantically searching for him.

Spence was the first to reappear from the deep water, the boy in his arms. Camden and Jackson flanked him on either side and the three of them towed the boy to shore. Jackson pulled the wet clothes from him, then grabbed his own clothing and used it to cover the boy, hoping it would bring him some warmth.

Meanwhile, Spence began mouth-to-mouth resuscitation, with Camden doing chest compressions. The three of them worked relentlessly, and after what seemed like hours, but in reality was only a couple of minutes, the boy began coughing. Spence quickly turned him on his side as water spewed from his mouth.

After struggling for several moments to cough up the remaining fluid in his lungs, he looked at his three rescuers with large green eyes. His confusion quickly abated, and he remembered what had happened and how close he'd come to losing his life.

"Y-you . . . s-saved me," he gasped, then started choking again. Spence patted him gently on the back. The kid couldn't have been more than ten or eleven years old.

"What were you doing in the water?" Camden asked as he glanced back out at the lake. He was looking for a boat or something.

"I w-was s-skipping . . . rocks on th-the . . . d-dock and s-slipped." His teeth were chattering so hard that Spence, Camden, and Jackson worried he'd break them. The three teens were also starting to shake as their adrenaline subsided and their wet bodies began to feel the chill in the air.

"Michael! Michael! Where are you?" a man was heard calling out only seconds before he walked over the small hill with several people trailing behind him. He spotted the four boys and came running toward them. "Michael, what happened? Are you okay?" The man dropped to his knees.

The people standing around him looked at the boy, whose clothing was half off, and then at the three nearly naked teenagers.

"What is going on here?" one man demanded, sending the teenagers a suspicious glare.

Before Spence could say anything, another person stepped in. "Aren't you three living in the Taters' house?"

Camden hung his head in shame. They despised living in the filthy foster home, but because they were together, they didn't complain. Each of them had been tossed from home to home practically since birth. During their two years together at this latest home, they had developed a bond rarely found in such circumstances.

It made the bad food, threadbare clothes, and their housemother's screaming fits all worth it. The three of them could face the world as long as they had each other. But if they complained, they would get separated and probably never see each other again.

"Yes, sir, in the Taters' house," Spence replied through chattering teeth as he tried to puff up his chest. As the oldest, he had to protect Camden and Jackson, even if that meant that he took all the heat upon himself.

"What are you doing with Michael?" another man asked, and his tone implied it certainly couldn't be anything good.

"They saved me," Michael said. His eyes gleamed with hero worship as he looked over at the trio.

"What happened, Michael?" the boy's father, Martin, asked as he embraced his son.

"I was skipping rocks and fell. I couldn't stay above the water. They pulled me out." Michael's eyes shone with unshed tears.

Martin looked from his son to the three boys, who were beginning to turn blue, and then at the crowd gathered around. The men's expressions changed from suspicion to awe in a few heartbeats.

"You're heroes," one man said as the rest of the group murmured their surprise and agreement.

Spence, Camden, and Jackson looked at each other before Spence spoke to the crowd.

"No we're not. We were just the first people here," he said with a shrug. Although relieved they weren't suspected of foul play, they still weren't good enough to be called heroes—at least not in their minds.

The men rushed into action: someone made a phone call, another person draped warm jackets over the boys' shoulders, while still another gathered their discarded clothes and handed them over. The normally unseen boys stared wide-eyed as everyone moved around in a blur, all the attention focused on them. None of them knew what to do or think. This was completely new for all of them.

They watched as an ambulance arrived and pulled up to the edge of the grass, then all four of them were carefully led to the vehicle. Spence, Camden, and Jackson were in such shock that they weren't able to speak—no one had ever worried about them before, and they couldn't quite process what was happening. So they sat in silence while the paramedics examined them.

They were taken to the emergency room, and then transferred to a private room in the back, where medical staff came in and out asking questions and checking their temperatures. After about an hour the man who'd been calling for Michael entered the room. Wrapped in heated blankets, the three boys were sipping hot chocolate and eating sandwiches. The man looked at them with tear-filled eyes.

"I don't know how I could ever possibly repay you for what you've done. I don't think you even comprehend what heroes you truly are. My son is going to be fine thanks to you. He's in the room next door sleeping," he said before pausing for a moment. "My name is Martin Whitman, and the boy you risked your lives to save is my only son, Michael. He's my entire world. We lost his mother two years ago and now all we have is each other." Martin's voice was choked.

The boys looked at him in surprise. They'd done what any other human being would do, hadn't they? But this man seemed to think they'd performed a great service.

"How long have you been living in the foster home over on Spruce?" Martin asked. Since Spence was the oldest—he was fourteen to Camden's thirteen and Jackson's twelve—he was the one to respond.

"We've been there for two years now."

Martin hesitated before he spoke again. "I talked with your social worker. She's on her way down here now. I'd like to make an offer to you boys."

They looked at him with distrustful eyes. They'd been in the foster-care system too long and had learned to trust no one but each other. They shared a common heartache—no one seemed to want any of them. Being alone was much better when you were "alone" with someone else. It had caused a unique bond to form—a brotherhood.

At least this man's eyes were kind. They waited in silence to see what he had to say.

"I'd like for you to come live with me. What you did today showed me more than I need to know about your characters, and I would be honored to adopt each of you. The judge here in town is a good friend of mine. He can give me temporary papers so you could come home with me right away. Then, if you like it at my place, we could make it permanent."

Spence took the lead again. "We've been lied to a lot. It would be pretty crappy of you to say something like this and then decide you hated us after a few days. They call us *throwaway kids* because we're older than kids who are typically adopted," he said with a slightly wobbly voice.

All of them were trying desperately to put up a brave front, but it was beginning to crumble as hope filled them. The pain that held all three of the boys in its grip was evident to Martin, whose heart filled with a deep sadness. What had they been through to be so wounded and so afraid? He hoped they never would have to carry that fear again.

"I understand that you don't know me, and it will take a lot of time to build up trust, but I don't lie and I never make a promise I don't keep. My father taught me to always be a man of my word. You three boys gave me the greatest gift today, one that only my wife had given me before now—the life of my son. Not everyone gets the kind of second chance you gave him. You deserve a second chance at life as well. I'd feel privileged to have you come home with me. You're not too old at all. My son is ten, right around your age. I think we could be a family if you give me a chance."

Spence immediately turned away when a tear started to slip down his cheek. The others pretended not to see and gave him a chance to pull himself together. They never cried, at least not where anyone else could see. They'd learned long ago that tears didn't matter from a throwaway kid anyway.

Martin Whitman did something then that no one had done for so long that the boys had forgotten what it felt like. He wrapped his arms around Spence and gave him a solid hug, and then did the same to Camden and to Jackson. All three boys were shaking with emotion by the time he let go.

Martin stood and walked to a nearby restroom so he could compose himself and give them a moment alone to discuss his offer.

"What do you think, Spence?" Jackson asked with a hopeful expression.

Spence looked at both Jackson and Camden, who stared back with a mixture of faith and disbelief. Though Jackson didn't want to get his hopes up, the thin layer of ice that encased his heart was beginning to thaw. He wanted to believe. He wanted this to be real. If Martin took them all, they would never be separated.

The rational part of him knew that a brighter tomorrow would never come. But for the sake of Camden and Spence, he put a confident smile on his face.

"I don't see what it would hurt to give it a try," he said.

Ultimately, the decision lay with Spence, though, since he was the oldest. They waited for his verdict.

"Why not?" he told them, trying to look composed, but excitement burned in his eyes.

Camden and Jackson beamed eager smiles his way, hopeful for the first time since they had been dumped at the state's doorstep when they were barely out of diapers.

When Martin emerged from the bathroom, Jackson and Camden looked at him with happy apprehension. Spence looked the man in the eye, issuing him a silent challenge: *this is me—take me or leave me.*

Martin smiled, not breaking eye contact for even a second, as if to reply that he would take him as he was, chip on his shoulder and all.

0 0 1

TWENTY YEARS LATER

"I promise you, Mom, I'm fine."

But Alyssa's mother kept on saying all the usual motherly things, full of worry and false cheer, not offering her daughter even the remotest chance of interrupting. Alyssa Gerard held her phone wearily against her ear. She had no more words to say, nothing that would make this nightmare end. A nine-hour flight was still ahead of her, then one connection, and she'd be home.

Or maybe not. Alyssa had waited in the crowded airport as her "on-time" flight was delayed again and again. It was already midafternoon, and she'd been in this boarding area for hours. Were there any other flights with open seats?

Not on this day of the year, New Year's Eve. She could either wait for her original flight, or give up— which wasn't going to happen. She was more than done with Paris, done with modeling, and done with people in general. This week had started out badly and kept on getting worse.

". . . and I know you'll really love it in Sterling . . ." Yes, her mom was still speaking, and yes, she should listen, but as she looked around at all the people in bright colors with what seemed like permanent smiles on their faces, she grew even grumpier and simply couldn't force herself to respond. Not that she needed to, as her mom was speaking enough for both of them. Alyssa should be happy, should feel like celebrating, but instead she was fighting tears.

". . . Martin is a wonderful boss. Your dad has never been happier . . ."

It was all over—everything had ended so much more speedily than it had begun. She'd set out at the tender age of fifteen, ready to change the world with all the millions she'd make, to see her name in lights, or at least to see her face on every magazine cover ever to grace store shelves and racks.

She'd gotten her dream . . . for a while. And then—poof!—it was gone. Her body tensed in anger as she found herself wedged between two large men who surely hadn't bathed in eons.

Her mother continued to yammer away, though Alyssa was long past listening.

". . . and you should see Martin's boys. They are so handsome . . ."

Shaking her head, she took a deep breath. To her left, a heated debate had broken out between a man in a dark blue suit and an attractive blonde. The exchange flung her back into her own head as she was forced to think about what had happened between her and her ex.

Her "trustworthy" manager, who'd also happened to be her boyfriend, had taken it all—he'd run away not only with her fortune but with her hopes and dreams and reputation. Now she was stuck in Paris on New Year's Eve, and all she could think about was how badly she wanted to be home, where she could lick her wounds in peace.

". . . your father and I are so excited to have you home. I only wish you'd been here last week. It was our first Christmas with snow . . ."

To top everything off with a nice, fat cherry, her parents had decided to move out of the thriving Texas town she'd grown up in and hare off to the backwoods of Montana, settling in a place she had never heard of before—Sterling. Her mother swore up and down they'd visited an aunt there several times when she was a kid, but the place must be awful because she couldn't even remember it.

Great! Just great. She had to go home with her tail tucked between her legs, and it wasn't even home. They had snow in Montana? Lots of snow? Like the sort of snow that buried people alive, and they weren't found again until months later, when the spring came and the roads finally cleared? She had a feeling she was going to be one of those un-suspecting victims—huddled in the fetal position as she froze to death in her car.

That is, if she was lucky enough to find a car she could afford.

". . . I've had quite a time learning to drive in snow, but it can actually be fun . . ."

Alyssa had heard some of this before. She still wasn't interested in living in Montana, not that she had a choice. She'd never thought she'd want that twenty-year-old Toyota so badly, but she was pray-ing now that it had made the journey with her par-ents when they'd trekked north for her father's new job. Alyssa didn't even have enough money left to buy a five-hundred-dollar "preowned" lemon to get her to and from whatever job she'd manage to find back in the States.

". . . your dad sold the car, but I'm sure we can find you something when you get here . . ." Great. She didn't have the Toyota.

She could try to start again, try to make a go of a modeling career from scratch, but the reality was that she hated the industry, had hated it almost from the beginning, and now, at twenty-four, she was considered old in this world of the rich and beautiful, the sleek and connected. Connections that her manager/boyfriend had managed to sever irreparably.

"Honey? Are you still there?"

Alyssa jumped. She'd been sunk inside her own head so heavily that she'd forgotten her mom was on the phone.

"Mom, I love you and I promise I'm doing fine. I really appreciate the ticket home. But they're speaking to the passengers, so I have to hang up now."

With a little grumbling, her mother finally allowed her to disconnect her cell, though by then Alyssa had missed the agent's message. Scanning the seating by the gate, she promptly spotted a nice, quiet corner, one with no loud *or* sweaty men nearby, and made a beeline for it.

A few minutes later she heard a commotion and she glanced up to see an unhappy passenger arguing with one of the customer service agents. This wasn't anything new. Alyssa wasn't thrilled with the delay, either, but she'd been traveling a lot over the years and knew it was par for the course.

Would the passengers rather fly in an unsafe plane? Alyssa would prefer to fly with her mind at ease, and to land the same way. Delays were never fun, but she wasn't going to argue with people who knew a lot more about the airplanes than she did.

When several other people surged around the guy who'd gone ballistic—his voice was rising by the minute—and gained the "courage" to yell at the agent along with him, Alyssa tried not to watch. But it was like passing a wreck on the freeway. You knew it was ridiculous to slow down, but no matter how much you lectured yourself not to twist your head, it just seemed to happen.

As Alyssa focused on the clamor, she felt the air stir next to her as someone sat down. No rank odor assailed her, so she didn't pay attention to her new neighbor; she was busy watching two policemen walk to the customer service counter. The noise finally began dying down when the officers told the passengers that the next person to cause a problem would be escorted off the premises.

Nothing more to see there. She turned her head idly and then started in surprise; her eyes surely widened to the size of small saucers. Sitting next to her was a heart-stoppingly beautiful man—and she never used that term lightly. His thick, dark hair was cut just a little longer than was conventional, brushing the top of his ears. His solid jawline and high cheekbones gave him an air of natural sophistication, and the straight, smooth shape of his nose perfected his features.

But what really caught her attention were the sultry dark brown eyes with their perfect almond shape, and thick, long lashes that most people in her former industry would pay thousands of dollars to acquire. The man was positively delicious, which sent an instant shot of awareness through her stomach. And she had no business gazing his way.

Something was making him unhappy. His flawless lips were clamped in a straight line and his eyebrows bent inward in a scowl. When Alyssa finally exhaled, she found herself sitting up a little bit straighter. His scent was now dancing inside her, and—mmmm—whatever cologne the man was wearing was meant to seduce. Meant to make women turn their heads. And it was doing the trick on her.

"Mr. Whitman, is there anything else I can do for you?"

Alyssa turned to find one of the airline's agents hovering around her compelling neighbor. The name was familiar, but she couldn't place it.

"No. Leave me."

Wow! He *was* an unhappy man.

Alyssa decided that staying silent would be the wisest course of action. But she had never really been the silent type, and for some odd reason, this stranger's disgruntled mood made her feel less sorry for herself. It looked as if his day was going worse than hers. And *that* was saying a lot.

"I'm so sorry about the delay, Mr. Whitman," the agent said. "We'll be boarding within the next twenty minutes." When he didn't respond, she shifted on her feet before shuffling away.

The man's cold dismissal would make anyone uneasy. The little show that had just taken place told Alyssa that she should stand up quietly and find another seat. But she wouldn't. Not when she was suddenly so entertained right where she was.

The man was retrieving his laptop from his computer bag when the device slipped and he jerked his hand out to catch it; in the process, his elbow leapt over the armrest separating him from her and jabbed her in the ribs. She couldn't help giving out an *oof* of pain.

002

Cold.

  Untouchable.

  Forbidding.

Those words described Jackson Whitman perfectly. It was the way he wanted to be viewed. It was safe—it protected him. After the loss of his daughter, he was done. Done with love. Done with playing nice. Done with it all.

People skirted around him, steered clear. Most people, that is. Certainly not his meddling family, who couldn't get it through their heads that he was now a lone wolf and preferred it that way. Of course, if they ever *actually* gave up on him, would he like that? He wanted to think that he would, but he knew the truth, knew he needed them. No one, however, would ever hear him say those words aloud.

Okay, he didn't need *companionship*; he didn't need long talks or people to be in his face. Sex, on the other hand—oh, yes, that need bubbled up inside him like molten lava boiling for an eternity in the confines of the earth, begging for release.

Right now, sex should be the last thing on his mind, but his neighbor, the woman he'd just managed to elbow, was making him unable to think of anything else. As he took in her pale blue eyes, sleek yet curvy body, silky reddish-blond hair, and ripe parted lips, sex was his only thought. Thrusting that thought away, he opened his mouth to apologize when her lips turned from an O to a smile.

"Well, that's certainly a new greeting," she said with a chuckle.

What the hell was she talking about? "Excuse me?"

"An apology would be expected, but you don't seem to be the sort of man who goes around apologizing, if your interaction with the airline employee is any indication of how you normally speak to strangers."

She wasn't being rude, exactly. She was just being . . . he couldn't quite put his finger on what the hell she was being. Jackson was used to women batting their eyelashes, licking their lips, leaning in to give him a clear invitation with a close-up of their cleavage. He wasn't used to anyone mocking him. It took him several silent seconds to form two words.

"I apologize."

"Wow. You really need to work on that."

Again he was floored. It was just as she'd said: he practically never apologized for anything. And she'd just thrown his sincere—all right, maybe not completely sincere, but still . . . She'd just thrown the words back at him without even a nod of her head indicating acceptance.

"It wasn't as if I intentionally elbowed you," he pointed out.

"I would hope not, since we don't know each other, and I've never done anything to warrant being hit by you," she said, the same grin in place.

"No woman should ever be hit." He wasn't amused.

"Ah, so you're a gentleman."

"I wouldn't go that far." And miraculously, he felt his lips turning up just the slightest bit. Sheesh, he couldn't remember the last time he'd smiled. Too much had happened in the past five years to make him feel like grinning.

"That's good to know, Mr. Whitman."

How did she know his name? Suspicion entered Jackson's thoughts. Then he remembered the rep who'd been busy kissing his ass. Airlines annoyed him. He hated flying commercial, preferring to use his jet, but one of his brothers was using it this week, and he'd had little choice but to come to Paris any way he could. He'd have put the trip off, but with the holidays, he'd been under certain pressing deadlines.

Now, inevitably, the flight was delayed, and

here he was, sitting next to a distressingly intriguing woman. Dammit. Jackson didn't want to be intrigued, but it seemed as if his body had taken the reins from his brain.

That she'd mocked him gave him a measure of respect for her. It was refreshing to have a conversation with a woman who knew nothing about him, seemed to want nothing from him. He was tempted to change her mind on that front.

He loved sex.

Sex was healthy. It was vital. It's what kept this pathetic population going like the Energizer Bunny. Maybe this delay wouldn't end up being such an awful thing after all. But Jackson didn't jump into bed with women on a whim. Not usually, at least. He'd have to see how the next few minutes played out and then decide whether or not to bed her.

Yes, he was confident enough in himself to know that if he wanted her to share a bed with him, then she would indeed do so. He opened his laptop and pulled up a report. If she didn't speak again, maybe that would be the end of it. If she did . . . well, if she did, maybe he'd decide to prolong their conversation.

As he began working, a few minutes passed in total silence. So maybe their conversation was over; maybe that small stirring she'd caused in him had been nothing more than a fluke. But her scent began drifting over him. Fingers of jasmine and nutmeg twirled around his nose and slid across his cheeks. Taking a deep breath, he decided that work could wait for a while. There wasn't a lot of time before he and this nameless woman would board the plane.

As if his thoughts had caused the agents to actually do some work, an announcement came over the intercom, first in French, then in English. "Passengers outbound on Flight 28 with service to JFK, we apologize for the delay once again. We've been informed that boarding will begin in ten minutes. Please make your way back to gate K26 and we'll get through the boarding process quickly and have you on your way to New York in a timely fashion."

"Finally," she murmured, though she didn't seem particularly excited—most of the people in the terminal were clapping. She seemed to be practicing some sort of breathing exercises as she gripped her armrests. Was she afraid of flying?

"Thousands of flights take off and land safely every single day," Jackson said, almost surprised by the sound of his voice as he attempted to comfort her. Why would he care if she was frightened? It didn't affect him.

She turned her head slowly his way and her eyes were wide. "Yes, I know."

He waited, but she said nothing further. "Then why the panicked expression?"

"Probably because even though I know that flying is much safer than a car or boat, my brain won't listen to reason. Being thirty-something thousand feet in the air in a big metal machine is just unnatural," she replied before taking another long breath.

"I wouldn't say that boats are unsafe." Why had that popped from his mouth?

"Have you not watched *Titanic*? Or *Poseidon*? I'd say the passengers on those boats weren't too thrilled about how their ocean cruises ended," she said.

"The *Titanic* disaster could have been prevented, and *Poseidon* is fiction."

"Well, a lot of plane crashes could probably have been prevented, too, but with my luck I'm going to be on a flight that goes down in a fiery blaze of glory. Or simply disappears from radar, never to be seen again."

For some reason, she amused him. One minute she was all mocking and happy-go-lucky, and the next she seemed like a frightened teenager. Whatever she was, she wasn't boring.

"Why did you come all the way to Paris if you hate flying?"

"For work."

Her breathing had started to grow easier as they continued chatting, and that brought Jackson surprising pleasure. He liked that he was calming her, that the conversation they were having was taking her mind off her fears. Jackson performed billion-dollar deals on a regular basis. Deals of serious import and excitement. Calming a frightened woman wasn't in his job description and shouldn't matter to him in the least. But the fact was that it did matter.

"What kind of work?" he asked.

She tensed again.

"Nothing important," she said, then added, "I'm Alyssa, by the way. Alyssa Gerard."

She held out her hand and he looked at it as if it were a snake. With a strange reluctance, he held out his hand and clasped her fingers. He should have known better. As their fingers brushed together, a vibration of awareness rocketed right through him. That was all it had taken, one simple touch. This woman was dangerous.

Good thing he liked danger.

Just then his phone rang and he lifted it, his eyes not letting hers go. After a moment of listening, he gave a curt "No comment" and hung up. Damn reporters!

"Excuse me."

Without looking back at her, he stood and moved purposefully through the throng of eager passengers. Jackson always purchased two seats when he was forced to fly commercially. The last thing he wanted was to end up sitting on an eight- to twelve-hour flight next to some annoying stranger. In this case, his extra seat was an advantage.

"I want Alyssa Gerard moved to the open seat next to mine," Jackson said, handing over his boarding passes.

He always booked himself into the last row of first class, giving himself even more privacy. This trip, which hadn't begun well, was shaping up to be a lot more pleasant now that he had a sexy companion to pass the time with.

A predatory smile transformed his features, making the agent helping him blush. Now *that* was the reaction Jackson was used to receiving from women.

003

When Alyssa was called to the counter as preboarding was announced, she wondered what possibly could be going wrong now. Maybe her seat assignment had been lost or given away and she would be stuck in Paris forever.

Instead of being anxious, though, she turned her thoughts back to the stranger who'd bolted. But, today of all days, why was she thinking twice about the man? Maybe all the trauma had made her lose her mind, and it would be a mental ward she landed in instead of New York.

Having men lust after her was something Alyssa was used to. Most guys wanted to sleep with her, that was for sure. But it wasn't because they were in love with her. They either wanted to use her because they liked what they saw—not her, just her looks—or figured that it was a fashion model's duty to warm their beds.

It was almost inevitable in the world she'd been a part of. Modeling certainly hadn't brought her the life she'd expected. Her young dreams of fame, fortune, and glamour had earned her sackcloth and ashes, and she hadn't done anything wrong.

When she'd refused man after man, whether a coworker or a boss, she'd struggled in her career. Why should they deal with her when their working world abounded with exotic beauties who would do anything to further their careers?

It had taken her much longer to get the big break she'd been looking for, and then the ride hadn't lasted long. The one person she'd trusted . . .

A shudder ran through her. She refused to think about Carl Avone, her ex-boyfriend and manager. He was scum and wasn't worth the precious brain cells it would use to think of him again.

"Ms. Gerard, you've been upgraded to first class. Here's your new ticket."

Alyssa stood there in disbelief and stared at the agent, not moving to take the ticket. "Are you sure you have the right person?" she finally asked.

"Yes, ma'am." The woman didn't blink as she pushed the ticket closer.

"Seriously, I've had a hell of a week, and if I get on the plane in this seat and then they boot me out, I'm probably going to end up causing a riot," she warned the woman. She was impressed when the agent kept her smile in place.

"I assure you, Ms. Gerard, that the upgrade is legitimate."

Still suspicious, but not willing to appear ungrateful, Alyssa grabbed it and looked at the seat number with the words *de première classe*—"first class"—written in bold letters across the bottom.

Since she was left with virtually nothing, her parents had bought her a ticket to get home. There was no way they could afford a last-minute international first-class ticket. Feelings of guilt assailed Alyssa as she stepped away from the counter.

What if she was stealing someone's seat? Her name was printed on the pass, but how could she have been upgraded? She didn't even have a frequent-flier number. Her manager had always booked all her flights. Once in a blue moon she'd been placed in business class, which was heaven itself. But she'd never, *ever* flown first-class. It was a luxury she'd always wanted to enjoy.

First-class passengers were offered preboarding, and with only a small amount of hesitation she joined the line, feeling frumpy in her worn fitted jeans, wrinkled blouse, and baggy sweater. She'd been in a hurry to leave her small apartment and catch her flight home, and she had dressed quickly, packing the rest of her clothes for the journey.

Since she'd shared a place with several other models, it had been depressingly easy to move out; she owned only what she carried in her suitcases. Being a model, she had worn a lot of borrowed clothes to promote companies, and she played down her everyday appearance—she hadn't wanted to be recognized when not on the job.

None of the furniture had belonged to her, and she'd hung nothing on the walls. Sadly, she hadn't had so much as a single trinket in the apartment. The more she thought of her life as a model, the more she was grateful it was over. It just would have been nice if her exit from the business had been her choice. She would have come to the same place eventually, but she should have had a nice nest egg to fall back on.

As she entered the first-class cabin and spotted her seat, a smile of anticipation crossed her lips. Oh, this was definitely the way to fly! There was so much *room*. Plenty of space for her carry-on bag, her feet, her entire body. She might actually be able to catch a few hours of sleep. Not that she wanted to miss out on a moment of this experience, but she was exhausted from the sleepless nights this week, and then those frustrating hours of waiting in the terminal.

A blanket, pillow, and headphones were sitting in the large seat, and a bottle of water waited for her on the adjoining table. Putting her bag under the seat in front of her, she sat down with a wide smile as the flight attendant approached.

"Would you care for a drink?"

It had been hours since she'd ingested a single thing, and Alyssa desperately wanted something to eat and drink, but she didn't want to be a fool and ask whether there was a charge. All she had was the small emergency cash fund that she'd stuffed into her purse that morning, and she was holding on to *that* as tightly as humanly possible.

"Not right now," she replied. She'd have to look through the airline magazine first, find out whether precious dollars would be required.

"Let me know if you need anything before take-off." With that, the pleasant flight attendant turned around and assisted other first-class passengers who were gradually filling up the cabin.

After grabbing the magazine, Alyssa was thrilled when she found the page describing first class. Not only were the drinks free, but so were the two meals she'd receive. Meals! Not just pretzels! Her stomach rumbled when she read the options.

"Mmm, this will be a nice flight," she murmured, feeling giddy and finding that she was having to stifle an excited giggle.

"I certainly hope so. It's been delayed long enough."

Alyssa's head snapped up to encounter a side view of Mr. Whitman as he slid into the aisle seat next to her.

"You're sitting here?" she asked, dumbfounded.

"I hope so," he said with a smirk as he placed his bag underneath the seat in front of his.

"Would you care for a drink?" The flight attendant was back, her smile just a bit more radiant than when she'd spoken to Alyssa a moment earlier.

"Yes, please. A gin and tonic," he answered, barely glancing at the woman.

"I've changed my mind," Alyssa said before the attendant could turn away. "I'll have a vodka and orange juice."

"I see you're in a much happier mood," her neighbor said.

Why was she sitting here? And why was he speaking to her? The last she'd seen of him had been the back of his head as he'd practically run away from her. So, of course, being a woman who didn't seem to have a filter when it came to speaking her mind, Alyssa had to make a comment.

"Do you always have that smirk on your face?"

He seemed startled by her question, but then he chuckled.

"I guess I do," he said before pausing for a few moments while he just looked at her with those intense eyes. "I never did introduce myself," he finally said, not holding his hand out this time. "Jackson Whitman."

The flight attendant returned with their drinks and Alyssa took a grateful sip. She definitely had to make the most of this. She'd never be able to afford first class again, and she hoped to heaven that it wouldn't kill her when she had to go back to the pits of coach.

Jackson pulled out some papers and read quietly while he sipped his beverage. Alyssa found her eyes glued to the small window next to her, the activity going on outside the plane oddly fascinating.

Bags were loaded, small carts darted around the tarmac, then the jet bridge was pulled back, and soon the airplane was gliding easily away from the gate. After the plane began moving forward, it wasn't long before they were racing down the runway and then lifting into the air.

This part had always made her clutch her seat in fear in the past, but now it was different. Maybe it was the smooth ascent. Maybe it was the comfort of her seat, or maybe the vodka had helped ease her fears. Whatever it was, her heart pounded only a little harder, and the hairs on the back of her neck weren't standing straight up.

Yep. This was going to be a great flight. Okay, it *would* be as long as she didn't think about the fact that they were high in the sky over a huge body of water that would prove harder than cement if they plummeted into it.

Nope. Alyssa wasn't going to think that way. The

one and only time she flew first-class was not going to end with her becoming fish bait.

When the flight attendant brought an appealing plate of appetizers and placed it on her tray, Alyssa decided the night was just going to get better and better. Jackson seemed engrossed in his papers—he picked food off his plate without paying attention to what he was eating—but Alyssa didn't need him to entertain her.

He might be used to this life, and people might think a model was used to it, too, but only the lucky ones got this sort of treatment. She hadn't been in that mix. So she was going to enjoy every second and dream about it later.

If only her eyes would quit straying to the sensual man beside her, she'd have been a lot more pleased. But, hey, when a man looked that good, it was a law that he had to be looked at, right? Man candy, her mother would call him.

That thought made her giggle aloud, causing the man she was thinking about to turn his head, and suddenly she was caught by those simmering brown eyes.

004

Why wasn't he striking up a conversation with this woman? After all, Jackson had been the one who'd ensured that she would sit by him. He'd been reading the same line on this damn document for the last thirty minutes, his thoughts on the petite blonde next to him.

Of course, she wasn't really blond; she was more—what was it called?—strawberry blond. There were natural highlights running through the silken strands of her hair, and he had a powerful urge to run his fingers through it. Never before had he wanted so badly to pull a woman close and slowly bring their mouths together. Sure, he always wanted sex, but this strong sensation in his gut was absurd.

Jackson stopped pretending to read and instead gave in to what he wanted to do. He reached confidently across the short distance between them and let his fingers glide down her long tresses, startling her.

Yes. Her hair was as soft as it looked. He always loved when women grew their hair out, loved how it would fall across their naked backs in a plunging gown, or how it would fall forward against their cheeks. And there was nothing sexier to him than a woman straddling his lap, her hair cascading down to cover her luscious breasts in a game of hide-and-seek. He shifted in his seat as his pants grew tight at the thought of sharing such an intimate moment with a woman he'd only just met.

"You never did tell me why you were working in Paris," he remarked.

How much time had he spent staring at her, even burning into her with his greedy gaze? It was probably a good thing she'd been looking out the window earlier, though he had no clue what she was seeing now. They were over the ocean and it was dark. It had to be that she could feel his look, could feel this intense energy rushing between them, and it was making her nervous. Well, it was about to become a lot more intense.

"I don't want to talk about it," she said when she turned his way again and raised her eyebrows in a flirtatious yet pointed extension of her words.

"You will find that I'm not easily dissuaded." His eyes still held hers, his hand moving away from her skin as he reached for a mojito shrimp in pineapple sauce.

He was intrigued by the shuddering breath she took. Though she was trying to look as if his touch hadn't affected her, it was nothing but a show. When their fingers had entwined themselves earlier, he hadn't been the only one who'd felt the spark. No, Alyssa was doing her best to keep her distance with her snarky comments and short sentences, but she, too, was intrigued.

He wanted to know how intrigued.

"Do you always get what you want, Jackson?" There was a challenge in her eyes.

"Always." He was sure in his answer.

"Sadly, you won't be able to say that after tonight," she said, her lips turning up in a winning smile.

"No, Alyssa. I can *guarantee* you that you'll talk." He leaned close enough to make her squirm in her seat.

She said nothing, just put a tender scallop into her mouth and chewed. Jackson laughed as the flight attendant cleared their trays, refilled their drinks, and said the main course would be right out.

After they were served, Jackson found that he was enjoying her pleasure in the food far more than he was enjoying his own dinner. Hell, he couldn't taste it, really, because his brain was engaged elsewhere. This plane ride was becoming one big adventure to him, in great part because it was clearly exciting to her. He watched her delight in everything around her.

"Have you flown first-class before?" he asked once they'd both finished their meals.

"Never. But I'm telling you, this is the *only* way to fly."

"Yes, it makes it more pleasant when you're stuck on a commercial flight."

"How else are you going to get around?"

"On a private jet. It's much more enjoyable than even the best first-class cabin."

"Isn't that a bit excessive?"

"Why would you think that?"

"A big jet for just you?" she replied incredulously, making him almost feel guilty about it.

That was insane. He had nothing to feel guilty about if he wanted to travel alone by private jet. "You're not going to start spouting off about saving the whales or something, are you?" It wasn't that Jackson was anti-nature. It was just that he worked hard and he enjoyed life's luxuries. He couldn't stand it when people tried to make him feel ashamed over that.

The key word there was *tried*, though. They might preach to him, but it was easy for him to tune their words out. If he wanted something, he took it. That was who he was and he wouldn't apologize for it.

"No. But still . . ." Her voice faded, leaving her sentence unfinished.

"There are pilots being paid. A staff to run it on the ground, and many others who are employed because of my jet. There's nothing wrong with owning one. Bill Gates has a few," he pointed out.

"Yeah, what's up with that? One seems excessive, but to have more than one . . . What? Do you need a different color to fly in for different days of the week, or to match your outfit?"

Jackson sat dumbfounded as she spoke, then he laughed again. "Perhaps I will point that out to the board. Tell them that one just isn't enough."

"Rich people baffle me. They don't even think for a minute about how lucky they are, about how easy they have it. All of this," she said, holding her arms wide, her hand coming within inches of his chest, causing his breath to hitch, "and still, it's not enough. I made decent money the last few years, and luckily I sent some back to my parents. If I hadn't—" She stopped when she realized she'd been revealing something of herself.

Jackson *really* wanted to know what that was. Yes, he could have a background check done on her the second they touched down, but he wanted to hear it from her, not from his investigator. He wanted to know her—but only for tonight.

"So, you think the wealthy are just a bunch of pompous asses?" he asked, interested instead of offended.

She tilted her head and paused briefly. "I wouldn't say *that*. I mean, there are a lot of amazingly wealthy people out there. Do you know the amount of money Bill Gates donates? Oprah gives away so much it's staggering. And lots of celebrities give millions anonymously. I'm just saying that the wealthy, especially the ones who are born with a silver spoon in their mouth, should take a moment to appreciate what they have."

"And I take it you weren't born wealthy?" he asked.

"No, but I wasn't poor, either. My dad always worked hard, provided well for our family. We got a family vacation somewhere new and exciting every summer. My parents made sure I never missed out on anything; they paid for sports and clubs and so on. My mom was able to stay home when I was little, and I love her more than any other person on this planet. So, I wasn't rich by any means, but neither was I poor."

"That sounds like a pretty great childhood," he said.

"I'm not complaining. I'm just saying that *really* rich people should have a little more appreciation for all the extra luxuries they take for granted. A *lot* more appreciation, in some cases."

"Point taken," Jackson said.

She had no clue about his story. The very strange thing was that he *wanted* to tell her. Would it change her opinion of him? Did he want it to?

Jackson shook his head, confused yet delighted by the woman fate had led him to sit next to in the terminal. Had their flight been on time, he never would have met her, never would be having this conversation.

Jackson wasn't a man who believed in fate. He could, however, appreciate good timing. And though he'd been furious earlier because of all the problems he'd encountered while simply trying to get home, right now he could kiss the mechanic who had delayed their flight. Or at least he could kiss the woman sitting right next to him. Not only *could* he kiss her, but he most certainly planned on it.

The two of them continued chatting as their plates were cleared and the lights dimmed. Conversation around them began to die down, and they seemed to be in their own little world, alone in their small area in the back of first class.

To be sure, activity continued around them, some people reading, some chatting, but it seemed everyone was preparing for the rest of the long flight. Some had already nodded off. When the flight attendant asked if the two of them would like any help in folding their seats down into beds, Jackson noticed the blush that stole over Alyssa's cheeks.

Hell, yes, he was more than ready to have their private cave made, their beds laid down, and bedding brought out in which he'd be able to hide certain activities if he was very discreet. He couldn't do too much, but maybe he'd finally steal that kiss.

Alyssa avoided his eyes as she grabbed her small carry-on bag and made her way toward the bathroom. He wouldn't mind if she reappeared in some mouthwateringly sexy little number.

Of course, he knew that wouldn't happen in a public place. He had an imagination, though, so when she stepped from the bathroom in the same clothes, her hair brushed and her teeth sparkling, he chose to picture a sexy red nightie that hugged the curves he knew were lurking underneath her baggy sweater.

She might not admit the connection that had sparked between them, but it was real and he was more than willing and *able* to exploit it to their mutual benefit.

Maybe after this flight he'd go back to regular commercial flying. He never would have met Alyssa had he been on his private jet. Slowly, as she arranged her blankets and climbed into her roomy flight bed, Jackson removed his tie and then unbuttoned his shirt, shrugging it from his shoulders. He was immensely pleased when her wide blue eyes stayed glued to his chest.

Jackson was well aware of his great physique and worked hard to keep in shape. A healthy body was essential to a healthy mind. And tonight he planned to make sure Alyssa's dreams were filled with colorful images of their limbs entangled together.

When he climbed beneath his own warm bedding and turned to face her, she gazed at him through half-closed eyes. He could see her internal struggle as she tried to decide whether to turn away and attempt to sleep, or continue facing him and move toward the next step they were destined to take.

They were partially concealed by the darkness of the cabin and the blankets that covered them, but Jackson was very aware of passengers all around them. The sound of quiet talking was their white noise, and though he and Alyssa were on a plane filled with people, it felt sinfully intimate.

"You've managed to elude my question about your job. Now it's just you and me and we have hours before we land," he said, smiling as he watched her take a deep breath.

Jackson had a feeling she wasn't the type of woman to jump into affairs. Good. But that should send up red flags; maybe this just wasn't meant to be.

No. He refused to believe that. Seeing the curious light shining in her eyes as she looked at him, he knew they were just beginning whatever it was the two of them had started. This was the perfect storm of circumstances. And Jackson wasn't a man to let such an opportunity pass him by.

005

Alyssa faced Jackson in their intimate cocoon, and she felt as if the rest of the world had disappeared. She'd expected him to turn away, expected this strange pull between the two of them to disappear, but he hadn't—and in defiance of the howls of outrage coming from her brain, she was gazing into his eyes and having a most difficult time not looking at his sculpted chest. Damn him for letting his blanket sit so low on his waist.

How was she supposed to have a normal conversation with this man when her only thought right now was sex? It was actually almost comical. Here she was, twenty-four years old, just out of a terrible relationship with her one and only sexual partner, and still incredibly naive when it came to the nuances of sexual behavior.

It seemed the world thought she must be a sex aficionada, though, because all models knew the ins and outs of sex, didn't they? How could they possibly make love to the camera and not be experienced in the bedroom?

Sadly, almost all of her experience had come

from watching every romantic movie out there. When she'd finally caved in and had sex for the first time with Carl, she'd been disappointed. It had gotten slightly better after a few times, but she just didn't get all the hype. Why had this messy animal act caused so much drama throughout history?

Romantic movies had also been her best resource for proper facial expressions when simulating the throes of passion. Her favorite scene of all time was from *Top Gun*. When Maverick looked deeply into Charlie's eyes as the music played, Alyssa had felt her first stirring of desire. Whenever she'd been on a photo shoot that required sultry looks, she'd just pictured that love scene.

Great. Now "Take My Breath Away" was running through her head while she was lying in the dark next to the hottest guy she'd ever spoken to.

She'd never looked at male models as if they were real men—they were simply bodies she was posing with. The same couldn't be said about Jackson. He was all man, and he obviously knew it.

"Have I lost you, Alyssa?" Jackson asked, startling her.

"What?"

"You seem to be lost in your own thoughts."

"It's been a rough day. A rough week, really." Now, why had she said that?

"Really? It would help, then, if you told me why you were in Paris. What do you do?"

"I recall telling you that it was none of your business."

"And I recall telling *you* that I get what I want."

From the look in his eyes as he stared at the top of her blanket, she suspected that he was talking about a lot more than work.

She tugged on the blanket, pulling it just a little bit closer to her chin. It wasn't that she was a prude. She'd just never felt a desire so strong that it made it worth the time or energy to fall into bed with a stranger. But now? Whoa! After just a bit of conversation with Jackson, she was ready to climb into his small bed, straddle him, and have her every fantasy fulfilled.

It wasn't helping that she was going to some Podunk town in the middle of Montana she'd never even heard of, where the chance of meeting eligible bachelors was probably nil. Texas hadn't been the greatest of places to live, at least not in the summertime, when the heat and humidity were off the charts, but at least the state had a large population. Alyssa had heard that cows outnumbered people in Montana. If she ever hoped to get married and start a family, she would be hard-pressed to find a man where she was going—population: negative five.

Okay, maybe she was being a bit overdramatic,

but after traversing the world for the last few years, the idea of landing in Montana wasn't exactly a dream come true.

"We have all night," Jackson reminded her.

"You sure are persistent. What if it's something that I'm greatly upset about? Or maybe, just maybe, I don't know you and don't want to share my life with a stranger." That was pretty cut-and-dried. The problem was that she found herself wanting to share everything with this man. This stranger.

Probably not very wise.

"I read people. I do it for a living, Alyssa. I find companies that are failing and I overtake them, then fix them or rip them apart. I know how to read people better than you could imagine."

"And you're reading me?"

"I've been reading you from the first moment our eyes met."

From the expression on his face, she had no clue what he'd come up with in his assessment, and she found herself desperately wanting to know. So of course she refused to ask. Still, it wasn't like her to back down.

She gave him a sassy smile. "Maybe I'm reading you right back."

"Good. I'm an open book."

"Liar."

If it wasn't his idea, he didn't speak to people.

She'd seen him in action. What she didn't understand was why he was speaking to her now. What did he find so fascinating about her? She was, all in all, a very uninteresting person.

"Still, I have nothing but time . . . for now," he said, showing how persistent he could be.

"Yes, and then the clock strikes midnight and we both fade away," she countered.

"Technically, the clock should strike about eight or nine when we land."

"I hate traveling backward in time. I start one place on a certain date, and when I land, it's the day before, or two days later. Why can't every place just be the same time zone?"

"That would be interesting," he said. "It could be pitch-black out and still be high noon. Or we could watch the sun rise at midnight."

"Let's just reset time." Dang. He must be floored by the fundamental stupidity of her remarks. But she was so tired . . .

"You can put me off, but I won't give up," he told her as he fiddled with her blankets, making her stomach quiver as she waited for the brush of his fingers. When it didn't happen, when his knuckles never brushed against her flesh, she felt disappointment.

"Fine! But I'm warning you that it's a horrendous story that no one would really be interested in hearing. Then again, since I won't ever see you again after tonight . . ." He wasn't giving up, so what could it hurt to talk to him?

He just continued to gaze at her with those soulful brown eyes of his as he waited for her to continue either her rant or her story.

"I'm a model. Or I guess I should say I *was* a model. To make a long, boring story much shorter, but still just as uninteresting, my manager, who also happened to be my boyfriend, was having an affair with several other people besides me, including my wardrobe guy. However, I'm the one who got spotlighted. I'm the one labeled, and I'm the one who lost everything when he ran off with my money, my reputation, and my self-respect." Her voice dripped with self-loathing.

"Whoa, wasn't expecting that," Jackson said.

"To make matters worse was how I found out. He cleaned out my account, ended my contracts, and left me high and dry in Paris. I'm currently returning home with my head shamefully low, preparing to eat crow in front of all those who told me the modeling world wasn't where I should be."

"How could he end your contracts?"

"That's just another part of my own stupidity. I signed the documents without even blinking because I trusted him, and didn't know he was ending my contracts instead of extending them. I was a fool and I'm paying for it now."

There was a pause as he processed her words, then he focused on something she'd said a minute earlier.

"Why would anyone tell you not to go for your dreams, that modeling was stupid?"

"Because modeling is short-lived and most people don't make it. I really struggled for a while, but then things started to come around. Romance sparked between my manager and me, or so I thought, and I landed a big contract with a makeup company. All of that has been taken away now. I'm twenty-four, way too old in the modeling world to start over, and I have nothing. No college degree, no work experience to list on a résumé, and no money. The people who told me to get an education instead of modeling were right. I'm sure they'll enjoy telling me so."

"Why is it such a scandal? It sounds like he was a cad."

"Because he was married . . . and before you give me that look, I didn't know he was married. I also didn't know he had been taking pictures of me that if ever leaked to the papers would horrify my parents. He framed me to take a fall because all along he was only there to use me."

She took a shuddering breath. Why was she spilling her guts to the guy? It felt freeing to speak about it, though, to tell her story and let it go.

"If you really don't want to quit, you don't have

to. Sure, he has what sounds like blackmail material, but the truth will come out. It just may be a long ride while you go to trial."

"You sound like this is something you've gone through," she said, her curiosity piqued.

"I know the law. Without seeing any documents, I don't know your exact situation, but it sounds to me like you have a good case to get your contracts back, at least."

"Yes, I was told the same thing. However, I'm done with this world. I'm tired of the lights, the fake people, the drama. I was ready to come home a year ago, but I didn't want to accept failure. Carl just forced me to make the decision I wanted to make anyway. The only part that really sucks is that he got away with almost all of my money."

"Have you hired an attorney?" he asked.

"I'll worry about that when I get home. This just happened. Right now all I want to do is go home, get some advice from my mom, and take a breath. Then I'll regroup and try to figure out what I'm going to do next. It just feels like I've gone nowhere, done nothing with my life," she said.

Jackson looked at her for a long moment, his eyes seeming to see right into her very soul. "I think you're downplaying what you *have* accomplished."

"How so? Are you not listening?" she replied with an edge of irritation.

"I'm listening. You got to travel the world. You made good money, even if it was stolen from you. Landing a big account in the modeling world isn't an easy task, so, again, you accomplished something impressive. Okay, you trusted the wrong person. Many of us have made that mistake."

"Have you?"

Jackson was quiet as he looked at her, collecting his thoughts. "I've made many mistakes, and, yes, I've trusted the wrong person before. It's something you allow to happen once. Trust me when I say you won't be fooled again by someone like your ex-boyfriend."

"I think I would be a fool to trust you." This she somehow knew with every fiber of her being. Still, a shiver passed through her while she gazed at Jackson with a rapidly building attraction kindling inside her, and she couldn't seem to turn away. It was absurd. She didn't know him, couldn't possibly know him after talking for only a few hours.

There was hot chemistry between them; that was more than clear. But there was a long way between chemistry and actually knowing the man. Was it his eyes? Though he tried to appear cold and calculating, there was a softness in their endless brown depths that spoke of honor and hardship and led her to believe she could trust him.

"You're wise to think so," he said.

"What is happening here?"

A couple of seconds passed before she realized she'd voiced her thought aloud.

"We're connecting," he answered, his hand lifting again as he held her captive with his gaze while his fingers trailed down her cheek and then caressed her bottom lip.

She fought the need rippling through her and tried to lighten the mood. She should turn away, but she couldn't stop speaking to him, couldn't end their night just yet. So she had no other choice but to put on a smile and challenge him.

"Okay, I've told you my pathetic sob story. Now it's your turn to tell me something about you."

He smiled, a secretive smile that said he wouldn't give her anything of himself that he didn't want to give. A smile that had her hand twitching with a need to run her fingers across that impressive expanse of his chest. That had her wanting to take a taste of those lips. Wanting to learn what he was hiding.

Shaking her head, she remained stubbornly silent, refusing to reveal anything further about herself until he gave up something—anything!

"I was once a completely different man," he said, then was silent.

She raised her eyebrows expectantly. "You're persistent in your silences, Jackson."

He laughed. Oh, the sound of his soft laughter tickled her nerve endings, making her want so badly to close the gap between them.

"I was once married, to my college sweetheart. We had a daughter." Jackson went silent as he looked at Alyssa.

She didn't want to say a word, too afraid he would stop talking. She could see he didn't even understand why he was telling her this, and the pain radiating from his eyes clearly made it obvious this wasn't something he normally shared.

"My daughter's name was Olivia. She was three months old when she died. For years I didn't think I'd ever forgive myself for letting it happen."

"Oh, Jackson . . ." What should she say? There was nothing that could make that kind of pain disappear.

"I was the fire chief. When I was finally able to enter that building and found her lifeless body, I was done with it all." He spoke in almost a monotone, his eyes looking over her head as if he wasn't even seeing her.

"What happened?"

"It's a long story involving a bitter divorce and a fight for our daughter. My ex wasn't a good woman, and she didn't want our child. She was smoking in the apartment, fell asleep, and the building caught fire. I was young when I married, naive, with stars in my eyes. All I'd wanted was to settle down, have a family, and live happily ever after. I discovered it wasn't going to happen. I will never love again, certainly never marry again, and I would never subject a child to the trauma of parents who hate each other."

"You had to have loved her if you married her." That's how the world survived: people falling in love, getting married, and bringing a new generation into the world.

"I did. And I learned that love isn't enough to counter greed, dishonesty, and selfishness."

"Not everything is so black-and-white. Just because your wife turned out to be someone different from what you thought doesn't mean all women are deceptive," she said.

"Ha. All women want something, Alyssa. What is it that you want?"

She was instantly offended, and though she shouldn't respond to such a crass question, she did. "I want to be happy, to have a family someday and live the American dream. I have to regroup, but just because I have to start over doesn't mean that I'm giving up on life."

"Give it a few more years."

"You seem so sure, Jackson," she said with sadness. "Where is the man who was just giving me a pep talk a few minutes ago?" He ignored her question, so she continued. "Yes, what you went through is horrible, but that doesn't mean you have to change into another person entirely."

"At one point in my life, all I wanted was to be a hero. Now I realize that people don't want to be saved. They want to take and take, just like your manager took from you."

"It's too bad you feel that way," she said with a sigh, thinking that opening up hadn't been such a great idea. She decided to try to switch things up, to try to salvage their conversation. "You said you buy and sell companies now?"

"Yes. It's boring, it's easy, and I have a knack for it."

"If it's so boring, why do it?"

"Because it's something to do. I have been investing for years; this was just another form of investment."

"You're right, that does sound boring," she said with a laugh, and he raised his eyebrows.

"Are you mocking me, Alyssa?" Oh, the sound of his voice whispered right through her entire body.

"I find I quite enjoy mocking you. I have a feeling not too many people do it, Jackson."

"You're certainly right about that. Besides you, I think the only other people who would dare to challenge me or *mock* me are my father and brothers," he said with a real smile.

"Tell me about them."

His eyes sparkled, making her stomach twist knowing she'd hit his sweet spot. "I have three brothers: Michael, Camden, and Spence. They're a pain in the ass, but we have each other's backs no matter what."

"And . . . ?" He sure didn't speak much.

"And that's all. They are great. My dad is great. I love my family."

"Getting information from you isn't very easy," she said.

"Don't you like it that we both have an air of mystery about us, Alyssa? Isn't that what makes this so exciting?"

She felt caught. Did she admit how exhilarating all of this was for her? Or did she stay cool and collected? Was she making a huge mistake here by flirting with this man? Her entire world had been flipped upside down, yet lying here beside Jackson seemed to drown out the disappointment, the sadness, the emptiness. Didn't that mean she was using him? Wasn't that wrong?

But in any case, wasn't he using her just as much? It was more than clear that he, too, felt an attraction. That was something she was used to—men wanting her. It was the unfamiliar desire awakening within her for this man that was catching her by complete surprise.

Could she surrender to the desires of her body and continue down this road with him? It wasn't as if they could have sex. They were on a plane filled with people. But what would a little harmless flirting do?

"Yes, Jackson, I do like the air of mystery."

"Then let's stop all this talking about our past. Why don't I tell you exactly what I want to do with you right now?"

As he spoke, he shifted closer to her, bringing his lips within inches of her own. Would she allow a kiss? Was she even capable of denying this man when she wanted to taste him so badly?

Not giving her a chance to think anymore, he caressed her face, brought his mouth to hers, and connected their lips, sending jolts of electricity through her body. As his lips moved across hers, she felt an unfamiliar pressure build deep within, a feeling she knew would only grow stronger the closer she got to this man.

"I knew we would set off sparks, Alyssa," he murmured as he pulled back, looking at her with clear desire in his eyes.

Fear filled her as she realized the power this man could have over her. What was she thinking? She was playing with fire. Hadn't she been burned enough?

"This isn't wise, Jackson."

"We don't always need to be wise," he informed her.

Luckily, he backed up, gave her some space. They continued speaking and soon her fatigue was overwhelming. She fought against that inopportune drowsiness as the two of them talked about neutral topics, nothing too intimate, but enough that as she got to know him a little bit more, learned what made his lips twitch, or his eyes sparkle, she found herself becoming increasingly infatuated with him.

When she fell asleep, Jackson less than a foot away, he filled her dreams—just as he'd assured her he would do.

006

Alyssa opened her eyes slowly to a hushed silence. Damn. She'd wasted precious time with something as useless as sleep, and now she didn't know how much longer she had until the plane landed.

Stretching quietly in her seat, she sat up and looked over at the peaceful expression on Jackson's face. He looked almost like a different person. He was just as handsome as before, but his guard wasn't up as he slept. She wondered what this man dreamed of.

The barest hint of stubble dotting his square jaw and angular cheekbones rendered him even more striking than when she'd first laid eyes upon him. Despite an almost desperate need to reach over and touch him, she slipped from her warm bed and went to use the bathroom, where she took her time brushing her teeth.

When she came back, Alyssa tripped, landing right in Jackson's lap. His beautiful brown eyes instantly snapped open, and then she couldn't pull her gaze away from them.

"Good . . . morning?" he mumbled, and her blood ran hot at the scratchy timbre of his voice. It was so deep and rich, it must have originated clear down in his toes.

"I'm sorry," she said, trying to get off him, but his arms locked around her. Oh, this man would star in her dreams for many nights to come. She was surprised and delighted to know that one chance encounter would shape her, change her, from this point on. No, she wouldn't moon over him forever. But hereafter she'd compare every man she met with him.

And they'd all come up wanting.

"I could get used to waking up to such a beautiful woman. I'm going to kiss you again." That was her only warning before Alyssa found herself flipped beneath him, gazing up into his sparkling brown eyes, their only shelter the thick blankets that covered them.

She was caught. Completely caught.

The very next moment, the warmth of his lips covered hers. And Alyssa wasn't disappointed. Jackson's lips were sure and confident, just like him. It wasn't a casual meeting of mouths. It was hunger, raw and untamed. It was passion and ecstasy. It was everything she'd hoped for and more. It was unlike anything she could have ever possibly imagined. The kiss he'd given her before she went to sleep was just a friendly good night. This kiss was pure seduction.

His tongue traced her lips, then pushed against her teeth so she would open to him. There was no hesitation, no doubt. He knew what he wanted and he demanded her submission. And she gave it to him willingly.

This man wasn't used to losing, and right now he wanted her. And for once, she wasn't afraid to accept what he was offering. With a hunger she didn't know she was capable of feeling, Alyssa lifted her arms and clasped his neck, then pulled him closer.

Their tongues dueled, both of them fighting to deepen the kiss, almost attempting to climb within one another. No kiss had ever inspired such an animal hunger inside her. Carl had made her believe she was frigid, incapable of passion.

Now she knew that was nothing but a lie. She felt anything but cold right now. She felt heat, longing, a fierce appetite for more, for everything. She just couldn't get enough. Jackson swallowed the low groan that rumbled from her mouth, greedily taking that as he took everything else she was giving him.

As his tongue slowed and began slipping in and out of her mouth, her core boiled over. He was telling her with his mouth exactly what he planned on doing with the rest of her body, and the blood rushing through her veins in response told her that her answer had to be a firm yes.

When he shifted to the side and his hand slid

beneath the thick blankets that provided some semblance of privacy, she quivered beside him. His
fingers danced over the top of her blouse, gently
moving along the plane of her stomach before going
higher.

As his kiss continued on and on, not stopping
even long enough for her to draw needed breath,
she reached for him with her entire body, writhing,
angling, desperate for him to move his hand up a
few more inches.

Her nipples tightened as they anticipated the
healing touch of his palms running over them. And
he didn't disappoint her. With the sureness that she
was learning was deep-seated in Jackson's very na-
ture, he slid his hand inside her shirt, his fingers as
hungry as his mouth against her skin.

He roamed over the mound of her breast, and his
palm soothed her nipple, making her back arch as
she reached for him. She hated that she'd left her
bra on; she was desperate to have his flesh against
hers, to feel nothing between them.

Her fingers wound into his hair, and she tugged
hard. All she could feel was a burning need, and if
he didn't make the ache go away, she was afraid she
would melt where she was and be no more.

The stubble on his jaw scratched her smooth
cheek, leaving his mark there for all the world to
see, but she didn't care. Let them think what they

wanted. As long as he pleasured her, nothing else mattered. Nothing existed beyond the two of them and their overpowering desire.

His fingers slipped beneath the barrier of her bra and he finally pinched one swollen nipple. Oh, that was good, but now she desperately wanted his mouth where his fingers were, wanted his kiss to extend over the rest of her body. She was his, and he could do with her what he wanted.

With a low growl in his throat, Jackson withdrew his hand, making her whimper into his mouth. He pulled tighter on the blankets, ensuring that if anyone walked by, it would look only as if two lovers were sharing a kiss. At least Jackson was protecting her as he lit her body ablaze. When the haze cleared, she'd be thankful for this—perhaps.

Sliding over just a little more, he angled his chest so he'd have access to her breasts, and with the blanket firmly in place, he unclasped the front of her bra, allowing his hand to cup a swollen breast. Then he lifted up, his heated gaze capturing her own half-closed eyes. She was in a trance and couldn't understand why he'd stopped kissing her.

"Beautiful," he whispered as the look in his eyes made her fly even higher. It was both a relief and a cause of pain as he rolled her nipple tightly between his fingers, making her core pulse with need.

When he'd learned the shape of her breasts, his

hand drifted down her body, and when he swiftly undid the button and zipper of her jeans, she didn't so much as think of protesting. When he slipped inside the snug material to conquer the insignificant obstacle of her silk panties, she gasped.

Alyssa arched into Jackson when he found the place where she ached most and rubbed his fingers against her. He moved his lips up her neck and captured her mouth again as he stroked her heated flesh, sending her higher and higher.

This man could play with her all he wanted, as long as he continued building the flames of her desire like he was. There was nothing unsure about Jackson's technique. She sought completion in his arms.

Flicking his fingers across her swollen bud, he whispered, "Let go." His kiss deepened, and he grabbed her tongue with his lips and sucked as his fingers dived into the slick folds of her body.

She did as he asked—she let go, exploding in his arms, having to cover her mouth so the rest of the passengers didn't know what was happening right next to them. Trembling as she slowly drifted back down to him, Alyssa was barely coherent. When the trembling stopped, she opened her eyes and gazed at him. Intense heat gazed back at her from his dark brown eyes, but deep satisfaction also burned within his depths.

"We're only starting, Alyssa."

She didn't understand what he was saying until the lights popped on, making her nearly panic as she realized how disheveled she was.

"It's okay," he assured her as he slid his hands easily inside her shirt, pulled her bra into place, and clasped it, covering her up.

Thoroughly mortified, Alyssa scrambled to sit up at the same time she was fastening her jeans. Next she ran her fingers through her hair and hoped she didn't look like a scarecrow.

An announcement came over the intercom to let them know they'd be landing in two hours. Without looking over at Jackson, Alyssa stood, quickly escaping to the bathroom, desperate to hide from him. Looking in the mirror, she was shocked when she saw the reflection staring back at her.

Her skin was flushed, there was irritated redness on her chin and cheek from his stubble, and her eyes were shining. She'd never been so pleasured by a man, and she'd never felt like this before. What did he mean, they were only starting?

They were soon going to land. He would go his way and she'd go hers. This had been only a small interlude on a long flight. It couldn't go any further than that, could it?

After brushing her hair for the third time, Alyssa realized she couldn't stay in the bathroom for the rest of the flight, so she reluctantly opened the door. But what was she going to do or say now? She'd never been in this position before.

He must be thinking that because she was a model she was easy—that this was something she did on a regular basis. He didn't know her, didn't know how out of character this was for her. She had always been a good girl, and surprisingly enough the modeling world hadn't hardened her the way it did so many others.

Her behavior with him didn't fit the kind of person she was, dammit. If he thought they were going to just continue where they had left off, he was going to be sorely disappointed. But . . . but . . . despite everything, Alyssa was amazed that she didn't really want him disappointed. She wanted his last image of her to be a positive one. How she would accomplish this, she had no idea, but she'd just have to figure it out.

Their time was quickly running out . . .

007

Alyssa made her way down the aisle, refusing to meet anyone's eyes. She knew the other passengers didn't suspect a thing, but she felt as if they were all focused on her and knew exactly what she'd just been up to. That scarlet *A*—or maybe *M*, for *mile-high*—was surely growing larger and larger on her chest.

If Jackson was expecting more of a make-out session before the flight was over, he would be highly disappointed. As she sat down, her bed now made back into a seat, he didn't even glance up, though, but simply read his document as the flight attendant placed a tray before him with a light breakfast. Yes, it was actually evening, but for their bodies, still on Parisian time, it was closer to morning.

It didn't take long for Alyssa's food to be set in front of her, and she moved her eggs and sausage around on her plate. She was sure it was excellent, but she knew better than to try to eat anything when her stomach was feeling so nervous. Barf bags weren't her idea of fun.

She had to admit to being a bit disgusted as she

glanced surreptitiously over at Jackson. He didn't appear as if he'd slept in his clothes. No. He looked just as good as when she'd met him in the Paris terminal. He'd even managed to shave while she'd been away from her seat, working fruitlessly on her own appearance.

He had on a new shirt, and he didn't seem in the least affected by their sex play. It seemed she was the only one still thinking about it. If only she could act as if he hadn't had his fingers inside her body less than thirty minutes ago.

With the clock ticking down, she stubbornly refused to say a word. If he wanted to pretend they hadn't spoken for hours on end, that they hadn't nearly made love, that they hadn't had an almost magical encounter, she would follow his lead.

When an hour later the plane began its descent into JFK, her nerves sputtered and sparked. Would he even say good-bye?

This distance he'd suddenly placed between them confused her. Heck, she confused herself. Maybe he was disgusted with her, thought she was too easy. She herself wasn't exactly happy with what she'd allowed him to do. And now she felt lost as they approached the landing strip.

When the wheels touched down, her heart sank. The flight was over. It was time she accepted that Jackson had merely found a way to entertain himself on their trip. She'd been the show and the encore. That he hadn't "gotten off" didn't matter. Maybe it had been on his bucket list to make a woman fall apart on an airplane. Well, he could certainly put a checkmark on that one.

It wasn't just their make-out session that was making her feel so dismal all of a sudden. It was because of the hours they'd spoken, the way he'd listened to her, the things he'd shared—now all gone.

She'd fallen almost instantly under his spell, and she hadn't quite figured out how to pull herself away from it. Trying to decide whether she should bid him farewell—*Live long and prosper*—Alyssa was shocked when he turned toward her with gleaming eyes.

JACKSON MIGHT HAVE appeared to be reading the document on his laptop, but he'd been staring blankly at the same line since Alyssa returned to her seat. It was déjà vu all over again—since he'd met her in the terminal at Charles de Gaulle, he hadn't gotten a lick of work done. And what was with this sudden, uncharacteristic indecisiveness?

As the plane touched down, he was completely at a loss. All he knew for sure was that he didn't want the journey to end quite yet. He needed to spend the rest of the night with this woman, and he didn't care what it would take to get her to agree to it. He was just unsure of what to say next—almost a first for him.

Jackson Whitman was *always* sure of what to say. Until today.

This fascination he had with her should have been setting off all sorts of alarms in his brain, but he chose to ignore his instincts. He needed to finish what they'd started, right? This wouldn't be anything more than a night of great sex. He wouldn't lie to her, wouldn't fill her mind with visions of happily ever after; that would be despicable. He'd be straight with her and tell her again that they weren't finished. He'd leave off the *yet*, though—no need to be *too* blunt.

Jackson normally chose women who knew the score, who wanted what he wanted. Occasionally, he'd run into a woman who angled for more than a night, but he was quick to put the kibosh on that.

He was good to the women he bedded; even those who pushed for more didn't complain when the night was over. Sure, most, if not all, would have wanted him for at least a few more nights, but he was strictly a one-night kind of guy. That way feelings never had a chance to get involved.

He'd already shared too much with Alyssa, which should have been the ultimate red flag—but for some reason he found himself not caring.

"I have a room for the night."

"What?" Understandable that she'd be startled, since he hadn't spoken to her since their earlier make-out session.

"I want you to spend the night with me." He couldn't be clearer than that.

"I don't think that's a good idea," she said, her hand tangling in her hair.

His fingers joined hers as he tugged her closer and kissed her, short and sweet, enough to deepen her breathing. "I think it's an excellent idea," he said, not allowing her to look away.

"I don't normally do what we were doing . . ." Her cheeks flamed as she admitted this.

He should stop now. He knew he wouldn't, though.

"Come with me, Alyssa. I promise you won't regret it," he said, using his most persuasive voice.

"What time is it?" she asked.

That threw him off track. What did the time matter? Glancing at his phone, he looked back up. "Eight in the evening. We're early."

"It's New Year's Eve."

"What does that matter?" He was confused.

"We're in New York City on New Year's Eve. I'm going to Times Square." Her tone of voice told him that he could take it or leave it. She hadn't said whether she would go with him to the hotel room, but he was more than happy he'd reserved the penthouse suite at the W Hotel, right on the square.

"That's where the room is. Anyway, there's no way you could get into Times Square at this hour, even if you wanted to—they closed it off early this afternoon. If you want to see the ball drop, your only option is a room with a view . . . and my view is excellent."

Her eyes widened, and still she said nothing, which was making him practically twitch. When she was silent as he helped her gather her carry-on and the two of them stepped from the plane, he would have killed to know her thoughts.

"I've missed my connecting flight, but I really should see if there's another one tonight," she finally said, making his heart thud. She left him standing there as she went to a ticketing agent.

When she came back, she sported a smile on her face. "No flights tonight, and not even a fee for the rebooking. I don't leave till tomorrow morning." With that, she picked her bag back up and began heading toward the exit.

"Do you have bags?" he asked.

"Yes." Without further words, they went to baggage claim. He wanted to demand to know her answer about the hotel room, but he wouldn't beg, so he stood impatiently by her side as the baggage carousel turned.

It was another hour before they managed to get the bags through customs, and neither said a word the entire time. All he wanted to do was get her into his bed. He couldn't possibly make small talk. Not with what he had planned for her this beautiful New Year's.

"Do you want to watch the show, Alyssa?"

Jackson pulled her into his arms and gave her a look that could in no way be misinterpreted, but he wanted her sure before he had her all alone in his hotel room. Holding his breath, he waited for her answer.

008

As Jackson's hands gripped her shoulders, a spark raced through her body. Hunger? Most certainly. But something . . . more. Something that made her want to retreat a step, made her want to shield herself.

Jackson Whitman was a dangerous man. When their gazes collided, she didn't know whether it was the spirit of the impending New Year or the magic of the moment, but suddenly he was leaning forward and she had no desire to escape. Her only desire was this.

Alyssa sank deeper and deeper into Jackson's arms while he continued his expert assault on her lips. His hands glided across her back, and she embraced him tightly. Would one night of pleasure with this man be a good farewell to a crumbling career? Or the finishing touch to a very bad week?

Could she go through with a one-night stand? Could she really finish what they'd started just a few hours earlier? The way she felt right now, yes, she could, so she smiled, lifted her finger to his lips, and ran a long red nail along the moistness that was still clinging from their kiss.

"Are you coming back with me, Alyssa?"

"Yes," she replied, her stomach tightening at what she was doing. If she went down this path, there was no going back. She could either try to get to Times Square on her own, then rush back to the airport for her morning flight, or go with him . . . Hell with it, this was New York City on New Year's Eve. It wasn't as if she'd ever see this man again. She could make a fool of herself and have no regrets.

Jackson moved immediately, taking her out front to where his car and driver waited. The streets would be crowded, traffic impossible to get through for people who wanted to stand around in Times Square, but they'd be at the hotel, a part of this fantastic city on this fantastic night—and they'd be alone.

Alyssa scooted inside the SUV, and though her nerves were unsettled, she still had no desire to back out—until she looked at the man she'd met just half a day earlier. And now some doubts began creeping in, sending alerts to her brain. This could be a serious mistake.

As if knowing her qualms, he reached out and pulled her to him. The second his hands circled her, pulled her on top of his lap, she knew she was right where she wanted to be. His mouth descended and all doubts disappeared.

His hands reached beneath her sweater, scorched her skin as he kissed her with hunger. Her breathing heavy, her blood racing, she was ready to get to that hotel room. Losing all track of time, she was startled when he pulled back. "We're almost there."

Slipping off his lap, she adjusted her clothing, praying no one knew exactly what the two of them had been doing on the long ride to their hotel. Though she knew thousands of others had to be engaged in exactly the same behavior at the exact same time, she was still embarrassed and blushing when they emerged from the vehicle. The crowds pressed in on all sides, but hotel security met them at the car, forming a buffer against the crush.

"After you," Jackson said, and Alyssa walked through the wide glass doors and into the hotel.

"You must have unlimited connections to get this place on New Year's Eve, Jackson," she said, maintaining a poker face.

"The W is the newest addition to Times Square. I reserved ahead just in case any of my family wanted to come."

Checking in took minutes, and then they were riding the elevator to the top floor. She was immediately drawn to the balcony in the beautiful suite, to the noise rushing up to her from the seemingly endless mass of people below. "I can't believe there are over a million people right here."

"I don't get the appeal—why would anyone want to be down in that crowd? Way too many people for my liking. I'll order something for us to eat."

Time was lost as she stood on the balcony, waiting, as so many others were, for that ball to begin its descent in about an hour. Soon Jackson joined her, wrapping a warm blanket around her shoulders, and a waiter followed with their food. He set up a table right there on the balcony, with a white tablecloth gently stirring in the light breeze, candles lit, and plates dressed to perfection. The balcony heater made it bearable to sit there on this freezing cold night. The view made it worth it. It wasn't long until they were alone again.

"Wine?"

"Yes, thank you." She accepted the glass he handed her, then leaned back and sipped the dry wine while looking over the side of the balcony. Nerves seemed to be the only thing she could feel right now.

"What are your hopes for the New Year, Alyssa?"

"To be free," she said with a sigh. The more her reality sank in, the more she realized that was true. But she didn't have to wish, or make a New Year's resolution, because she already was free. The thought made her practically giddy. To be sure, the good wine was a fine contributor to her mood.

"Free from what?" he asked.

"That is something for me to know . . ." She smiled—but she wouldn't tell him everything about her.

"Hmm, you're aware, I take it, that you've been very mysterious tonight," he said with an easy smile before he added, "I love to solve mysteries."

"I don't think you could solve me, Jackson."

"Challenge accepted. I'll give it my best shot."

"You can try," she said, accepting a refill of her wine and feeling more relaxed by the minute.

"I want to make your body sing tonight, Alyssa. It's killing me to wait even one more minute."

"Ha! You must think you're a smooth talker, Jackson."

"And you're good at avoiding what's right in front of us."

"Well, I will say this: my day is ending much better than it began." This night would be her final good-bye to her old life, and then maybe she wouldn't arrive at her new Montana home as innocent as she'd left Texas nine years ago.

"I hope I can take some credit for that," he drawled.

"You get *all* the credit," she said, tossing him what she hoped was a come-hither look.

It must have worked, because sparks flashed in his dangerous brown depths. He set his glass down, then moved closer to her. "I'm going to kiss you again," he whispered, sending a bolt of heat straight to her core.

"Finally," she replied, and the air left her lungs as he reached over and pulled her close.

She knew that if she was going to have any objections, now was the time to express them. Once his lips touched hers, it would all be over.

The countdown began for the ball to drop, and Alyssa missed it all.

. . . four . . . three . . . two . . .

009

The further things went with Alyssa, the deeper Jackson fell. What particularly surprised him was his need to hold her, to caress her, to make this night never end. That should have scared him into stopping.

He didn't do long-term relationships. Hell, he didn't do relationships, period! He just took care of his body's sexual needs. But with Alyssa, something was going wrong.

Or right.

He had to have this woman. Alyssa obviously wanted a hot, sexy night, and so did he. They'd both walk away with no regrets. Slowly, surely, he pulled her into his arms, enjoying the lowering of her eyes, the deepening of her breath. She was turned on; the foreplay on the plane had ensured that. It was time for both of them to forget all about their respective woes and go together to the highest reaches of heaven.

Tilting her chin, he tasted her lips with a flick of his tongue before he captured the bottom one with his teeth and bit down lightly, just enough to make her moan and turn the beautiful pink lip red.

"Jackson," she sighed, sending an ache straight to his groin, his body demanding he take more.

He pulled her against him, letting the balcony rail hold them both. He explored her satin-covered back as he deepened the kiss and discovered every nuance of her mouth, taking what he wanted—and giving back even more. Her hands moved slowly up his arms; her elegant fingers glided across his shirt, leaving a trail of fire everywhere she touched. A groan escaped his throat as he undid the buttons of her blouse, then slowly peeled it downward, off her body, leaving her back bare to his touch.

Pure, flawless silk. He'd known her skin would be soft—known she wouldn't hesitate to give sound to the pleasure she was feeling, not after what they'd shared earlier, not now that they were alone and free to do as they pleased. Now she didn't have to muffle her pleasure. Her cries of passion would only add fuel to the flames burning inside him.

Knowing they needed privacy, and that if he wanted to take her clothes off he would have to get her in a warmer place, he moved them inside, never breaking the connection of their lips as his hands continued to strip the clothes from her body, exposing more and more of her skin to his wandering hands. After unfastening her bra, he pulled back to behold her perfection.

The air caught in his throat as he took in the luscious mounds of her naked breasts, the pink nipples hard, an invitation for his touch. Gliding over the deep curve at her waist, he ran his hands upward, then cupped her in his palms as his thumbs whispered over her peaks.

"Oh, Jackson," she gasped, her head falling back, her breasts thrust forward.

She demanded more, and he was glad to oblige. Squeezing a breast with one hand, he bent his head down, captured her sweet nipple, and suckled, his teeth scraping across the sensitive surface.

Hearing the exquisite sounds of encouragement from deep in her throat, he relished her flavor, moving from one side to the other until both peaks were glistening and well loved.

He needed her lips again. With his hands now around her back, he raised them quickly, clasped her neck, and brought her mouth back to his, leaving her in no doubt that he was pleasuring her, possessing her, owning her.

She grabbed the front of his shirt, and he wanted to complain when her exquisite breasts left his chest, but as she began undoing his buttons, his protests faded. *Yes*. He needed to be skin to skin with her.

He tugged off his cuff links, and the heavy gold flew off, neither of them knowing or caring where. Running her fingers down the insides of his arms, she pushed the offending shirt away, then drew back momentarily with half-closed eyes to take in the sight of his naked chest. A smile tilted the corners of her mouth.

Leaning forward, she kissed his neck before taking her time and exploring him the way he'd been exploring her. He reveled in the feel of her slender hands running across his skin, of her mouth skimming over his chest, her tongue grazing his skin. She kissed his jaw, then circled his lips with her tongue. Her kisses seemed almost hesitant, as if she didn't quite know what she was doing, but he knew that couldn't be right. She was beautiful, confident.

He knew she'd had at least one lover—and doubtless more—and he was sure she had plenty of experience to bring to his bedroom. Needing her in bed *now*, he wrapped his arms around her waist, gripped her luscious behind, and began walking. Gasping, she threw her hands around his neck so she wouldn't fall.

"Bedroom. Now," he growled, barely able to speak because his erection was throbbing so desperately.

"Mmm, good," she said as she pressed closer, the peaks of her breasts rubbing gloriously against his chest.

He strode to the suite's bedroom, set her down at the side of the bed, and stepped back to take in the full view of her as she stood before him in nothing but a gleaming white pair of minuscule panties.

"I have to say this is the best New Year's I can ever remember," he said.

She shifted, apparently embarrassed to be on display. A model could be embarrassed? No. He couldn't allow nerves to intervene in what they were about to do. If she decided to walk out and leave him in this condition, he might very well explode. Still, he knew he couldn't take her if she wasn't sure.

"You're not having second thoughts, are you, Alyssa?"

She paused, and he could swear his heart stopped. "No. Can we . . . um . . . can we just turn off the lights?"

"Why would you want to turn off the lights? You're beautiful and surely you're used to being in the spotlight—after all, you've been a model for some years."

"That's why I hate the lights. I hated being looked at as nothing more than a sex symbol. I want to be looked at as just me, but that hasn't happened in a long time." She shifted on her feet, and he knew he was going to lose her if he wasn't careful.

Without any further hesitation, he moved over and flicked the lamps off, grateful that there was still a glow of light coming in from the hallway.

Jackson undid his slacks as he walked back toward her, and he let them and his briefs fall to the floor. He pulled her back into his arms, his arousal pressing against her and leaving no doubt whatsoever about how much he wanted her. "I want you because you fascinate me, but don't doubt for a minute that you are desirable." She sighed into his mouth as he joined their lips together again, then she ran her hands down his chest and over his stomach. He was practically shaking when she went lower.

"Oh, Jackson, this is nice," she said as she wrapped her fingers around his thick shaft.

"If you keep doing that, we won't get to the fun part," he warned her as her thumb slid across the slick head of his arousal.

"I thought you were more of a man," she taunted, and his muscles locked up.

He would show her a man. With a quick movement, he shifted his arm beneath her knees and lifted her in the air, then laid her down on the bed, quickly covering her body with his.

"Yes, that's exactly what I want," she told him, spreading her legs as she rubbed against his hardness.

He tore her panties away and nearly thrust inside her before he froze, his body shaking with need.

"Protection," he groaned as he stood up and snatched a condom from his wallet. Where was his brain? He'd almost forgotten, and that was a mistake he'd never made before.

Rejoining her at breakneck speed, he sheathed himself while she nibbled on his shoulder. When he ran a finger down her slick folds and it came back coated in her arousal, it was his turn to groan—she was more than ready for him.

Turning so he was lying flush against her, his chest cushioned by her breasts, he positioned himself and felt her heat nearly scorching him. With a quick movement forward, he slid inside—and almost lost the last hold on his control.

She was too tight—he wouldn't last. Her body tensed, and he waited. She was small and he wasn't, so he knew she had to adjust. When she began twisting about beneath him, it was his cue to move—and move he did.

Grabbing the backs of her legs, he settled more fully inside her, pushing in and slowly pulling out of her heat. Within minutes, he was picking up the pace, listening to her moans of pleasure, feeling the pressure build in the movements of her body as he stoked both of their fires higher and higher.

She cried out as her core began convulsing around him, and she pulled him farther inside her, made him give up his struggle to last any longer. His head rolled back as he pumped repeatedly inside the safety of her heat.

Time stopped as he collapsed against her, barely able to take his weight off her as he tried to catch his breath. Normally this would have been the time he'd get up, go to the bathroom, dress, and make it more than clear that it was time for her to go. But he couldn't persuade himself to get out of the warm bed. With her delectable body draped partway over his, they lay there panting, and neither of them said a word for several long moments.

As he drifted off to sleep, Jackson felt a contentment unlike anything he'd ever felt before. His last thought was that he wasn't even close to ready to let this woman go.

WHEN ALYSSA HEARD the soft sounds of Jackson's deepened breathing, she carefully untangled her limbs from his and inched away. He reached for her, and she held still, standing naked by his bed, waiting to see what he'd do. But slumber held him firmly in its grasp, and she was free to leave.

But not free enough to ever forget her fascination with the impressive cut of his muscles, bare for her to see in the light shining through from the hallway. Every inch of her body ached—in the best possible way.

And yet not all of her hurt was good. Surprised by the poignancy of the moment, she was feeling more pain than she'd expected at the sad fact that she'd never see this man again. But there wasn't time to dwell on that. She pulled her clothes back on—well, everything except the ruined panties, which she tucked into a trash can to be thrown away with all the other New Year's trimmings.

After taking only a moment to clean herself up, she collected her purse and slipped from the room. It was four in the morning. The traffic from the New Year's revelers had cleared, and that was a major blessing. It was time to go home. Time to return to being Alyssa Gerard, just a normal woman with no clue what to do with the rest of her life.

Hailing a cab was easy, and just as quickly as she'd slipped into this stranger's life, she slipped out. Alyssa was very proud that she looked back at the hotel only once before it disappeared from view. Using the last of her cash to pay the cabbie, she entered the airport and made her way to her gate.

It was time to start over. And this time she was going to make no mistakes.

010

Why wasn't he smiling? Jackson normally enjoyed a function like tonight's. New York in early March was at last beginning to shed its layer of snow, and even the wintry days were a respite from Montana's frozen beauty. There were a number of women to choose from for an easy night of pleasure, the food was always excellent, and it gave him a chance to catch up with old friends.

But tonight it was taking all of his willpower to stand in the beautiful room, wearing his custom tux, while he sipped a glass of wine. He didn't want to be there, didn't want to fake a smile, and didn't want to talk to anyone. Maybe he should just leave.

"You made it. I thought for sure you'd find an excuse not to be here."

Jackson turned to find Lucas Anderson walking up to him, his beautiful wife, Amy, by his side.

"I tried to get out of it. But my father guilted me," Jackson admitted with a crooked smile.

"Why am I not surprised?" Lucas said with a laugh.

"Because you know me well and know I've been less than social the last couple months. How is the clan in Seattle?"

"Everyone is doing well. My father's here somewhere, but Amy and I are hoping to sneak out early, so we've been staying on the perimeter. He can see that we've made a showing, and then we can escape," Lucas said. "And you've been less than social for a few years, but you seemed to be getting a little better about coming out until a couple of months ago."

"Sometimes a person just has enough," Jackson said. The thing he liked most about Lucas was that he knew his friend wouldn't push the issue, or ask him why he didn't feel like socializing. The last thing he wanted to do was tell a sob story, or try to explain to someone else what he couldn't even explain to himself. "I have a meeting with Congressman Jones and then I'm going to slip out myself. I've been in New York for a week now, and I'm more than ready to return to Montana."

"I know how that is. I'm glad I do a lot less traveling these days."

"I don't know, Lucas. It's nice to get away from home every once in a while," Amy said.

"I'm more than happy to go anywhere as long as you're with me, darling," Lucas said with a brilliant smile for his wife.

Amy laughed. "He's still a smooth talker."

The three of them moved over to the open bar and refilled their drinks, then found a table and sat down.

"The fashion show will be starting soon. I'm hoping to find a new dress," Amy told them.

"Something low cut," Lucas added with a waggle of his eyebrows.

"Would you behave?" Amy said. "This is a black-tie event."

"Yes, Lucas, please behave," Jackson told him with a real smile.

Their table soon filled up, and Jackson joined in with the small talk, but the only saving grace of the evening was the presence of Lucas, someone he actually enjoyed speaking to. Soon the show started, and Jackson had to grit his teeth as model after model walked down the runway, decked out in the newest fashions from Paris.

When the show was coming to a close, a red-haired woman stepped onto the runway in a stunning emerald gown and made her way smoothly down the aisle. The chattering at their table continued, but Jackson tuned them all out as his eyes locked in on the model.

As she drew closer, he let out his breath and felt his stomach knot up. For just a brief moment, he'd thought the woman was Alyssa. It had taken only a second for him to realize his mistake, but just thinking she was in the room with him had made his blood run hot.

It had been *two months* since he'd woken up to find her gone. Instead of the normal relief he should have felt, he'd had the urge to chase after her, demand she come back. He wasn't finished yet.

But after the initial urge, Jackson had told himself it was better this way. She was just a woman he'd met on a plane. They were never going to have more than a night together. That's what he wanted, what he needed.

So why was the sight of a redhead walking down a runway sending pangs of longing through him two months later? Obviously, their night had been a good one. That didn't mean he should still be thinking about her, though.

Jackson shook his head in frustration and focused on the man to his right. What was he saying? When Jackson realized where the conversation had gone, fury rushed through him. It seemed he wasn't the only person who'd noticed the model had looked like Alyssa.

"It was quite tragic, really. Alyssa Gerard was going places," the man said as he lifted his glass and sipped his wine.

"Oh, come on, now," a woman piped in. "Aren't all models doing what she did? I mean, they all sleep their way to the top. They don't care if the man—or woman, for that matter—is married. They just care about their careers."

"She did a show for my company last year. I was impressed with her poise and attitude. She seemed different," another woman said.

"Ha! That's all an act," the first woman stated, making Jackson's temper rise a few degrees.

"I don't think I remember an Alyssa Gerard," Lucas said.

"She was nearing the end of her career," another person remarked.

"Except she did have that cosmetics contract."

"Well, she must not have slept with the right people if it took her so long to land that one."

And Jackson was done. When he stood up so quickly that his chair scooted back several feet behind him, the people at his table went silent, obviously wondering what had antagonized him. Let them wonder.

"Excuse me," he almost growled, then turned and walked away.

He nearly turned around to at least tell Lucas and Amy good-bye, but he couldn't even do that. Not with the black mood that he was in. It was better for all of them if he left without delay.

He hadn't wanted to come, hadn't wanted to socialize with anyone. And now he wasn't even in the mood to meet with the congressman. It could wait. Jackson didn't know why he couldn't get Alyssa from his mind, and didn't know why he'd become so upset when others had spoken ill of her, but he was damned upset.

Once outside the building, he immediately reached into his inside pocket and pulled out one of the cigars he carried, just in case he felt the urge to have a taste of the sweet tobacco when attending one of these events.

"Trying to skip out early?"

Turning, Jackson found himself standing with Joseph Anderson. His father had been friends with Joseph for as long as Jackson could remember. There were times they didn't see Joseph much, and times he was around more often, but Jackson had always liked and respected the man.

The years Jackson had spent in foster care had taught him early not to trust people. His father, Martin, had helped heal him, and Joseph had shown him that there were more people in this world he could trust. Money hadn't corrupted Jackson's father, and it hadn't corrupted Joseph Anderson. They both did great things for many people.

"I'm starting to get a headache," Jackson said as he reached for his lighter.

"Are you going to be rude, boy, and smoke that alone?" Joseph asked with a scowl.

"I wouldn't think of doing that, Joseph," Jackson said with a smile as he reached into his pocket, pulled out another cigar, and handed it over. He was glad he'd run into Joseph, or vice versa—it was hard to remain in a black mood with this man around.

"Mmm, good quality," Joseph said after he accepted Jackson's lighter and took his first puff.

"I don't smoke one very often, so I only get the best," Jackson said.

"What caused that angry look on your face?"

Busted, Jackson thought. There was no way he was telling Joseph anything about Alyssa Gerard. He'd spoken to Joseph's sons, and they were pretty sure their father had quite a bit to do with their sudden desire to marry.

Jackson in no way wanted to be shot by Cupid's arrow. Sure, he was thinking of Alyssa Gerard a little more than he was comfortable with, but that was just a slight infatuation. It would pass.

He ignored the fact that his feelings for the woman hadn't diminished in two months. He knew he was lying to himself—he was desperate to find her, but for that very reason, he knew he couldn't. If he'd really wanted to find the woman, no problem—money had its advantages. So he obviously didn't want to find her, right?

"I'm fine, Joseph. Just can't stand this black-tie

atmosphere," Jackson finally said when he realized he hadn't answered Joseph's question.

"Ah, Jackson, it's nothing more than a song and dance. All the players move in perfect sync together and then they go on their merry way. When you get as old as me, you learn to care about what matters, and just let the other stuff go."

"That's some good advice, Joseph. I'll remember that for next time," Jackson said as he looked out at the busy New York street.

"Are you heading back home?" Joseph asked.

"Yes. I've never liked being in the city for long. I enjoy the fresh air, where I can work for days without seeing another soul. Of course, if I'm in hiding too long, my brothers will hunt me down," Jackson said with a laugh.

"Ha! As well as they should. Family is everything, boy. Don't you be such a hermit that you forget the value of a fine family. I know that there are times I drive my brood crazy, but let me tell you, I would die for any one of them, as they would for me. My Katherine had to stay home this trip and I'm anxious to get back to her," Joseph said in his typical lecturing voice.

"You've been lucky in your marriage, Joseph. Not everyone can say the same," Jackson said almost bitterly.

"Oh, Jackson, don't let one bad experience dictate the rest of your life. You'll find the woman you are meant to be with for eternity, and when you do, you will never let her go."

"I think I'll leave matrimonial bliss to you, Joseph."

"That's what my boys thought, too," Joseph told him with a wink.

The look in Joseph's eyes made Jackson squirm. He didn't want to be on this man's radar. "I had best get going. I've already called my pilot," Jackson lied, feeling a need to flee.

"Hitting a bit too close to home, boy?" Joseph said.

"Of course not," Jackson said, and he stuck out his hand to shake Joseph's. "I look forward to seeing you the next time you visit."

"It won't be long. I've promised your father I'll be there soon." Joseph's words almost sounded like a threat, and Jackson wasn't so sure they weren't.

With a final good-bye, Jackson walked to the sidewalk and hailed a cab. Leaning back, he tried to push thoughts of Alyssa from his mind. By the time he reached the airport, he still hadn't succeeded.

This was utter nonsense. He would forget about the woman, one way or another.

011

"It's been a long time, my old friend."

"I apologize for that," Joseph Anderson replied. "I should have been here sooner." Joseph sat back and enjoyed the view from Martin Whitman's front porch. With spring just beginning to reshape the meadows, the scenery in Sterling was spectacular.

"Yes, you should definitely get out here more often. We can't let so many years escape us again."

"I don't know how the time passes so quickly. It seems like just yesterday that I was proposing to my Katherine, and now my kids are grown and have families of their own. It keeps me very busy," Joseph said with a laugh that erased years from his aging face.

"That's why I asked you to come all this way," Martin said. "I've noticed how your family is flourishing, while my own sons have given me a lot of grief. I thought our family was going to expand when Jackson married and his wife got pregnant. But after Jackson lost Katy and Olivia, he hasn't been the same. I still grieve the loss of my grand-daughter, but I want him to be happy again. I want all my boys to have as full a life as I've been blessed with."

"I agree with you. It's time for your boy to live again. His daughter would want that for him. When I saw him a couple of months ago, he seemed very unhappy. We need to change that."

"He still holds on to the past. I haven't seen a whole lot of happiness in him in a long time. We need to focus on the future," Martin said, a sparkle lighting his eyes. "I need your help in putting the pieces of our quilt back together again."

Joseph perked up instantly. "What can I do?"

Before Martin could speak, a female voice broke in. "My, my, my, if it isn't the infamous Joseph Anderson. Are you slumming it with peasant folk like us, coming all the way out to the backwoods of Montana?" Martin's ten-thousand-square-foot ranch house and his prosperous oil fields wouldn't be considered slumming it in any circles, but he was used to Bethel's dry wit.

Joseph turned toward her with a delighted smile. "You know I've been sporting a broken heart for you all these years, Bethel. That's why I've stayed away."

Bethel Banks chortled as she stepped onto the porch along with her best friends, Eileen Gagnon and Maggie Winchester. The meddling women were lifelong friends of Martin Whitman and Joseph Anderson. "If I thought there was a lick of truth in that statement, I might have to fight Katherine for you, Joseph, but since I know you're over-the-moon in love with your wife, I'll just take the compliment and replay it in my head a few thousand times."

"It's good to see you, Bethel," Joseph said, getting up and giving her a hug. "And it's been years, Eileen and Maggie. You are both still shining beauties." He embraced the women.

"What did we interrupt?" Bethel always got right to the point.

"We were discussing how ornery my boys are," Martin told her. This was a topic he and Bethel had been discussing often.

"Your boys aren't nearly as much of a pain as my granddaughter," Bethel said with a disgusted sigh.

"Now, Bethel, little Sage can't be no trouble at all," Joseph said, remembering a mischievous little redheaded girl in pigtails, with mud on her cheeks and a continually scraped knee.

"That girl isn't so little anymore. She's nearing twenty-five and happy as can be down in California. She's got one year of medical school left, and then I'm hoping to persuade her to take her residency here. It's a mighty fine hospital. I'm enormously proud of her, but it's time for her to come home. I want to live long enough to see my great-grandkids," Bethel grumbled.

"Ha, woman. That tone may work on your grand-daughter, but we know you a lot better than that," Joseph said. "I do agree, however, that it's nice to have little ones filling the halls of an otherwise empty home. Each of my boys has married a fine woman, and I have a large gathering during the holidays now and at any other time I can get them all to the house at once."

Martin leaned forward in his chair. "Then you really must share your secrets, Joseph."

"Well, my old friends, we just have to bring the kids together, and then love does the rest," Joseph said with a twinkle in his eyes. Joseph was growing a little too confident in his matchmaking skills, since he'd yet to have a miss.

"We can give little Sage a bit more time," Martin remarked, "but I think I've spotted a mighty fine match for Jackson. This girl is full of sunshine. For a while I was hoping some sparks would fly between her and Camden, but Camden has his heart set on another woman. He just won't admit it yet."

"Who are you talking about?" Eileen asked.

"For which boy?" Maggie said at the same time.

"For Jackson. He's who we're focused on, right?" Joseph was getting a bit confused.

"Yes. Sorry. First Jackson, then one of the others," Martin said with a chuckle. "Do you know the Gerards?" Martin asked.

"Yes, of course," Bethel replied. "Real nice family, moved in a few miles down the road about six months ago. Texans, I think."

"The father works for me and he's a real good man. Four months ago their daughter joined them here. For a while there, it looked like she was needing someone to mend a hurt heart, but over the last month she's started to get her feet on more solid ground, and she's a real pleasure to speak to. She works down at the Country Saloon."

"Oh, yes, I've met her. Quite a delightful girl," Eileen said. She leaned forward to join in with their plans.

"I just need to get her and Jackson together and I know the fireworks will start. He keeps himself so busy with work that he rarely experiences the joys of life anymore," Martin said.

"How do we get him there to see her?" Joseph asked. He loved matchmaking, but he knew a fundamental rule—you had to get the kids together if you wanted to make fireworks start.

"That part's easy, if I may say so myself. I *bought* the Country Saloon," Martin said. "And I put it in Jackson's name. It's his birthday present." He sat back and lit a cigar, mighty proud of himself.

"Well, my old friend, you didn't need me at all," Joseph said, chuckling. "You're doing just fine on your own as a matchmaker."

"I can get them in a room together, but I don't know what to do next," Martin said.

Joseph beamed. "Now, that's where I can help you out . . ."

The five friends spent the better part of the afternoon plotting away. By the time their children knew what hit them, it would be too late for them to fight. Jackson Whitman and Alyssa Gerard were about to be struck with Cupid's arrow. Well, if Cupid came in the form of five meddling elders.

012

Jackson sat outside the Country Saloon, gritting his teeth. What in the hell had his father been thinking? Sure, Martin's intentions might have been noble, but Jackson didn't want to run some out-of-the-way bar. He was too busy to mess with something so . . . simple and yet time-consuming.

When he'd tried to give the business back to his father, the old man had gotten all choked up, as if his feelings were badly hurt, and Jackson, of course, had backed down immediately. He was only kidding, he told his dad. Oh, yes, he absolutely *loved* the gift.

So now he was stuck with ownership of a bar and grill he wanted no part of. He'd promised to meet his family there half an hour ago, or he wouldn't have even bothered coming tonight. All he was going to do was hire a manager or two and tell them to do whatever they wanted with the place. Hell, for all he cared, someone could light a match and have a big bonfire. He'd even provide the hot dogs and marshmallows.

Since that was unlikely to happen—and as former fire chief, he was rarely amused by the idea of arson—Jackson would make an appearance every once in a while so his father knew he appreciated the ridiculous gift, but other than that, he couldn't possibly care any less about the place.

Still, when he saw a full parking lot and a group of people laughing as they moved arm in arm toward the entrance, he couldn't help but be a little impressed. When he opened the front door, he was blasted with music and ear-shattering laughter. A familiar-looking band was onstage, but he couldn't quite place them. Impressive, he thought; the local talent must have improved greatly.

Though the old log cabin wasn't much to look at from the outside, it had atmosphere and a surprising amount of space. It housed a bar, some dining tables, and a ridiculously large dance floor. That made no business sense. How could a bar and grill so far out in the boonies attract enough people to fill it?

Come to think of it, though, his brothers had mentioned going in quite often. If Jackson hadn't been filled with grief for so long, he might have joined them occasionally. Maybe it was time for him to get out more than just when he was searching for his next one-night stand.

"There you are, Jackson. Took you long enough," Camden said as he grabbed his brother's arm and guided him through the large crowd.

"I think the building has exceeded its limit of allowed occupants," Jackson said. He had to raise his voice to be heard.

"Ahh, the fire chief is sitting over at table nine with the guys. If he ain't saying anything, we'll just let them have some fun," Camden replied.

Jackson walked over to a table full of firefighters. "What are you doing down here when you have a beautiful wife at home?" he asked Hawk Winchester.

"We just finished with a wreck down on Market Lane. Besides, Natalie is out with the girls tonight."

"You let her out of your sight? From what I heard, the two of you are disgustingly clingy."

"Ha! How could you hear anything when you never get out?"

Jackson almost flinched. As if knowing he'd hit a sore spot, Hawk smiled before adding with a wink, "Don't knock it until you've tried it."

"Yeah, right. There's no way I'm taking that walk down the aisle *ever* again."

"Don't give up, Jackson. I thought the same thing until I met Natalie. Now I can't imagine life without her."

This was getting too serious, so Jackson shook Hawk's hand companionably before walking away with Camden.

"There'd better not be another fire alarm tonight," Jackson told his brother.

"I hope not, 'cause half the department's here," Camden said as they reached their overcrowded table. "Of course, it's not every day that Little Big Town comes through."

"Ahh, that's why they sounded so familiar. I'd just thought the local talent had improved while I was traveling. What's such a big band doing here? This doesn't seem to be a typical place for them to play."

"Lots of bands stop in. It's the best-kept secret around these parts," Camden told him.

A sense of unease, an uncomfortable tightness, began to spread in Jackson's chest. A place that attracted big talent would also attract reporters. He wanted nothing to do with reporters. That persistent woman—what was her magazine's name?—was constantly trying to get him to do an interview for a story about eligible bachelors. He knew that was an excuse. She really wanted to dig into his past, his ex-wife and child, and why he'd dropped everything and became a business shark instead of fire chief. It was none of her damn business.

"Don't worry, son," Martin said as he stood up and shook Jackson's hand. "They don't announce they're coming, and they aren't here every night. They just like stopping by and playing at a place where they're basically left alone."

Jackson laughed. "Are you a mind reader now, Dad?"

"A father knows what his boy's thinking."

"Hey, Jackson, I can't believe you dragged your sorry ass out for once."

"Look who's talking, Spence. You're hardly ever home anymore, what with your being a big-shot Seattle doctor now," Jackson fired back at his brother.

"Yeah, but I get homesick every once in a while," his brother replied.

"All right, quit the bickering," their brother Camden said with a grin. "Let's get drunk."

"That's the best advice I've heard all night," Jackson said. "Where's the waitress?"

"Taking care of this crowd," Martin said.

Jackson looked out at the throng and couldn't help but smile when he spotted his baby brother, Michael, out on the dance floor doing a poor two-step with a brunette who appeared to have drunk a bit too much.

"She'll be back in a minute," Camden said, so Jackson swiped his brother's untouched beer and took a swig.

"Good thing I didn't want that one," Camden growled.

"I'm saving you from getting plastered and embarrassing yourself," Jackson said, then took another long swallow.

"Always thinking of others," Camden said.

"Are you boys ready for another round?"

All the noise in the room ceased—at least for Jackson.

He knew that voice. He hadn't forgotten it in four months, though he'd tried like hell to put her from his mind. Slowly, as if someone had pushed the slow-motion button on an invisible remote, he twisted his head around.

And his eyes connected with the pair of pale blue eyes that had been haunting his dreams for months. Her mouth was turned up in a smile, and she seemed happy, content. She didn't look as if she'd lost a single night of sleep over him and their night together.

Then their eyes met and her smile vanished. If Jackson had thought this was some trick of hers, that maybe she'd found out about who he was and had followed him back to Montana, her reaction would have proved him wrong. She looked shell-shocked.

Jackson didn't know how long the two of them faced off, the sizzling connection between them undeniable, but when a passing patron bumped his shoulder hard and the music came back on at the same time, he managed to tune back in to his surroundings.

"Whoa, want to quit ogling poor Alyssa?" Camden said with a deep laugh.

Not funny. Jackson shot him a glare that had Camden's eyebrows almost hitting the ceiling.

"Do you two know each other?" Martin asked.

His dad was always so damn observant, Jackson thought wryly.

"Um . . . no," Alyssa said quickly. She turned her eyes away from Jackson and focused on Martin, and a semblance of a smile brightened her countenance again. Her upturned lips could easily convince most men of anything she wanted them to believe, but though she had let her guard down for only a second, Martin hadn't missed the way she'd looked before the shutters went up.

"Yes," Jackson said in open contradiction. There was no way in hell he was going to allow her to deny their night together. He hadn't forgotten it, and he wasn't going to let her forget about it, either.

"Well, is it yes or no?" Martin grinned as his eyes bounced between the two of them.

"We met on a flight from Paris," Jackson said before she was able to deny knowing him again.

After taking a moment to compose herself and her feelings, Alyssa ratcheted up her smile. "Oh, yeah, I forgot all about that." She looked at him sidewise and laughed oh so sweetly. "What was your name again?"

Either she was one hell of an actress or she *had* forgotten all about him. Jackson considered neither option acceptable. He felt incredibly annoyed, though he didn't understand why—he should just be grateful she didn't seem to want anything from him. He hadn't planned on anything more. He most definitely hadn't planned on ever seeing this woman again.

So why did his muscles tense and his heart race? Why did he want to haul her to the nearest bed—hell, a freaking table would do—and remind her of exactly *who* he was? She'd certainly known his name back in New York. She'd screamed it as he played her body like a piano.

Before he could control the animal impulse, Jackson was sliding his chair back and gripping her arm. "We'll be right back," he told his family, then tugged Alyssa after him. The two of them were going to talk—*right now.*

Alyssa tried to dig her feet in. "I can't leave. I have a full bar."

"It can wait, sweetheart," he practically growled.

"No it can't," she said, and she struggled against his hold.

"I'm the owner. I said *it can wait,*" he snapped, then lifted her up, cradled her against his chest, and walked out the front door.

013

Oh no, oh no, oh no. Panic? A heart attack? Alyssa couldn't diagnose her condition as Jackson caught her up in his arms. The shock at his aggressiveness had left her temporarily speechless. But once they made it outside and he set her down in front of a large red truck, she found her voice.

"Who in the *hell* do you think you are? You can't go around kidnapping people like that!" she yelled as she raised her index finger and stabbed him in the chest as hard as she could.

He ignored her remarks. "When did you get here?" he asked, his breathing heavy as he stood tensely in front of her, blocking any chance she might have at escaping before they finished this conversation.

"You *knew* I was in the middle of a change in careers, and I *never* told you where I was from or where I was going!" she shouted. "Why? Because I didn't want to see you again after that night. So why don't you pretend like we didn't just see each other and scurry off to wherever you normally go?"

"A career change? And this is what you're choosing to do?"

"I don't appreciate that tone of voice. There's nothing wrong with serving a hungry crowd," she snapped.

"Yeah, but something tells me you aren't the waitress type."

"I don't like to be pegged. And I most assuredly don't want to talk to you about my personal life or my choices. Make yourself scarce. I have a job to do." She tried to edge around him.

"I don't think so, Alyssa. I asked a question and I expect you to answer it." He grabbed her arm and tugged her back to him, then boxed her in against the truck.

"Just like you kept pushing when we were on the plane? You don't know when to quit."

"You're certainly right about that."

"You can't force me to speak to you, Jackson!"

"Ah, so you do remember my name," he said, a satisfied smile appearing on his lips.

"I . . . I . . . Just go away." This was not good. She was starting to unravel, and that was no way to deal with a man like Jackson.

"Not gonna happen. I want to know what you're doing here."

"Do you own this town?"

"No, but I do own the bar you're working in," he said—quite smugly, in her opinion.

She was really hoping she'd heard him wrong.

There was no way he could be her boss. She'd been working at the Country Saloon for nearly four months, and she hadn't seen a sign of him.

"No . . ." Alyssa's anger started to diminish as worry set in.

"Oh, yes, Alyssa. Just took ownership last week. I wasn't too thrilled about it, but now . . ." He paused to crank up a deadly smile. "I'm beginning to grow attached."

"We had *one* night together, Jackson. One. That doesn't mean we're going to be friends. It doesn't mean we even have to talk to each other. As a matter of fact, you said you didn't do commitment. Top all of that off with my being drunk that night and doing something completely out of character, and let's just say that it was fun, but then be on our way." She hadn't been drunk, but she'd rather *he* thought she had been.

As he stood in front of her, so tall and broad, his smile not faltering in the slightest, she began to chew on her lip. What was she going to do now? This was a nightmare. Sterling was a small town, a town where everyone knew everyone else.

The nearest serious city, Billings, was only thirty or forty minutes away, but that was a lot of commuting, especially when the roads were covered in snow. Granted, people did it all the time, but she was deathly afraid of traveling over ice.

Besides, her car wasn't up to driving in bad conditions.

She could get a place in Billings, but she was trying to save as much as she could before she had to take time off from work. Of all the people in this huge country . . . Yeah, just her luck. The one man she'd had an insane fling with happened to be from the unbelievably small town her parents had decided to move to.

"Are you going to give me the silent treatment now, Alyssa?" No one could have missed the irritation etched on Jackson's face.

"I wasn't the one who demanded a conversation. I have nothing to say to you—nothing at all. Why don't you take a hint and disappear?"

She felt horrible when he flinched. But she must have imagined it, because just as quickly as she thought she'd stabbed him with her words, he grinned at her and winked.

Bastard.

"Fine, Alyssa. You want to pretend we didn't add to the New Year's fireworks, be my guest," he said as he released her from the cage of his arms.

She wasn't sure whether he was letting her leave or not, but she took a tentative step away, and then another, and then picked up her pace when he didn't follow.

"We could make those fireworks again—one

more time," he called out after her, and she hated herself a little when her stomach turned cartwheels at the thought.

After rushing back inside, she made a beeline for the tiny bathroom in the private employees' lounge. She could hardly fit in the thing, but at least she wouldn't have to worry about customers knocking on the door and yelling about how badly they had to go.

She barely made it in time to empty the pathetic contents of her stomach. When she was finished, she washed her face, then slid down a wall and sat on the floor with her head in her hands.

This wasn't in her plans. None of this. How could her life have changed so drastically in one freaking day? She'd already lost her job, her money, her pride. And then she'd decided to sleep with a complete stranger. He'd worn protection, dammit! How could she have gotten pregnant?

None of that mattered. The reality was that she was carrying Jackson's baby, and within another month at most she wasn't going to be able to hide that scandalous fact.

Her fingers moved down over the tiny bump that was just beginning to show on her lower abdomen. No one knew for now, not even her parents. Or did they? She was beginning to think that her mother might actually suspect more than she was letting on.

Alyssa had thought she was being quiet and careful when her morning sickness had made its grand appearance, but lately, her mom seemed to be trying to force-feed her. At least Alyssa hadn't been called on it, and she was grateful for that. She didn't know how to explain herself just yet.

Her parents were going to be so disappointed in her. She'd left home thinking she was going to be a star, and instead she'd come back with nothing— okay, that wasn't true. She'd come home with an unplanned pregnancy.

And now the father, whom she'd never planned to see again, who was supposed to be a stranger passing in the night, was here, right in the middle of butt-freaking nowhere. And he'd made what he thought about marriage and families more than clear during their night together. He said he wouldn't bring another child into this world. His ex-wife had done a number on him.

When the dizziness passed, she sat back and thought about her dumb luck of finding him at the Whitman table . . . Then she froze and felt the color drain from her. She crawled back to the toilet and heaved again.

Jackson *Whitman*.

His family and the Winchester family controlled Sterling in its entirety. Yes, it was a small town, but the Whitmans' bank accounts were anything but small. Their oil plant provided employment for most of the small town and surrounding areas. Hell, her own father worked for them. As she sat there thinking, more unhappy details rushed in, overwhelming her.

Camden and Michael came to the bar often, and they loved to talk. She knew now that Spence was the doctor who rarely made it back home. That made Jackson . . . How could she not have put the pieces together? They'd said their brother bought and sold businesses, that he was reclusive. They'd said he was a good man, but he'd been hurt and they didn't think he'd ever wed again. Yes, they loved their brother, but they also thought he could be quite cold.

Also, not only was his family ridiculously wealthy, but he had enough of his own money to buy a small country. He owned properties all around the world. Most important, he'd lost his baby, and it had destroyed him. Would he want their child? Would he think it was a replacement for the one he'd lost?

"Alyssa? Are you in there?"

She turned as the knob on the door spun. Crap! She'd forgotten to lock it. The door opened, and one of her coworkers, Samantha, towered over her with concerned eyes.

"Are you okay? What's wrong? The fire chief is

out there. Do you want me to get him?" Samantha kneeled down and felt Alyssa's forehead.

Alyssa attempted a smile. "I'm fine, Sam. I'm sorry I took so long. I think I just ate something that disagreed with me, but I feel better now."

Samantha didn't look convinced. "I can see if Ben can come in and cover the rest of your shift."

"No. Just give me two more minutes, okay?" Alyssa pleaded. She couldn't go home. She needed the hours. Like all waiters and waitresses, she couldn't survive without the tips a packed bar would bring.

"If you're sure," Samantha said.

"I promise you I'm fine. Can you take over the Whitman table for me, though? You'll get all the tips."

"Are you kidding me? Of course I will, but are you sure you want to give that up?"

"Yes. Please. I'll take the slower side, since I'm not feeling that well."

"I saw that the reclusive Jackson Whitman came in tonight. Oh, my gosh, that man is beyond hot. I've wanted him for what seems like forever. It's a good thing that I don't ever plan on having children, though, because I heard he was brutal in trying to get custody of his daughter during the divorce. I bet if his ex hadn't died, Jackson would have made her life hell," Samantha said, loving nothing more than a morsel of juicy gossip.

"What do you mean brutal?" The fear in Alyssa's stomach made her feel like heaving again.

"He wanted his daughter, and nothing was going to stop him from getting her. When she died, he went slightly crazy. I seriously don't care, though. He's hot enough to make crazy work," Samantha said.

"Why would you be crushing on such a ruthless guy?" Alyssa asked.

"Have you not *looked* at the man?" Samantha was eyeing Alyssa like she was insane.

"Looks aren't everything, Samantha."

"Oh, please," Samantha drawled with a wave of her hand. "Looks are about eighty percent of it. Plus, the man is supposed to be a god in the bedroom."

Yeah, Alyssa could testify to that, not that she would ever in a million years share that information with Samantha. "Well, you better get out there and get some good tips," she said instead, needing this conversation to be over.

"Okay, I'm not going to fight you." Samantha beamed at her before rushing out. The Whitmans tipped like royalty. Everyone fought for their table, and the other members of the waitstaff were obviously jealous that the family seemed to prefer Alyssa. It really bit to give up those tips, but the farther she was from Jackson, the better. Maybe her luck would turn and he'd be gone when she came back out.

When she finally dredged up enough energy to rise to her feet and return to the circus in the saloon, she saw that her luck wouldn't win any prizes. Jackson was standing at the bar, and his eyes collided with hers.

Double damn!

Donning her best fake smile, Alyssa spent the rest of the night working her tables, staying as far from Jackson and the other Whitmans as she possibly could. Camden and Michael threw some questioning looks her way, but she just breezed by, apologizing that she had to switch tables and telling them she was terribly busy.

They weren't buying it any more than Jackson was.

After hanging out for a few drinks, the band left, and then the crowd began to thin out. Alyssa watched the clock, hoping she could get off her feet by 2 a.m. She'd worked a double shift, her stomach was rumbling, and she wanted nothing more than to crawl into bed, shut her eyes, and forget all about this miserable day.

But the saloon's patrons had other ideas, and at last call several people were still inside. Much to Alyssa's relief, however, the Whitmans had left. At least she was finished dealing with Jackson for the night.

Or so she thought.

014

Jackson paced the parking lot, his ears pricking up every time the front doors opened and closed. Everyone and her dog seemed to be coming out of the place, except for Alyssa.

Her answers hadn't satisfied him, and when she'd returned from the back room earlier that evening, after an absence so long he'd been ready to charge back there and find her, she'd looked pale. He hadn't intended to upset her—he just wanted to talk. Hell if he knew why.

But this woman was the first person to spark his interest in a long time, and he hoped to see where it led. No, it wasn't going to result in a happily ever after, but if the two of them could burn some sheets for a week or maybe even a month, how would that hurt anyone?

There was no ring on her finger, and no boyfriend had shown up at the bar—not that a boyfriend would stop him. Jackson couldn't see what the negative was if they saw each other just a few more times.

He obviously needed at least one more night

in her arms; that had to be why he couldn't seem to forget about her. It had nothing to do with her personality—he didn't know her. Sure, they had talked most of the night and shared a few laughs, and they'd made some pretty spectacular love. But that hardly made her special. It had to be all in his head. If he could just bed her again, prove to himself that it wasn't as great as he remembered, then he'd get over this ridiculous obsession.

When the door opened again, he nearly hollered in frustration.

"Oh, hi, Jackson," Samantha said as she sauntered over to him. "What are you doing out here? Having car trouble?"

The sultry look in her doe eyes screamed *Bed me.* He was tempted to kiss her, to see whether he could feel even a tenth of the spark that he'd felt from just holding Alyssa's hand.

But as soon as the thought breezed across his mind, it dissipated into the wind. He'd known Samantha all his life, and he knew he didn't desire her. The only woman in that category was a sassy blond-haired, blue-eyed waitress who didn't want to give him even the wrong time of day.

"I'm waiting to talk to Alyssa," he said, letting Samantha know he wasn't on the market.

Samantha made a moue of disappointment before she gained control over her features. "She should be out soon," she replied, then ran a finger down his arm. "If you get lonely, call me," she said, and with one last heated look over her shoulder, walked away.

He didn't bother turning to watch the sway of her hips, although he was sure she was putting on quite a show. That, to be sure, Jackson was used to. It all boiled down to the same thing—he had something they wanted, whether it was his body or his wallet. He kept both in damn fine shape. But Jackson just wasn't for sale right now. Alyssa, and only Alyssa, was his current target. She'd certainly brought him plenty of pleasure, and not only in bed. He found it oddly exhilarating to be waiting for her, chasing after her.

He'd never had to do anything like that in his lifetime. When he wanted a woman, she said yes; that's just how it had always been. Then he'd gotten involved with Katy while he was a sophomore in college. They'd wed right after graduation, and hell began as soon as the honeymoon ended.

What a fool he'd been. He wouldn't be manipulated by a woman again, at least not as far as to put a wedding ring on her finger. As for heating the sheets, however . . . that was a completely different matter. He'd have to be made of stone to give that up, which he certainly wasn't. Okay, a few parts of him—one in particular—were pretty darn hard.

The lights over the entrance went dark and the large wooden doors opened a final time. Alyssa walked outside with Cody, the cook, at her side.

"Night, Alyssa. Drive safe," Cody said before jogging over to his truck and jumping inside. Not waiting for Alyssa to get into her car, the man drove off without glancing around the semidark parking lot. Irritation boiled up inside Jackson's stomach.

What kind of man took off like that and left a woman alone in an empty lot? Jackson would be having a chat with Cody first thing tomorrow.

Dammit! He hadn't wanted to get involved with this place, but now that he knew Alyssa worked there, he had no choice. Well, okay, he did have a choice, but he needed to follow this through, figure out what it was about her that had thrown him so off balance.

Her smile haunted him, the touch of vulnerability she'd tried so valiantly to hide. Those were the images that popped into his mind when he thought of her and their night. And then, of course, the vision of her lying beneath him as he sank inside her—how she'd writhed beneath him and moaned.

Jackson preferred the greedy, self-absorbed women who buzzed around him like flies around a jam jar. They were easy, and they were easy to forget. But the woman walking toward him was the exact opposite.

She was the girl next door. The one he would have built a tree house with as a child, the one who would have been right there playing cops and robbers with him. This girl, standing before him in all her womanhood, so feminine, so real, had a hold on him that he couldn't shake.

"Hard night?" he asked, and she screamed and dropped her purse.

"What are you doing? Trying to give me a heart attack?" She squatted down and began picking up the scattered contents of her purse.

"You shouldn't have been left here alone, Alyssa. Your coworker should have waited to make sure your car would start," Jackson replied as he bent down and began helping her. When he picked up a prescription bottle, she snatched it from his hand and tucked it safely back inside her large tote with a look of panic in her eyes.

What the hell was in that bottle?

"Are you hungry?" he asked. When she looked at him as if he'd lost his mind, he figured she was probably right. Wasn't he essentially stalking her?

"No," she said, but her stomach rumbled loud and clear in the early morning quiet.

"Sounds to me like you are," he countered with an obvious grin.

Alyssa glared at him. "I'll have something when I get home."

"Why don't we drive out to the truck stop? It's not too far away."

"Look, I don't like being a mean person, Jackson, I really don't, but I'm just *not* interested in starting something up with you. Believe it or not, having one-night stands isn't something I typically do, and I would rather forget all about our night together. I don't have a whole heck of a lot of pleasant memories from that time," she told him with a tired sigh.

"What happened to make it so bad?"

"You're not listening," she said, her eyes narrowing as she stood up.

"Fine. You don't want to see me. Is it because there's nothing between us?"

"Yes. I feel nothing." Now he had her.

"Liar."

His softly spoken word infuriated her. "Look, Jackson, contrary to popular belief, you aren't all that. Take a hint and save some pride." She turned away, done with the conversation.

"One kiss. If there's nothing, I leave you alone."

He waited to see if she'd take the bait.

She turned around and stared at him contemptuously. "I'm not going to play such a childish game."

He could barely see her, let alone the way she looked at him, in the shadows cast over the parking lot by its lone light. He would have to fix that.

"Fine. Then I'll come back tomorrow . . . and the

next day . . . and the next . . ." He leaned against his truck with his arms crossed, looking as if time were nothing of consequence to him.

"You're being ridiculous," she said, but he could see that he was breaking her down.

He knew he should just leave, let this go. But he couldn't seem to force himself to do that. Sad. "It's up to you, Alyssa. One kiss and I go away . . . If there's no spark, that is."

That was the catch. They both knew there were going to be sparks. He could almost see her doing calculations in her head. He waited. He'd issued the challenge, and it was now up to her whether she'd accept it or not. His hardening body prayed that she would. He'd sleep much better if he could have just one taste.

Who in the hell was he kidding? One taste was never going to do it. Maybe he should take back the challenge, because it would clearly leave him even harder than he already was. Even though the kiss was sure to start a five-alarm fire, she wasn't about to climb into his bed. Not tonight, at least. No, he couldn't back down, because he knew he'd get her there soon.

"One kiss?" she asked, taking a tentative step toward him.

Jackson would never admit how much his heart was thundering from that small step, her tiny concession. "Yep. One kiss."

"And then you'll go away?"

She was now only a couple of feet away, and her chest was already heaving. Good sign—she was having a hard time controlling her breathing. He was having just as difficult a time controlling his, and he hoped to hell that she didn't notice.

"Yes. I go away . . . *if* there aren't any sparks."

She paused, only a foot away now. He could feel her hot breath on his face as she gazed up at him. One kiss. He had to keep his word. If he tried to push it beyond that, there'd be no chance she would trust him later. He'd have to sing some old church hymns to keep his word, but even if he died just a little, he would keep it.

"Fine," she said, and she tipped back her head and closed her eyes tight while her fists were clenched at her sides.

Jackson found himself almost laughing. The image immediately brought to mind Missy Elwood from the second grade. They'd decided to kiss and she'd looked just like that, horrified that her lips were about to touch a boy's.

He leaned forward and whispered in her ear: "Breathe."

The shudder that passed through her body brought him immense satisfaction. He let his lips trail across her cheek in a soft caress before he reached her mouth. Taking his time, he ran his tongue along her cold lips, the taste of her going straight to his groin, lighting a fire unlike anything he'd ever felt. *Oh, this was good.*

Keep it light, he reminded himself, though his body screamed at him to pull her roughly into his arms. Cupping her neck and stroking her smooth skin with his thumbs, he tilted her head and nibbled gently on her bottom lip.

With a sigh, she opened her lips, and when he immediately deepened the kiss, invading the soft recesses of her mouth, heat shot through his body. But finding himself nearly at the point of no return, he pulled his head back, kissed her one more time on the corner of her mouth, and ran his thumbs across her cheeks. He waited for her eyes to open.

Her lashes fluttered, and then he was looking into the shadowed gaze of her soft blue eyes, smoky with the same passion he was feeling.

"I'd say that's a hell of a lot of spark," he murmured, pulling her against him for just a second so she could feel what that kiss had done to him.

Her eyes widened as she tried to catch her breath, but she didn't say a word. After they shared a few moments of heavy breathing, she turned and walked to her car, unlocked it, and sat down.

"Drive carefully, Alyssa. I'll see you tomorrow," he called out as he leaned against his bumper and watched her start the car.

She wouldn't even look at him. They both knew that he could easily prove how much power he wielded over her. She seemed defeated for a moment, which, to his surprise, caused him pain. When he was about to apologize, she turned her head and rolled down her window.

"I've had better, Jackson Whitman," she told him coolly, and he couldn't help the grin that flashed across his face.

There was the fighter he liked. "I'll just have to keep on practicing," he said before she drove off. Jackson liked having the last word.

"You can try," she said, then peeled out of the parking lot.

Hot damn! She'd gotten the last word after all. Jackson was whistling when he jumped into his truck and drove away from the bar's parking lot. Life had just gotten a heck of a lot more interesting.

". . . and then he just grabs me in front of my customers and hauls me outside like he owns me!"

Alyssa was wearing tracks in her parents' living room carpet as she paced back and forth. After getting home the night before, she hadn't slept for more than a few hours, and of course those hours she had slept, she'd been tossing and turning because her dreams had been filled with Jackson.

Yes, she'd thought about him endlessly over the last four months. How could she not when he'd left her with a permanent reminder of their night together?

"What's his name?" her mother asked calmly.

"That doesn't matter. I met him once, a long time ago. We flew together," she said, leaving out the night of hot sex after that flight. "We weren't supposed to ever see each other again, and then, of all the places in the world, he comes strolling into the place I work. But that's not bad enough—oh, no. He then has to manhandle me and try to force me to talk to him. Well, I didn't want to talk to him."

Teresa couldn't hide her smile. "It sounds like you're pretty riled up over this."

"Wouldn't you be riled up?" Alyssa asked, stopping with her hands on her hips.

"It doesn't sound like you're upset, darling. It sounds as if you might be mad because you like this man."

"Mom! That is a horrible thing to say. I don't like him. I don't even know him. He's . . . he's . . . he's just a pig," she spit out.

"Okay, then don't talk to him again."

"Ugh, I hate when you try to make it sound so black-and-white. It's not like I didn't think of that. I told him I didn't want to talk to him, and then . . . and then . . . well, what happened then doesn't matter," she said, barely stopping herself from telling her mom about the bone-melting kiss he'd tricked her into.

There was no way she was telling her mother she'd been foolish enough to fall for his kissing taunt. She'd wanted that kiss—badly—which meant she should have run as fast as she could have the other way.

It was just that she knew he wouldn't go away if she didn't kiss him. Well, to be fair, she knew he wouldn't go away either way. So why had she kissed him? Had she really thought there would be no sparks? Of course not. The sparks from New

Year's were still rushing through her and it had been four months.

That kiss had awakened her in ways she had not wanted to be awakened. This man was danger, and she couldn't have anything to do with him. She wanted desperately to place her hand on her stomach and barely managed to stop herself. It wasn't time to tell her parents. She knew she didn't have much longer, but she just didn't have the courage to tell them yet.

Alyssa knew it was really wrong not to tell Jackson about the baby now that he was here, and her only excuse was fear. Yes, he wanted her. He'd made that more than clear, but she knew he'd been married and knew he didn't want to go through that again.

He'd also lost a child. Alyssa couldn't allow him to try to replace his lost child with her baby. And Jackson was wealthy, more than wealthy. He could buy anything and everything he'd ever wanted. Wouldn't that mean if he took her to court, they would see it in the child's best interest to be raised by him? That would just destroy her, and it would be completely wrong to treat her child that way.

Oh, this was so complicated. If she could just go to bed, pull the covers up over her head, and hide away for the next five months, she would do exactly that. But that's what a coward would do, and Alyssa was anything but a coward.

There was a knock on the door and Alyssa turned to stare at it, but could make no further move. Even her basic motor functions seemed to be compromised at the moment.

"Don't worry, I've got it," Teresa said, chuckling again and setting Alyssa's teeth on edge.

Bethel Banks walked in. "Sorry we're late, Teresa. I had to wait for my special Chex mix to finish crisping up," Bethel said.

"It's well worth the wait. I've tried to get Bethel to give me the recipe, but she won't budge," Eileen said with a stern look at her friend.

Maggie came in last. "Oh, these two have been bickering the entire ride."

"You're not late at all. I was just talking with my daughter. I've got the game table all set up," Teresa told the newcomers.

"Oh, wonderful," Bethel said, then went up to Alyssa and enveloped her in a warm embrace. "Alyssa, you look more and more beautiful each time I see you."

Alyssa smiled as the women fluttered in—until she arrived in Sterling, she had never met three little old ladies quite like these. The first time Alyssa had met the "troublesome threesome," as they were known around town, she'd been overwhelmed. Small-town people seemed a lot more friendly—and nosy—than their big-city peers.

It hadn't taken her long to fall in love with the women, though. They were just so kind, and they remembered everything. Alyssa had once been eating a cookies-and-cream candy bar and mentioned how much she loved white chocolate, and the next time the three had come over, they brought her a gift basket filled with various chocolates. It was something so simple but so sweet.

Since her hormones were all out of whack, the gesture had made her cry, instantly concerning the three women. She'd assured them she was fine, just very tired from her late shift at the bar.

"Are you going to play with us today, Alyssa?" Eileen asked.

Once in a while, Alyssa would join them in their weekly card game—she actually enjoyed herself. Although they all looked like sweet women, they were definitely sharks when it came to card games.

"I wish I could, but I have a double shift today," she said, her feet already aching at the prospect.

"You work too much, darling," Maggie remarked. "How are you supposed to find a good man and settle down if you're always hanging out in a bar with a bunch of drunks?"

"I'm not looking for a man. I like my life just the way it is," Alyssa told the women for what felt like the hundredth time. Was their mission to ensure that Sterling contained no single adults over the age of eighteen?

"Oh, pish posh, we all need someone," Bethel said.

Alyssa had heard this same response just as many times. "You ladies have a wonderful time. I need to shower and get ready for work."

She made her escape up to her room to gather clothes. She knew the four women downstairs would immediately start picking apart her love life, or lack thereof, the minute she was out of hearing range.

Before Jackson Whitman had stepped back into her life, she'd been just fine as a single woman, even a pregnant single woman. Seeing him again had all sorts of thoughts rushing through her, though. That wasn't a good thing. She'd best avoid him at all cost—not that she thought he would make that an easy task for her. After all, he was now her boss. Great.

With a sigh, she climbed into the shower and hoped she would have the strength to get through the day. If she just took it a day at a time, she'd be fine, wouldn't she? One minute, one hour, one day at a time. That was her new motto.

016

"Your usual?"

Jackson glanced up with a winning smile, and before he could even say yes, Alyssa was setting down a Diet Coke and a bowl of chips and salsa. She took her pad and pen out of her apron pocket and said, "The special tonight is beef lasagna with a side salad and fresh baked bread." Nine times out of ten he just got the special.

"Sounds good. Why don't you join me?"

"Sorry, just had dinner." Alyssa turned on her heel and headed back to the kitchen.

Their routine had been the same for two weeks now. He came in, ordered dinner, tried to get her to join him, and got turned down.

He figured he should be over the constant rejection, but her attitude made him more determined than ever to win her over. He'd have abandoned his mission as hopeless if he'd seen disgust or even boredom in her eyes.

But that's not what he saw at all. The sparks between them could have set off an entire New Year's fireworks display. Her breathing was always a little shallow when he was near, and her heart was obviously racing. She was just as attracted to him as he was to her, but for some reason, she'd put up a "No Trespassing" sign, and nothing he'd done so far had managed to breach her barriers.

But, hey, he didn't give up, and he had all the time in the world.

He sat in the corner of the bar with his laptop and allowed the music and ambience to give him welcome relief from the monotony of the reports he had to read. Working at the saloon rather than at his house had the added benefit of letting him watch Alyssa bring him drinks and snacks. She'd tried to send other waitresses when there was more than one on the job, but he'd quashed that right away, saying he wanted only her to serve him.

What choice did she have but to obey? After all, he owned the place and she was his employee, making the situation even more tense. And it wasn't like jobs were easy to find in small towns like Sterling. He didn't like pressing his advantage to get her attention, but he had to use what he could right now. At first she'd been almost hostile. The last two days, however, she'd switched her game, and she was now plastering on a smile.

It was about time for them to speak alone. Damn! He couldn't wait.

"I see you're stalking the pretty waitress again," Camden said with a laugh as he invited himself to sit across from Jackson and have dinner.

"It's not stalking. I told you how we met. Anyway, I'm trying to work here, Cam," Jackson growled. He hardly wanted his brother to witness his failure with Alyssa again, not after that first night.

"Yeah, it's a lot of work to watch a girl's ass as she walks away."

"You're a pig."

"Yep. Haven't tried to convince anyone otherwise."

"Hey, Camden, you drinking your usual?" Alyssa asked with a much friendlier smile for his brother than she'd given him. That didn't please Jackson in the least.

"You know what I like, beautiful," Camden said with a wink.

Even though Jackson knew his brother was laying it on thick to get a rise out of him, he still felt the urge to give the guy a shiner. Yeah, sure, that would really impress Alyssa. Camden was safe for now.

"Hmm. I thought for sure that would rile you," Cam said, leaning back and getting comfortable. He wasn't planning to leave anytime soon. "You must be mellowing in your old age."

With a defeated sigh, Jackson closed the lid of his laptop and ate a tortilla chip.

"I know you're trying to piss me off. I also know you won't go after her . . . since she's already claimed," Jackson said.

"Interesting," Camden said, helping himself to a chip.

"There's nothing interesting about it. I like her, she likes me. Case closed."

"From where I sit, there's not a whole lot of love going on between the two of you."

"That's just what it looks like, Camden. She's fighting the attraction. As soon as I can figure out why, then we'll get on to the next phase."

"Here you are." Alyssa appeared with Cam's drink, then took his order. "I'll be right back with your salads. How's your difficult case going?"

"Not as well as I'd like," Cam said.

How did she even know which cases his brother had? When had they become so chummy? Jackson didn't like this at all.

"Sorry, Cam," Alyssa said. "But we both know you'll pull it off. You always do."

The pat she gave Cam's shoulder made smoke come out of Jackson's ears. Worse, she turned and walked away without even glancing in his direction.

"When the hell did you two become so close?" Jackson asked.

"Look, I really was just teasing you earlier, Jackson. I have zero interest in Alyssa. She's a client of mine and we've become friends over the last few months. I come up here a lot, especially after a really trying day at the office. She's a good listener. But I'd better warn you that a lot of the locals come in just to talk to her, and several of them *do* have crushes."

"Who's she suing?" Jackson wanted information now.

"You know I can't discuss that. Come on, bro, don't be dense. If she wants to share with you, she will. I can tell you this: she's gone through some hell of her own and she's strong. I respect her."

"I know she's strong, Cam. What I can't figure out is what in the hell I'm doing. I don't want a permanent relationship, but I can't get her out of my head. If I could just have one more night with her—just one—I think I would be cured." Jackson huffed in frustration.

"My deluded brother . . . She's not a disease you have to find a cure for," Cam told him. "She's a woman, a damn *fine* woman at that, and maybe you like her a hell of a lot more than you're letting on. Just go for it. Tell her how you feel. Maybe honesty would be the best policy at this point."

Alyssa dropped their salads off without saying a word and then disappeared again to tend to her other customers. It was a fairly slow night and Jackson hoped she'd get out of there at a decent hour, giving them a chance to talk without interruptions.

"I can't just lay it out there. I don't even know what it is I'm feeling," Jackson said.

"You know. You just don't want to analyze it. You've been alone a long time—you've punished yourself for long enough. Don't give up because it feels like you aren't allowed to be happy. Your daughter wouldn't want this."

Jackson's face blanched at the mention of his daughter. "I can't. If I move on, it will be like she never existed. If I find happiness, then I am living while my daughter isn't allowed to."

Cam's response was gentle but insistent. "She was a baby. It was tragic, but it's been five years, Jackson. It's time."

"That's not what this is about, dammit. It's not about my daughter. This is about Alyssa and me. The two of us made a connection on New Year's Eve, and I just want to see if we can do it again."

"And I think you're delusional. I don't care how spectacular the sex is. You don't go this crazy over a woman unless there's something more to it than incredible chemistry."

"I don't know her enough for it to be anything more than chemistry," Jackson insisted.

"Are you trying to convince me of that or yourself?"

The two of them paused when Alyssa came back with the rest of their dinner. Jackson couldn't turn his mind off, couldn't quit thinking of Alyssa, but he did know that he was going to wait until she got off work, because tonight they were having a real conversation, even if he had to kidnap her to do it.

"It's probably just because she's playing hard to get," Jackson said as he chewed without tasting his food.

"I don't think it's that, either, bro. You would have lost interest by now if that were the case. I think you have some real feelings for this girl, and you're lying to yourself about it so you can tell yourself that it's okay. Let go of the past and try to grab some happiness," Cam said.

Jackson was silent after that, not knowing what to think. Camden finished his meal and left soon after, allowing Jackson to become lost in his work. Now that he had an established routine, he was able to read more than one line of a report in Alyssa's presence. That was good. He quickly tuned out everything around him and entered the world of finance, the world he'd managed to create—where the players were controlled by him and the one with the most money and power always won.

017

Alyssa watched Camden leave and then let out a sigh of relief as Jackson got lost in his laptop. He might not have known it, but the hunger burning in his eyes, his constant but gentle pursuit, and his almost daily presence at the saloon were wearing her down.

He was so damn handsome—too good-looking to be let out on an unsuspecting public. And there was such mystery to him, which made her want to dive right in and learn everything about what made him tick. Add to that the most spectacular sex a woman could even begin to imagine, and she was hooked.

But she couldn't let herself get infatuated with the man. She had to keep her distance. The second he found out about their child, the game would change. He wouldn't be interested in taking her back to his bed. He'd only want to plant her in front of a judge and take away her baby. With his past and his wealth, that was the only thing that made sense.

She wouldn't allow that to happen. Although she wasn't exactly ready to be a mother, especially a single one, the longer this pregnancy went on, the more attached she grew to the tiny being growing inside her. She wouldn't let Jackson use her baby to replace the one he'd lost.

"Alyssa, some of the customers have requested that you play the piano."

Alyssa turned to find Kevin, their head bartender, standing there at the waitstaff's station.

"You know I hate doing that," she said, but it wasn't true. She loved to play the piano. It just made her self-conscious when Jackson was in the room.

"Aw, come on. We're slow tonight," he pleaded.

"Fine."

Her heart beating erratically, Alyssa sat down at the piano and played a number from memory. It didn't take her long to forget where she was as her fingers glided effortlessly over the keys, and her eyes took on a dreamy look. She played one of her favorite ballads from *The Phantom of the Opera*, "Angel of Music." As she finished, she opened her eyes and saw Jackson standing near the bar, a look of wonder on his face, and she felt a blush fill her cheeks.

Enough with the sad ballads. Next she began "Bennie and the Jets," and soon the remaining customers in the bar sang along. Alyssa found herself beaming as she belted out the words in the chorus.

"She's got electric boots, a magic suit . . ."

As she finished, she raised her head and saw that Jackson hadn't moved from the bar, his gaze intense as he watched her. Her fingers trembled as she stood up. This connection between them had to be a fluke. It couldn't be real.

Jackson pushed off the bar and moved toward her. "I could listen to you play all night, Alyssa."

"I enjoy the piano." Obviously. What a lame statement.

"You were meant to play. We need to try a duet." His eyes were intense and his double meaning was clear.

"I think our time for duets has passed, Jackson."

"It sure as hell doesn't feel that way to me."

"Jackson . . ." His name came out almost as a sigh, and she saw shutters close over his eyes seconds before he turned and strode away. Was she making a mistake to keep throwing him over? He wasn't backing down, and the attraction between the two of them remained undeniable.

More confused than ever, Alyssa took a few minutes alone in the back room before returning to the bar. Tonight, for some reason, she had to struggle harder than usual to keep her distance from the man, and he was making it more and more clear that he wasn't letting go of their one night together.

Even worse, she was beginning to wonder what was wrong with her. Why wasn't she accepting the offer he was extending to her? Just then she felt a stirring in her stomach and her hand trailed downward. It was as if the baby she carried was reminding her of his or her presence.

Oh, yeah. Jackson had no clue that he was going to be a father. That was a pretty dang good reason to keep her distance.

After another hour of slow business, it was time for Alyssa to leave. There was no need to keep a cook, two waitresses, a bartender, and a busser on the clock when there were fewer than a dozen customers, most of whom were sitting at the round bar in the middle of the place.

She'd normally be the one to stay—she needed all the hours she could get—but Samantha had a few of her favorites there tonight, and Alyssa's feet were aching, so she bowed out gracefully.

"I'm walking you out," Cody said when he saw her grab her coat.

"You know you don't have to do that every time I leave," Alyssa said with a chuckle. She seemed to have her own personal bodyguard all of a sudden.

"Yes I do. Mr. Whitman will hang me by my toes if I don't. Besides, he's right. A woman should always be accompanied outside," he said as he offered his arm.

Wanting to be irritated, but deciding Cody's behavior was quite sweet, Alyssa accepted his arm.

"We're sneaking out the back door. I want to be long gone before Mr. Whitman tries to corner me again," Alyssa said, feeling like a thief in the night.

"No prob, Alyssa." Cody opened the back door, and the crisp spring air came as welcome relief to the stuffiness inside the saloon.

"Thanks for doing this, Cody. You're a sweetheart," she said as they reached her car. She leaned over and gave him a kiss on the cheek.

"I like to, Alyssa. Besides, it gives me an excuse to have a smoke and play a game of Flappy Bird," he said with an almost childlike grin.

Before Alyssa could launch into an antismoking lecture, they were interrupted by one of her regulars, who was a little drunker than usual. "Where are you off to in such a hurry? I was waiting for you to come back with my next beer when Samantha showed up instead."

Hank stood at just under six feet, with graying hair and dull gray eyes that looked a little too vicious when he'd had too much to drink. His normally happy smile was gone, and in its place was a leer that creeped her out. It wasn't helping that they were standing in a nearly empty parking lot.

At least the lighting was better now that Jackson had fixed it. She had to admit he was true to his word—when he said he was going to get something done, he did it, and did it fast.

"I'm off work now, Hank. Do you have a ride home?" she asked, hoping and praying that he wasn't going to get behind the wheel of a car.

"Nah, I can drive just fine. Come on, I'll show you." He stepped a little too close.

"Why don't you let me call you a cab?" she said as she reached into her purse.

"I said I don't need one," he snapped, swatting the cell phone out of her hand.

Alyssa's temper flared as she stooped to retrieve the phone. "That was rude, Hank. And I hope it didn't break." It wasn't as if she could afford to replace it.

"I'll buy you a new one if it did, sweet thing," he said, and he reached for her.

"What are you doing, Hank?" This wasn't the man she'd gotten to know in the last few months. He must have drunk way too much tonight.

"I don't think you should do that, Hank." Cody moved closer to Alyssa.

"What in the hell do you think you're doing, kid? This is adult business. Stay out of it." Hank pushed against Cody's chest, making him stumble back.

Hank turned, snaked an arm around Alyssa's back, and pulled her up against his chest. "Fine. If you don't want me to drive, you can just sit in my truck with me," he said, and then leaned down and kissed her.

Alyssa pulled back and screamed. She wasn't

just pissed now, she was downright frightened. The man was beyond intoxicated, and she was clearly the next thing on his menu.

"Leave her alone," Cody yelled as he rushed back and tugged fruitlessly against Hank's beefy arm.

"You're like a pesky little fly," Hank growled. He released his hold on Alyssa so he could grab Cody by his shirtfront.

"Don't!" Alyssa screamed, but it was too late. Hank pulled back his free hand and slammed his fist into poor Cody's face. Blood immediately began pouring from the young man's nose and mouth as he slumped to the ground.

"You're disgusting, Hank." Flinging herself at him, Alyssa scratched his face.

"Now it's your turn," Hank said. He restrained her hands easily and dragged her to his truck.

Alyssa screamed again as he wrenched open the passenger door and tried to shove her inside. She wasn't getting into that truck. If she did, she knew it would be all over.

"Shut up and get inside," Hank roared, and he backhanded her so hard in the face that she went flying to the ground. Her head instantly began pulsing. She reached up to her face and wiped away blood.

Not even caring that her head hurt, or that blood was oozing from her mouth, Alyssa's hand immediately went to her stomach. A slight cramp had her worried. It wasn't bad, but she knew if Hank got his hands on her again, she might not be able to protect her unborn child.

"Get up!" Hank hollered.

He grabbed her hair and yanked, trying to drag her to her feet. Her eyes firmly shut, Alyssa locked herself into a ball and hoped to heaven that he'd give up. With her head pounding and her scalp aching, she couldn't concentrate on fighting him. Tears stung her eyes.

When he let go of her hair, she cringed, waiting for the next blow. But it didn't come. Instead, she heard a groan and then what sounded like snapping twigs.

"You worthless son of a bitch! How dare you assault a woman!"

Alyssa opened her eyes and looked over to see Jackson's fist slamming into Hank's jaw. The man dropped, then lay on the ground in a heap.

"You broke my arm," he whined.

"I should break a lot more." But instead of following through on that, Jackson dashed over to Alyssa. "Are you okay?" he asked, then shook his head. "Of course you're not okay. I'm sorry I didn't get out here sooner. I only just found out you left."

A moan caught his attention, and that's when he saw Cody. "Ah, Alyssa, you *and* the kid? That bastard better get some major jail time for this." Jackson grabbed his cell phone and dialed the sheriff.

"Send an ambulance, too," he said before disconnecting the call.

"Where do you hurt, Alyssa?" he asked as he felt her arms and legs.

"My . . . my head is pounding, but I think I'm fine. Please check on Cody. He got hit hard."

"Dammit! *You* got hit hard, too. You're going to have a black eye and a bruised cheek. I want the paramedics to check you."

"I'm fine. Please, please check Cody," she insisted. She felt a stirring in her stomach and knew her baby was okay. A couple of Tylenol and her head would be all right. She hoped the same could be said about Cody.

"He's fine, I'm sure. I'm more worried about you," Jackson said, though he looked over at the boy as if torn.

"Cody . . ." she insisted, and Jackson let out a frustrated breath.

Several people came out of the bar at that moment, then froze at what they saw. "See how Cody's doing," Jackson ordered, and they ran over to the kid. "He's not alone now."

Alyssa watched as Cody began to stir. "I tried to protect her," Cody choked out as blood sprayed from his mouth.

"That's right, Cody. You tried. You did good," someone assured Cody.

Alyssa sagged with relief when Cody spoke. He was going to be just fine. She began to tremble as the reality of the situation settled in. This could have been so much worse. Sure, she and Cody would both feel a bit of pain, but it didn't look as if there would be major injuries.

When the ambulance pulled up, one man rushed to Cody and one moved over to Alyssa. "Where do you hurt, ma'am?" the paramedic asked after he kneeled down and began taking her pulse.

"My head is throbbing, but I'm sure I just need Tylenol," she said shakily, then looked over at Jackson, who wasn't going anywhere. She needed them to check the baby, but she didn't want to say it in front of him. Still, she couldn't risk her baby's health just to keep her secret. "Please make sure my baby is okay," she practically whispered, refusing to look in Jackson's eyes. She was hoping he wouldn't hear, but there was no way that was possible, not with how close he was to her.

The paramedic did an exam on her and, after about ten minutes, said everything sounded good. They could take her to the hospital if she wanted, but if she would rather go to her regular physician in the morning, that would probably be fine.

"I'll go to my doctor tomorrow," she said, still not looking at Jackson.

What was going to happen next? Fear now overwhelmed her, but at least it made her physical pain less acute. The ambulance finally departed after Cody refused to go with them, and the sheriff took statements from her and Cody and then arrested a groaning Hank, Alyssa found herself sitting on Jackson's tailgate, wondering what she was going to say next.

"We have some serious talking to do, Alyssa," Jackson said, his brows furrowed.

"I'm so tired, Jackson. I really just need to sleep," she pleaded. Now was not the time. She had to regroup.

Before he could say anything else, Alyssa watched headlights approach and sagged with relief when her father's truck pulled up. Her parents jumped from the cab and rushed over to her.

"What happened? Samantha phoned and said someone attacked you."

"I'm okay, Mom, but I want to go home," Alyssa said as she climbed down from the tailgate.

"Of course, darling. We'll talk after you've rested."

Jackson wasn't able to say a word as her parents led her to her father's truck. She knew she had to tell him something, but for right now she had a reprieve. And she needed that time, because she had no idea what her next move was going to be.

018

Alyssa awoke the next afternoon to find herself alone at last. Her mother had been hovering since the night before, then through the drive to the doctor's office and back that morning, but she still hadn't questioned Alyssa on the pregnancy. That showed how worried her mom must be.

What must her parents be thinking? Tears filled her eyes. She'd done this all wrong. She'd done everything wrong. She should have talked to them, told them what was happening in her life. Instead, it took a beating for her to confide in them just the smallest amount. She'd had to admit her pregnancy, but she wasn't ready to admit who the father was.

The baby was okay. That was all that really mattered. Her shame and embarrassment shouldn't factor into any of this. She rubbed the small bump in her lower abdomen. The baby was a part of her, and she would do whatever it took to keep the fetus safe until he or she was ready for this big world.

Little slivers of light stole through the closed blinds of her bedroom, telling her it must still be day. Hearing a noise, she turned to find her mom walking into her room, carrying a tray.

"Your coloring is looking better already, Alyssa." After getting her daughter and the tray settled nicely, Teresa sat down in the chair she'd slept in the night before.

"I'm sorry, Mama. I . . . just didn't know how to tell you," Alyssa said, fighting back tears as she finally said the words she should have said last night, should have said in the car earlier.

"You know better than that. You can tell me anything. I would have been thrilled to find out I was going to be a grandmother, whether you're married or not. I love you—you know that." Teresa took her hand and a tear fell down her soft cheek.

"I just didn't want you to be ashamed of me," Alyssa said as she fiddled with her fork.

"Nothing you could ever do would make me feel that way. You're my baby girl and I love you more than you could ever know. Until you have a baby of your own you won't fully understand that kind of love—but it appears you're well on your way to knowing the worry a mother feels when all is not right with her child."

"I'm pregnant and not married. I didn't know how to tell you."

"Do you speak to the father? Is he taking responsibility? Is it that ex-manager of yours?" Of course her mom would ask the most difficult question for her to answer.

"It's . . . uh . . . complicated, but it's not my old manager," Alyssa said.

"It can't be that complicated, baby girl," said her father, who walked through the door and joined them. "He either does the right thing or he's not a real man."

"Not everything is so black-and-white, Daddy."

"It sure is," Donald said. "He either wants to take care of his baby or he wants to run and hide and pretend it didn't happen—keep his head buried in the sand. I can't imagine you would be in the company of a man who would shirk his responsibilities."

"You're the perfect man, Daddy. No one could ever measure up to you." Alyssa knew her dad was one of a kind, and her mother had been blessed to find him. Not everyone was so lucky.

"I just know what's right and what's wrong," he said, brushing off her compliment as usual—he'd never been good at accepting praise.

"I know you do. I just really don't want to talk about the father right now." She knew it was unfair of her to ask them to remain in the dark, but she was so confused right now.

"We won't push you," Teresa said, then looked down at Alyssa's tray. "You need to eat your lunch, darling. When you're done, I'll help you get cleaned up." She stood and kissed her daughter on the forehead.

When they left her alone, of course her thoughts returned to Jackson. She hadn't spoken to him since the previous night when she'd left him standing in that parking lot. She wasn't a good liar, and she feared she'd end up blurting out to him that he was the baby's father.

If she knew him better, knew that he wouldn't try to take her child, she would be more than willing to share the responsibility of the baby with him. She wasn't a fool. She knew how difficult it was going to be to raise this child on her own.

But what if she told him and he decided he didn't need her at all? Yes, he desired her. That was more than obvious, but desire did not equal love. It wasn't like she was in love with him, either. She'd had one night with him, one fantastic night, and then she hadn't seen him again for months.

Sure, he'd been with her almost every day for the last two weeks, but he'd also made it more than clear that he was around because he wanted her in his bed and nothing more. Passion would fade. It always did—*always*. Unfortunately, she hadn't forgotten even a minute of their night together. Even months later, her impulsive night with Jackson had left her with an ache in her body that refused to go away.

When nighttime hit, she was grateful to feel herself drifting off toward sleep. At least that meant a few hours that she didn't have to worry, didn't have to make decisions. But such freedom would inevitably end too soon. One thing she knew for sure was that Jackson would come to her. She hoped she knew what to say when he did.

019

Pacing the long front deck of Alyssa's parents' house, Jackson felt as if he'd need to be admitted to the nearest hospital if somebody didn't answer the door, and soon. He'd barely managed to get any sleep the past two nights, and he wanted some answers.

How was Alyssa feeling? Was she going to the doctor? When had she gotten pregnant? Was there a man in her life? Why hadn't she said something sooner to him? What was the big secret? If there was someone in her life, he sure as hell hadn't met him, and Jackson had been around Alyssa nearly every day since he'd discovered she was in Sterling.

"Yes?" Jackson stopped and turned as he realized the door had opened and her parents were both there staring at him a bit skeptically. He must look slightly crazy, his hair mussed from the number of times he'd run his hands through it, dark circles beneath his eyes, and his clothes thrown on quickly, without his usual care.

"I want to see Alyssa," he said, hoping he didn't sound crazy, too.

"How do you know our daughter?" her father asked.

"We met months ago . . . and she works for me now, but there's more to it. It's . . . uh . . ." He didn't want to lie to the two of them, but he didn't know how to finish that sentence, because he really didn't know what was going on between him and Alyssa.

Her father looked at him for several long assessing seconds. "Donald Gerard," he finally said, sticking out his hand. "And this is my wife, Teresa."

"Jackson Whitman," Jackson answered, too tense to say anything else.

"Are you one of Martin's boys?"

Of course they knew the name. Everyone in Sterling, and half of Billings, knew the Whitman name, since his family was the largest employer in the town.

"Yes, sir, I am," Jackson replied.

Her father continued looking at him, obviously trying to size up the young man. Jackson didn't know what the verdict was going to be, but one way or another he was getting into this house to see Alyssa. He'd been the first one on the scene. He'd been the one to hold her when she'd been knocked to the ground. He had to see her, had to assure himself that she was fine. And he had to get some answers about the baby she carried.

"You can come in," her father said just when

Jackson was figuring the man wouldn't speak again. "I work for your dad. Your father is a fine man."

"Yes, he is," Jackson said, but he had to grit his teeth. He didn't want to make small talk about his father; he wanted to see Alyssa.

"Well, then, I guess it would be okay for you to visit."

Jackson thanked her parents and then went up the stairs after they told him her door was the second on the left. Stopping before he entered the room, he took a deep breath. He needed to be calm before speaking to her. For that matter, he didn't understand why he was so upset. Sure, he'd watched that asshole pull on her hair, and had seen the blood on her face. He would be concerned about anyone who'd gone through something like that. But what he was feeling was beyond concern. Jackson just couldn't figure out why.

Enough of this. Her door was open, so he stepped up to it and then felt his stomach churn when he saw how pale she looked. When she turned and saw him standing there, her eyes widened, but no words came out.

He walked slowly to her bed and took a seat in the chair her mother must have been warming earlier. Then, carefully, he picked up her hand. "Are you feeling any better?"

Her fingers trembled against his, but she didn't

pull them away. "I'm just scared, but I'm not hurting anymore."

"Everything will be fine. Hank is in jail, where hopefully he'll stay for a while. He was cursing at everyone the other night, but the next morning was a whole other matter. He couldn't believe what he'd done. It doesn't excuse his behavior, but I think he'll stay far away from you. My dad is friends with the judge, and I think he's going to have to take mandatory rehab."

"That's good to hear," she said. "Some people just shouldn't drink."

"I should have had security out in the parking lot. I've already called, and starting last night, there is a guard on every night shift."

"Jackson, this is in no way your fault. I've worked there four months and nothing like this has happened before. Hank just got out of hand . . ." She trailed off at the gleam in his eyes. It was obvious there would be no changing his mind about this.

Jackson sat there a few moments longer, debating whether or not to mention the baby. She just looked so fragile right now, that he didn't want to upset her. But he needed to know what was going on.

"Is the baby's father still in your life?" he blurted out. What if the guy came through those doors now? Jackson wanted Alyssa desperately, but he'd bow out if she was in love with another man and having the guy's child. It was the right thing to do. But he hoped to heaven the man wasn't in the picture, though he didn't want to think about how selfish that made him.

She gaped at him, and Jackson held his breath. It looked as if she didn't even want to talk about the guy. That meant he was long gone, right?

"Um, no. He's not a part of my life," she finally said, her cheeks turning pink.

"He's a fool, Alyssa. A real fool. I wouldn't leave your side if you were carrying my child."

"I thought you said you would never marry again, Jackson."

"What does marriage have to do with it?"

"So, if you got a woman pregnant, you would do . . . what?"

Jackson squirmed in his seat. It wasn't something he'd ever thought about. He didn't plan on getting a woman pregnant. He always used protection, so it was a moot point, wasn't it? She was silent, though, waiting for his answer.

"I don't know," he said. "I just wouldn't get someone pregnant."

Alyssa let out a sad sigh. "Not everything is that simple, Jackson."

"Well, is he stepping up or not? If he made a baby with you, he should be here."

She shifted nervously. "I don't want to talk about it," she said, her voice just above a whisper.

"This isn't something that goes away just because you don't want to talk about it."

"I can take care of myself, Jackson. I've been doing it for a long time." She clearly didn't like his patronizing attitude. She wasn't a weak female and she didn't want him to think she was.

"Yes, of course you can. But it's not easy to be a single mother." He paused, then something inside him seemed to blossom and he sat up a bit straighter. "I'll take care of you, Alyssa." He was almost as shocked as she was when he said those words.

"What are you talking about?" she asked, her eyes narrowing.

Hell, even he didn't know what he was talking about. How was he going to explain it to her? What he *should* be doing was backing out of her room and running as far as he could. His fascination with her should have stopped the moment he found out she was pregnant.

"You need to be taken care of. I can't seem to stop thinking about you, wanting you, so really, it's a simple solution," he said, as if that solved all their problems. A lightbulb seemed to have flashed on in his brain.

He wanted her desperately, with a passion that bordered on obsession. She was pregnant. It wasn't easy to go through a pregnancy alone. He would take care of her through the pregnancy, through the birth, and then . . . and then, he was sure by that time, he'd be ready to let her go.

He wouldn't have to feel any guilt over it, because he could tell himself that he'd done a good thing, that he'd stepped in when she was most vulnerable, when she needed him most. It wasn't as if he'd be the only one getting something out of the . . . relationship. Fear lodged in his throat when he even thought of that word, but he gulped it down. He knew that if he left now, he'd regret it.

"You're an ass, Jackson. Just when I think you're starting to show some hint of a real person inside that thick skin you wear, you say something like that."

Now he was confused. "What's wrong with admitting that I still want you? This is the perfect solution. I get what I want and so do you." He smiled, thinking he'd just had a marvelous epiphany.

"Do pregnant women turn you on?" she asked scornfully.

"*You* turn me on."

"And please tell me how I'm getting what I want. I would love to hear your thoughts on this one."

"I'll provide for you financially. Make sure you stay healthy. Take care of you."

The more he spoke, the more he seemed to feel that his plan was already set in stone.

"What if I don't want you, Jackson? What if there's someone else?"

"I don't care who the biological father is, Alyssa. He's obviously gone and doesn't seem to be coming back, so let me step in. We both win."

"Wow. And please tell me exactly what you think we should do?"

"Whatever it takes," he said, his eyes intense.

"Jackson, I don't—"

"Don't worry about answering me right now, Alyssa. You need to give your body time to heal. That's enough on your plate. I'll deal with everything else."

"I don't want you dealing with anything, Jackson!"

It was obvious he was upsetting her, which was the last thing he wanted to do. "I'm sorry. I'll go, but please tell me you'll at least think about my offer," he said, gripping her hand firmly as he looked into her frightened eyes.

"I need to rest, Jackson. I saw my doctor this morning, and he told me I need to be on complete bed rest for a few days just to be safe, and to assure the baby inside that it's still a safe environment, even after being knocked around a little."

"I'll let you rest. Just—just tell me this is something you'll think about."

"What do you want me to think about? I want to

be real clear on this, Jackson. Are you asking me to be your mistress? Your pregnant mistress?"

Now he was the one who paused. When she put it like that, it made him sound like a real ass. Was that what he was asking of her? "I wouldn't put it that way."

"Then tell me how you would put it," she said.

"I want to take care of you." The words came out almost weak, as if he knew it didn't hold up.

"I can't even think right now, I'm so tired. Fine. If you aren't going to answer me, and aren't going to leave, then I'm ignoring you."

With that, she turned over, leaving him to face her back, and then she closed her eyes. Jackson knew the chances of her falling asleep with him sitting there were unlikely, but he couldn't seem to make himself get up and leave. When a few minutes later her breathing deepened and she did fall asleep, he smiled slightly. She wasn't as uncomfortable around him as she said she was. Moving to the other side of her bed, so he could look into her face, he couldn't help but brush back the soft blond strands of hair that were covering her eyes, emotion clogging his throat.

She had to believe he was the lowest of the low. Then, as he considered the sort of man he'd been over the last five years, he flinched. He probably deserved any unpleasant thing she thought of him, and a whole lot worse. He knew he was hardened and cynical, but he couldn't help it. Life had made him that way. She was carrying another man's baby. He should leave, never look back.

While he continued battling whatever it was he was feeling, her parents stepped through the doorway. They approached the bed and stood next to Jackson, gazing upon their daughter.

"She's always been a fighter," Teresa whispered, a tender smile on her face.

"Yes, she has," Donald said.

"She certainly leaves an impression," Jackson told them. "All I've witnessed so far is her strength. I hope to get to know her a whole lot better."

"She needs good people in her life. There have been some who didn't have her best interests at heart," Teresa said, laying her hand on Jackson's shoulder. He wasn't sure if it was a warning or a blessing. He didn't know what he wanted it to be.

"Are you the father?" Donald asked bluntly.

"No. But I can take care of her," Jackson replied.

"What kind of man would leave her alone in this condition?" Donald asked. "You'd better not be playing games with her, especially not when she's so vulnerable."

"It's all a little complicated, sir. Your daughter is . . ." Jackson waited for the right word to form on his tongue.

"She's stubborn as hell and thinks she can do it all on her own," Donald said. "Look what that thinking caused. She could have lost the baby her mother and I didn't even know about until we were driving her home the other night." He spoke again after a brief pause. "What are your intentions with my daughter?"

Damn! Jackson really didn't know how to answer that question. Yes, he wanted her in his bed—that hadn't changed—and yes, he was willing to take care of her to help him reach that goal. But if he said that he wanted to bed the man's daughter, he was sure Donald would throw him through the second-floor window. And he'd deserve the harsh meeting with the pavement he'd receive.

"I hope to have a relationship with her." What sort of relationship, he couldn't say.

"Well, she didn't mention you once in the last two days," Donald said, not taking his eyes from Jackson's face.

"Alyssa and I have something. I know that for sure," he said.

"We'll see about that," Donald said, his eyes narrowing.

"That's all any of us can do," Jackson said, not breaking eye contact. He wouldn't show her father weakness, or he'd surely never be allowed to step foot in their house again.

"Alyssa needs to rest." Donald didn't say anything more and Jackson recognized the polite dismissal. He nodded his head and departed. He didn't want to; he wanted to take a stand and refuse to go, but that wasn't the kind of first impression he wanted to give Alyssa's parents.

Jackson was more confused than ever as he walked from their house and made his way to his truck. And as he drove away, he grew even more confused—there was no fear inside him, no regrets for what he'd offered. All he felt was fear that she wouldn't accept. He really wanted her to take him up on his offer.

Hell, maybe he should leave her completely alone until he could figure out what he was thinking. But as he parked in his driveway, he leaned his head against the steering wheel and groaned. He wasn't going anywhere—maybe not ever.

020

"Good morning, Alyssa."

Her parents were traitors! Alyssa stared at Jackson as he came through her door holding a box of chocolates and a beautiful bouquet of spring flowers. Why hadn't they given her a warning or asked her if she was okay with receiving visitors? Probably because the man could talk a saint into sinning. He was smooth. Too smooth for her to outwit.

She'd made no decision on what to say to him, or what not to say to him, and it was too early in the morning for her to try to keep her thoughts straight, let alone her words. He'd easily be able to talk her into anything if she wasn't careful.

She went for distant politeness. "Morning, Jackson. You didn't need to come back here. I'm fine." Show strength and he wouldn't ask any more questions, right?

"We never finished our discussion, so you must have known I'd be back." He stepped forward to hand her the chocolates and then set the flowers on her dresser.

"I should refuse to take these, but I have a weakness for chocolate, especially lately," she said as she opened the box and took one out, biting into the soft treat. "Thanks."

"Are you feeling better today?"

"Wow. We're both being so polite. It's almost like someone has died," she said, too tired to keep up this game.

"If you'd rather I get right to it, then why don't you answer a simple question," he said, sitting far too close to her.

"What?" she asked when he was silent for too long.

"Why didn't you tell me you were pregnant?"

That stopped her for a heartbeat. Then her brow furrowed as she looked at him. "I don't see why I should have. It's none of your business."

"I have been trying to get you into my bed for the past couple of weeks. Your being pregnant definitely is a factor," he said.

"I have been more than clear that I don't want to get back into your bed, Jackson."

"And I have been more than clear that I think you're lying to me. And until I feel otherwise, I'm not backing away."

"So it's all about you and your feelings? I have no say in any of this? You'll just camp out in my parents' house because *you're* not satisfied with what I'm telling you? If Martin weren't your father, I'd say you had a lousy upbringing."

He flinched. "Let's leave my upbringing out of this."

"Fine. Let's leave my pregnancy out of this."

"All your fancy footwork isn't going to change my mind, Alyssa. I want you to be honest with me. I want you, period."

The guy confused the heck out of her. "Even now? That makes no sense, Jackson. I'm pregnant."

"Yes, you're pregnant. It doesn't change how I feel, and why should it? I still want you."

"It must be very difficult for you to walk around all day," she told him sweetly.

Now he was the confused one. He looked at her and waited, and when she said nothing else, he finally spoke. "I probably don't want to hear this, but why would it be difficult for me to walk around?"

"Because you are so arrogant that all that weight from your huge ego has got to be quite a burden to carry around," she said with a big smile.

"Ah, baby, don't you worry one little bit about my ego or my feelings. I have a feeling I'll sleep just fine tonight," he said as he leaned over her, getting entirely too close for her comfort.

"Back off, Jackson," she said, leaning back as far as her headboard would allow.

"Why, Alyssa? Are you afraid of me?" he asked, coming just a little bit closer.

"No," she snapped, putting her hand against his chest to try to keep him away.

"I don't think you're afraid of me at all. However, I do think you're afraid of yourself and the way that I make you feel."

Bingo! He'd definitely gotten that one right. Not that she would ever, even under oath, admit that to him. How was she expected to keep him at bay when he muddled her thoughts so badly?

"Have you thought about my offer?"

"There's not a chance I want you taking care of me, Jackson. And I don't need you to. And it's not just that I have my parents to do a far better job than you ever could. There's more. When I first arrived her in Sterling, I was lost, I'll admit, and I didn't have a clue what I was going to do. But I've had time to grow stronger, to make plans. I am just fine on my own," she said with no little pride.

"What are your plans, Alyssa?"

She breathed a little easier when he backed away, though it wasn't far enough.

"I don't think that's any of your business, either, Jackson."

"Aren't we friends?"

"We don't know each other," she snapped. "How could we be friends? And for that matter, why would you even want to take care of me, whatever that even means?"

"I disagree. I think we're friends. We've spent a lot of time together in the past two weeks. To top that off, we have incredible chemistry, and we can be good to each other." He sat down and made himself comfortable, as if for a long stay. Then he continued. "And as far as taking care of you," he told her before pausing and lifting his lips in a brilliant smile, "it means that we live together. I watch over you, make sure you stay healthy and have everything you need. You quit working at the Country Saloon. It's dangerous. And in turn . . . well, you take care of me, too."

"Spell it out, Jackson. What you want is unlimited sex." She might as well make everything as black-and-white as he was doing.

"Well . . . yes, but you're going to enjoy that just as much as me."

He didn't even appear to be ashamed of that answer. What was he thinking? He was probably thinking that she was the type of girl who'd had a one-night stand with him and then went off and had another one with someone else and got knocked up. He probably considered her good mistress material. *That kind of a girl.*

"I have a home, Jackson, and I'm not interested in quitting my job. I like working there, love my customers—well, most of them, anyway. I love my coworkers. I can't possibly just sit at home day and night and twiddle my thumbs. I've worked hard from the time I was fourteen because my parents taught me that if I wanted the world, I had to take it in my own hands, not depend on another person to give it to me. And I'm not interested in being any man's personal mistress."

"There are also times when it's right to let someone else handle the weight thrust upon your shoulders. You're on your feet for hours upon hours at your job. You sometimes even work double shifts. That can't be beneficial to your pregnancy." He ignored the mistress comment for now. She had no doubt he wasn't letting the topic drop, though.

"Jackson Whitman, from the beginning of time women have been bearing children while still working hard. Women would work on their farms until delivery, and some of them didn't even manage to make it back in from the fields or the barns before the child was born. A little hard work certainly won't harm my child, and I resent you for trying to make me feel bad for having a good work ethic."

"Women of old also lost a lot of babies . . . and their own lives, too. Yes, they were tough, and they're still tough today, but they also know when they need to rest. They listen to their bodies. Your mother told me you were bleeding, Alyssa. Your doctor put you on bed rest for at least a few days. Isn't that enough to make you want to slow down?"

"I will have to chat with my mother about what she tells you," she said, furious for the invasion of her privacy. "And not that I owe you an explanation, but I will listen to what my doctor says, and after a few days, I'm sure I will be back in full health. I wouldn't risk my child."

"I'm not saying you would, and don't be harsh on your mother. We were just visiting and she's concerned about you," he said, not seeming as confident as he had before.

"When did you have a chance to chat with my mom?" She was confused.

"I sat in the kitchen with her for a few minutes. I like your mother."

Alyssa was about ready to explode. "You are so infuriating!" she snapped. "And I don't care what kind of dressing you put on this, Jackson, but you *are* telling me that if I don't take your offer of shacking up—a lovely idea in Sterling, where everyone notices everything and everyone talks about it incessantly—then I'm not a good mother. I think it's pretty despicable to use my fear for my child to try to get your way."

He was completely silent as he processed her words. He opened his mouth to speak when her parents walked into the room, interrupting them. She shot her mother a look that screamed "Traitor!"

"Mmm, chocolates," Teresa said, ignoring the

look as she reached into the box. "How thoughtful, Jackson."

"Yes, he's just a peach," Alyssa said, not wanting to share her chocolate with a traitor, and barely managing to keep her complaint to herself.

"I know the way to a woman's heart," Jackson said with a wink that had her mother smiling. "I hope you aren't being kept too busy taking care of Alyssa."

Alyssa sent Jackson another glare of warning. There was no way he was going to suggest that he take care of her to her mother. She could see him trying to go around her and getting the okay from her mom. Not that it would do him any good if he did. She was an adult who made her own decisions. Even if her mother approved of him, she couldn't possibly approve of her unmarried daughter living with a man.

"I enjoy having Alyssa back home and getting a rare opportunity to take care of her," Teresa replied.

"There are times I really would have loved to have a mother, especially one like you," he said, and Alyssa stopped herself from saying what she'd been about to say. It hadn't been nice, but guilt consumed her as she thought about him growing up without a mother.

"Oh, sweetie, everyone should have a mom," Teresa said, and then walked over and enveloped Jackson in a hug. Alyssa would have thought it all an act, but for one unguarded moment, he looked up and their eyes connected. What was in them couldn't be faked.

"Well, having a dad is important, too," Donald said, puffing out his chest.

"Yes, of course, sir, and my dad is truly a great man," Jackson said.

"You've been here two days in a row, son. I would really like to know exactly how close you and my daughter are, since you didn't answer my questions very well yesterday," Donald said.

Alyssa felt like screaming now. They were having a conversation about her as if she weren't even in the room. And her dad was acting like a nightmare from Victorian times. Oh, hell, in Victorian times no father would have asked a man his intentions when the daughter was knocked up and said it was by someone else. Her dad had carried this into lunatic territory.

Then she glanced at Jackson and didn't trust the look in his eyes, not one little bit. Jackson wasn't a slow man. If he could get Alyssa's father on his side, then he had a fighting chance with her. Both of Alyssa's parents were looking at him expectantly. She wanted to break in, wanted to end this conversation, but it turned out she didn't need to. Jackson's phone rang and he picked it up, as if grateful for the interruption.

After speaking for a moment into the phone, he flipped it closed and said, "I'm sorry. I have to go."

With that he walked from the room without answering her father's question. That was answer enough, wasn't it? Her dad must have realized that the man's intentions were anything but honorable.

Her parents looked at her, but they didn't say anything more about Jackson. And that was a good thing. She didn't want to hear another word about him. Why bother even thinking about him? The man had fled, and everything had worked out for the best.

If that was so, then why couldn't she explain this sudden ache in her chest? He'd left, that was what she wanted, or what she'd told herself she wanted. But as she gazed at the empty doorway he'd just left, she felt like crying.

Frustration made her turn her head away and put a false smile on her face as she began speaking of anything she could that wasn't related to Jackson. When the day dragged on and she still missed him, she knew she was in trouble. Big trouble.

021

He was a coward.

There was no doubt about it. There were probably scorch marks going out the doorway from Alyssa's room. Jackson couldn't think of any other time he'd ever run like that, but run he had. Alyssa was carrying another man's child, and he'd been propositioning her. And yet he'd tried telling himself he was doing the right thing. She was pregnant, after all. She needed to be taken care of.

But he knew he'd get so much more out of the bargain he was proposing than she would. How long did he really want whatever this was between them to last? Until the end of her pregnancy? A year? Years? Forever?

Was he a monster to take sex in exchange for security? Did she even need the security he could provide? She had her parents, and even though they were nowhere near as wealthy as he was, they obviously loved her and seemed more than willing to take care of her.

So where did that leave him? Was he just trying

to find excuses to be with her? Did he actually care about this woman, a woman he barely knew? Hell, he didn't know what to think about himself or anything else, for that matter.

One thing was clear, though: he was thinking in terms of more than a couple of weeks, of a commitment far longer than he'd ever expected to make again. It was togetherness of the sort that involved rings and vows and "till death do us part."

He'd sworn he would never enter into a real relationship again, let alone marry again. Commitments were a joke. The vows he and his former wife had made to each other ultimately ended up meaning nothing. Nothing! She'd walked away from him without so much as a backward glance. And then he hadn't been there fast enough to save his three-month-old baby from the fire her mother had started.

Jackson hung his head as he paced endlessly across the floors of his house. Alyssa probably figured she'd never hear from him again. He really didn't know anything right now. All he knew for sure was that his gut was churning and he was dazed and confused as hell.

His mind told him to run, to find some other woman, a woman who knew the score, or to find no one and hole up in his home and focus strictly on work. But his heart . . . The damn thing continued to send all sorts of ridiculous notions through his veins, and made him want to do the exact opposite of what his brain insisted was rational.

What was wrong with him? Why had he decided to sit in that exact place in the airport? Why had he decided to move her plane seat next to his? If he'd only waited in the first-class lounge or stood by the counter, as he normally did, none of this confusion would be oppressing him now.

No. To take away that night wasn't what he wanted. It had been spectacular. When he'd thought he would never see her again, he hadn't been filled with relief. He'd been . . . Jackson stopped pacing and gazed out his large living room window.

He'd been bereft.

Just admitting that to himself made him feel like a weaker man. He didn't need a woman in his life to validate his own happiness. He had his work, and he had his family, whether he wanted them around or not.

He had himself.

Why all of a sudden was none of that enough? Because he couldn't go a single day without thoughts of Alyssa. So what did that mean? His shoulders sagged. He knew the answer. It meant he was going back to see Alyssa.

What happened next, he'd soon find out.

ALYSSA HAD EXPECTED him to walk out, so why was she feeling so sorry for herself and lying like a limp rag in her suddenly claustrophobic bed? Maybe because she'd begun to have hope, if just the smallest trace of it, that he really did like her. And maybe it was simply because she was a fool.

He didn't want her. Yes, it was more than obvious that he wanted to spend a few more nights in *bed* with her, but that wasn't nearly enough. Of course, with the hormones rushing through her body, she might be able to spontaneously combust and light some bedding on fire all on her own. Her body was sensitive in the extreme, and to feel a man's touch would be divine. The mere thought of feeling Jackson sink deep inside her made her core pulse.

But she knew that wasn't what she should do. She'd been smart to keep her distance. The guy was clueless beyond belief, and he must really have a low opinion of her to have assumed so easily that the child was another man's.

Not that she'd told him anything different. But she hadn't exactly lied; she just hadn't told *anyone* who the baby's father was. That eased her conscience, if only a little.

"I can't seem to stay away from you."

Alyssa turned to watch Jackson stroll into her room as if he didn't have a care in the world. She was torn between relief, which she certainly didn't want to feel, and frustration, which she *should* be feeling.

"What are you doing here? I thought I'd seen the last of you. You ran so fast you left a cloud of smoke behind you."

"You thought wrong, Alyssa." He sat down in one chair and propped his legs up on another, making himself disgustingly comfortable, looking as if he weren't planning on ever leaving.

"I don't want you here."

"I disagree. I think you do want me here, but you're too stubborn to admit it."

"Well, then, I guess we're at an impasse, Jackson."

"You can always try to kick me out," he told her.

"Don't think that I'm weak just because I'm in this bed."

"I would never make such a foolish mistake as to think you anything other than beautiful, strong, and capable."

It was more than clear that this man was a smooth talker. Did he practice in front of his mirror? Probably. She had to remind herself that he was a powerful businessman, obviously good at coming up with lines in his life of constant schmoozing. He had probably used this same line so many times it flowed from his tantalizing lips without any help from his pea-sized brain.

"Jackson, this is a pointless game you're playing. You obviously know that I'm pregnant. I'm not on the market," she said, suddenly drained.

"I disagree. There's no ring on your finger, and I don't see a man anywhere nearby who's holding your hand."

"Maybe because I don't *need* a man to hold my hand."

"We all need somebody, Alyssa. Sometimes we're just too damn headstrong to admit that. Are you really so disgusted with me that you don't want to give us a chance? What we had that night isn't something that comes around very often. We were good together then and we could be good together again. You're different from any other woman I've met, and I think that if we gave it a go, we'd be exceptional."

"So, you want to get involved, get married, have a dozen kids and an endless stretch of sleepless nights?"

A twinkle lit his eyes. "I'm game if you are."

"Jackson! Can you be serious for once? I don't have time to play games. In less than five months I'm going to have a screaming, messy, sleep-deprived life. I know what I'm in for. I'm actually looking forward to it. None of my plans include carousing around town with a known playboy who never calls back the next morning."

"You didn't leave your number, so you can have no idea if I would have called."

"Would you have?"

He sat there as if really thinking about it. "I am almost positive I would have."

"You *think* you would have? Is it unusual for you to call a woman after you've already bedded her?"

"Okay, so I haven't done it in a long time. But that doesn't mean a man can't change."

"Yes, that's exactly what it means. The only reason you want to be with me is that I'm some sort of challenge. I unintentionally wounded your poor manhood when I slipped from the hotel room on the first day of the year. Yes, our night was great. Yes, I've thought about it," she said, and a satisfied grin splayed across his face. "No, I don't want to repeat it."

That wiped the grin off. *Good.*

"I think you're a liar. Whether you're lying to me or to yourself or to both of us, you are indeed lying. I think you want to spend a lot more nights with me."

"Even if I did, it wouldn't matter. I have another person to think about now. I no longer get to meet a stranger on New Year's Eve, have wild sex, and then disappear. Mothers don't do that."

"I know some pretty hot mothers who do indeed do that."

"Well, they aren't the ones I'll be spending my time with at PTA meetings," she snapped.

"You won't even know who you're spending time with at those meetings, darling. Everyone has secrets, and the older we get, the more savvy we are at fooling those around us."

Jackass. "I'm not your *darling*, Jackson. You're going to shoot my blood pressure right through the ceiling if you don't quit harassing me."

"Then quit arguing with me. I've decided I'm not going away. I like the idea of having a baby around."

"You don't get to make that choice." Those words sent fear spiraling through her. That's what she was afraid of. She was terrified he wanted to keep the baby around . . . and not her.

"I can make up my own mind, Alyssa."

"Well, you can't make my decisions for me. I've said it over and over again, and you just won't listen. Save what little pride you have left and scurry on out of here before I lose what shred of patience *I* have left."

"Do you like pizza?"

His change in topic threw her completely. Nothing she was saying had the smallest impact on him. He just sat there looking calm and in control. What would it take to drive this man away? And did she really want to drive him away, or did she just want to see whether he was strong enough to stay? He'd already run off once. What would stop him from leaving again?

"Everyone likes pizza," she finally huffed.

"Good. I have one on the way." He picked up her remote and turned the television on.

"We don't have pizza in Sterling," she pointed out.

"It's coming from Billings."

"What? Who does that, Jackson? Who has pizza delivered from that far away?"

"I wanted pizza, sounded good," he said nonchalantly. She didn't even want to think about how much it was costing him to get his pizza.

"I just had breakfast not too long ago."

"I hear that pregnant women eat a lot."

"That was rude!"

"How?" He stopped what he was doing to give her his full attention.

"Are you calling me fat?" she said.

"How do you translate my saying pregnant women eat a lot into your being fat?"

The puzzled expression on his face was almost endearing. Almost, not quite.

"Do the math. Eating a lot equals consuming a lot of calories, and that makes you fat." Did she have to spell everything out?

"I just don't get women." He turned back to the TV, ignoring the question and her ranting.

She'd really better come up with a game plan, and soon, or he was going to get his way from simply wearing her down, and she couldn't allow that to happen.

Alyssa said nothing more as he played with her television remote, flipping through the channels as if he didn't have a single worry. When he found an action film and settled back in his chair as if it were *his* freaking room, she almost lost her temper again.

"What. Are. You. Doing. Now?" she finally asked after five entire minutes passed without a word between them.

"Making myself comfortable. I'll talk to you more when you're being reasonable," he said before turning back to the big chase scene.

"That's it," she snapped. "And I'll talk to you when you learn to behave like a civilized human being and not a spoiled jerk who was clearly never taught manners." She picked up one of her pillows and tossed it straight at his head.

"Thanks, darling," he said, and he tucked the pillow behind his neck and kicked back just a little bit more.

Fine. If he wanted to hang around her boring room and waste his time, it was a free country. But she wasn't going to make it easy on him. Grabbing the remote from him, she flipped stations and found *Pretty Woman*, then leaned back and smiled.

Her triumph was a bit lessened when he didn't say a word, just watched the romantic comedy without complaint. What would it take to ruffle *his* feathers? Because he sure as hell knew how to rile her up.

The pizza was delivered a few minutes later, sending Jackson down the stairs to answer the door and bringing him right back to her room with a big cardboard box. When the smell of grease and cheese hit her nostrils, she hated him a little more because she began salivating.

She refused to give in and take a slice, not even when he set it on the little table right beside her, leaving the aroma to drift to her. By the time he had his third piece in his hand, she couldn't hold out any longer. Her resolve melted, just like the stupid cheese.

Oh, well, if you can't beat 'em, join 'em, right? At least for now.

022

"Wow, back again? Really?"

"You have a doctor's appointment," Jackson replied easily.

"I realize I have an appointment. That still doesn't explain why *you* are here."

"When I was on my way out yesterday, your mother told me you had an appointment, so she was going to have to cancel her volunteer work over at the library, reading to the children. I know how much the children enjoy it, so I volunteered to take you," he said, cheeky grin in place.

"And no one thought to ask me how I felt about this arrangement?" she snapped, now knowing for certain that her mother was up to no good.

"I have the day free and you have a ride, plus your mother gets to make the kiddos happy. Everyone wins."

"Everyone but me," she muttered as she scooted over on her bed and stood up.

He rushed up to her. "Do you need help?"

"No. I don't need help. I'm going to the bathroom to shower and change. And then I'm going to take the ride to the doctor because I don't want to bother my parents any further than I already have. But I'm not happy about it. Had I known my mother was volunteering, I would have asked one of the ladies to give me a ride," she told him before walking away and firmly shutting the bathroom door behind her.

It took her longer than she would have liked to shower and dress, and she wasn't pleased that it taxed her strength. Each day she was feeling better, and she really thought that it was more fear, because the doctor had told her she needed bed rest, than actual weakness. Still, she was doing all she could to be careful.

When she emerged from the bathroom, she found Jackson sitting on her bed, feet stretched out while he watched a movie on HBO. She tried to fight her irritation—and lost.

"You look like you're quite comfortable," she said as she moved forward and picked up her purse.

"This is a great bed. I can see why you like staying in it," he teased as he swung his feet around and then stood.

"At least you had the decency to take off your shoes. And I don't like staying in it," she informed him as she made her way from the room. "From what I've read, my doctor is a prize idiot, and I'm going to get a second opinion. Maybe the new doctor will tell me to keep people like you out of my bedroom."

"Ah, I have heard complaints about the temp guy. But, hey, everyone needs a vacation once in a while, but Doc Alf will be back soon."

"Doc Alf?" She'd never heard of him.

"Well, everyone just calls him Doc, but his name is Alfred, so then some of the more rambunctious kids—not me, of course," he said with a grin that told her he must have been a front-runner in this new game. "Well, some of the kids came up with Doc Alf—you know, from that old alien television show?"

"Why are we even talking about this?" she asked.

"You were the one complaining about your doctor."

"I guess the sooner Doc Alf gets back, the better," she said, ending the discussion.

Reaching the top of the stairs, she looked down them, feeling a little intimidated. It was ridiculous, she thought. Nothing was going to happen to her from climbing down a staircase. Her doctor wouldn't have her coming in this afternoon if he didn't think it was safe.

Before she could take the first step, she felt Jackson's arms wrap around her, and then she was being pulled into his embrace as he cradled her to his chest and then began descending the staircase, leaving her no choice but to grab ahold of him or risk falling forward.

"What in the world are you doing?"

"Making sure you don't overexert yourself," he said as he reached the bottom of the stairs and set her down, not even a little out of breath.

"I can walk just fine on my own, Jackson." She was the one out of breath.

It wasn't like she'd forgotten how it felt to be in his arms, but the memories had begun to fade. Now they were right back to being front and center with the feel of his solid arms around her.

If she didn't manage to get her hormones under control sometime in the next century, she might be the one propositioning him next. And that wasn't something she was willing to do.

"Ready?" he asked as he held open her parents' front door.

She answered in a monosyllable and said nothing else as she stepped outside, and then paused as she felt the fresh air and sunshine on her face. It had been only a couple of days since she'd been outside, but that was long enough. She'd rather live in a tent than be holed up for too long indoors.

"We've lucked out. It's a beautiful spring day," Jackson said as he wrapped an arm around her to help her down the front steps.

She chose not to fight him on this, or she feared he'd pick her up again. "I hate being indoors all the time. The summers in Texas were pretty miserable in the peak heat season, but I'd rather have hot, sunny days than too much snow. When I arrived here, the ground was so white that I didn't even know where the roads were. I was more than relieved when the stuff began melting away and the sun came out."

"Yeah, I guess if you're not used to it, it can be a bit overwhelming. But when you live here long enough, you learn how to adapt. There are a lot of fun winter activities to do here, too," he said as he opened his truck door for her and held out a hand to help her up.

She ignored the hand and grabbed the handle above the door and hoisted herself into his mammoth truck, then buckled up while he shut the door and went around to the driver's side.

"What kind of activities can you do without freezing to death?"

"There's snowboarding, snowmobiling, ice fishing, winter camping . . ." He paused and she jumped in.

"Winter camping? What in the world is that?" Nothing pleasant, she was sure.

"As much as you love the outdoors, you've never been winter camping?"

"No. Who in the world would go camping in the winter? That sounds like something miserable our ancestors had to endure while traveling to a new home."

"I know. We've actually laughed about that before. My brothers and I love to camp. The people traveling westward across the States would have thought we were crazy. Why would we leave homes with electricity and real heat to go up into the wilderness? It's simple, though. Camping is all about letting go of the world and going to an area that feels untouched. In the winter there are even fewer people, and for just a small moment in time, it feels like you're the only ones there."

"But what can you do besides freeze to death?" It actually did sound kind of nice to be away from everyone, and now she was curious.

"We've done all sorts of things, like snowshoeing, skiing, snowboarding, ice fishing, hunting. But the best part is the night. Sure, it gets darker much earlier in the winter, and it's so damn cold, but that turns out to be a good thing. We set up our shelters, build a huge fire, and talk for hours while having dinner and hot drinks. When we were young, our dad would scare the crap out of us with ghost stories and talking about alien abductions."

"Alien abductions?" she asked with a laugh. "Really?"

"Hey, don't knock it," he said with his own laugh. "I swear he had us convinced one night that a light in the sky was a UFO. I'm still not convinced otherwise," he added with a wink.

"Well, it sounds like I'm going to have to try winter camping," she told him as they pulled up to the doctor's office.

"I will be glad to take you," he said, shutting off the truck and jumping out, then rushing around to her side to open the door before she could.

"I think we will both be doing separate things by winter, Jackson." She needed to maintain some distance with this man, because each day she was with him, she was finding that task just a little bit harder.

"I'll just have to disagree with you on that."

She left Jackson in the waiting room and went back to see her doctor. The news wasn't good. He wanted her to stay off work for at least one more week. She'd developed a slight bleed that wasn't going away, and her blood pressure was high. It wasn't from being pushed down, he didn't think, just a symptom of pregnancy. Her second trimester wasn't being good to her.

Slightly depressed as she walked back out to Jackson, she climbed into the truck without saying much. For once, he didn't fill the silence with small talk. When they reached her house, she didn't try to fight him when he lifted her into his arms again and carried her up the stairs.

The trip had worn her out, and Alyssa quickly removed her coat and shoes and climbed into bed. Jackson hovered over her looking like he wanted to say something. She waited, knowing he wouldn't leave without getting off his chest whatever it was.

"I can see you're tired and depressed, but keep your head up. This won't last forever," he said, and she was surprised that was all. "I'll come see you again tomorrow, Alyssa."

With that, he bent down and softly kissed her, then turned and walked from the room, leaving her lips tingling and her body slightly achy. When after a half hour she wasn't able to fall asleep, she sat up in bed and grabbed her journal and pen from the nightstand drawer.

An hour passed before she was finished writing, and she felt much better after ranting in the safest place she knew of. Yes, she was still completely muddled about her feelings about Jackson, and she still wasn't sure when she would tell him the truth, but over the past few days she had figured out that she would eventually have to tell him.

Knowing the man made it impossible for her to justify keeping the secret.

023

"You have a visitor, Alyssa."

"Thanks for telling me this time," Alyssa muttered, but it was to no avail. Before Alyssa could finish speaking, her mother was gone and Jackson was strolling through her doorway, his arms full with two gigantic bags. It was more than obvious that her mother was in love with Jackson and Alyssa could see the wheels turning in both her parents' heads.

Their daughter was pregnant and alone. Jackson was making it more than clear to them that he was sticking around. Of course, they didn't know that he wanted to continue their affair and was willing to take her, baby and all, to do that. What they were hoping would last forever was in reality going to last only until he grew bored with the game. And, knowing him, that wouldn't take long.

She had to tell her mother the truth, but how could she do that? If she wasn't yet willing to tell Jackson that the baby she carried was his, how could she tell her parents? She was sure if they knew he was the father, they'd be marching the two of them down the aisle, perhaps with a shotgun at both of their backs. Neither she nor Jackson would be happy with that arrangement.

"What are you up to now, Jackson?" she asked as she pulled her blankets a little higher. This was even more perfect. She was lying in bed in her favorite flannel pajamas, her hair sticking out in all directions, and without a lick of makeup on. But who cared, right? She wasn't trying to impress him. She'd known he would show up. If she'd been concerned, she would have tried to doll herself up a bit.

Still, she lifted her hand self-consciously and tried to tame her hair. Bed rest wasn't conductive to feeling beautiful—or to getting better, from what she'd read. What she wouldn't give for a day at the spa. That was her first order of business when she could finally get out of the house again.

"I told you I'd be back, and this time I've brought goodies so you won't be bored. The doctor said one week, right?"

"No. He said that it would be a minimum of one week, but most likely two. You can't fire me because of this," she hastened to add. "I have a doctor's note."

"As much as I would rather you weren't working at the saloon, I won't fire you, Alyssa. I'm not a demon," he said as he finally set the bags down on the side of her bed.

Alyssa was dying to look inside them, but she hardly wanted to seem too eager. That would give him another leg up in their silent competition, with the prize going to the most stubborn.

"I see the sparkle in your eyes. Go ahead and see what I've brought. Since you so accurately pointed out that I don't know you, I've tried guessing. This way, if I made a few wrong choices, you still have a lot to choose from."

Damn him for looking far too adorable with his mussed hair and gleaming eyes as he sat at the foot of her bed.

Alyssa's curiosity got the better of her, and, pulling one of the bags closer, she took out several puzzle books—she loved the things, but she wouldn't admit it to him—plus more chocolates, caramels, fruit candies—every variety, it seemed—and finally a dozen novels, the covers all featuring gorgeous couples in passionate embraces with very little clothing on. The romances made her blush.

The next bag had lotion, more snacks, warm, fuzzy socks, and beautiful maternity pajamas. She wondered who'd helped him pick those out.

"You bought me pajamas?"

"Well, you *are* on bed rest. I figure it's what you'll be wearing for the foreseeable future. Hawk Winchester's wife, Natalie, told me that women like silky jammies," he said, and his own cheeks seemed to turn a little pink.

"Wow, Jackson, you really didn't need to do all

of this." Alyssa was surprised that she was having a difficult time not choking up.

"I wanted to."

"Thank you, but please, don't do it again. There's enough stuff here to entertain me for the rest of my pregnancy."

"I find I like getting gifts for you. The romance novels were a little hard to explain to the clerk. But once I told her what I was doing, she was more than happy to help, and said these were bestsellers with 'real steamy scenes'—her words, not mine."

"Want to read one? I've always thought men should read romance. Then maybe they'd know how to treat a woman, and learn what not to do."

"Baby, I don't need to read a romance. I know exactly what to do with a woman."

"Oh, you mean follow her around until she caves in to your demands? Yes, I see advice columnists tell that to stalkers all the time. And of course would-be lotharios are always told to hog the remote control in a woman's own bedroom."

But she did have to agree with him in part, though she had to think back almost five months. He knew just how to stroke a woman's body to give her the ultimate pleasure. The mere thought made her breasts tingle and her nipples harden. She was grateful for the thick pajamas and thicker blankets protecting her from his view.

"The lady doth protest too much, methinks," he said before pausing and looking concerned. "Is that what you really think?"

He could have been a gentleman and dropped the subject, but she was learning that Jackson was anything but a gentleman.

"No comment."

"I'll take the sparkle in your eyes and the quickening of your breath as definite proof that you have no problems with my skills as a lover."

"You are so cocky. Did that take years of practice, or is it something that just comes naturally to you?"

"Baby, when you're good, you know it."

"I guess that means you practice a lot."

The narrowing of his eyes gave her great satisfaction.

"You can fight me all you want, but I like being around you. I've decided to hang out—a lot. At least until you give me what I want," he said with a gleam in his eyes.

"Is that a threat?"

"Oh, no, Alyssa. I would never threaten you. I have only the best of intentions when it comes to us."

"Well, it's certainly not a promise."

"I'm like a fine wine: the longer I age, the better I am. You see, the more you're around me, the more you'll want to be."

"Did you honestly just say that?" Her jaw had dropped, and nothing she did could get her mouth to close.

"I have all sorts of lines, love."

"You actually seem proud of yourself for that, Jackson. I'm flabbergasted."

"I bought *romance* books. Doesn't that tell you how much effort I'm putting into our relationship?"

"First of all, we aren't in a relationship, and second, would you like a pat on the back for understanding the heart of a woman?" She spoke with enough sarcasm that even he couldn't miss it, thick skull or not.

"Well . . ." His tone implied he wanted a heck of a lot more than a pat on the back.

"Jackson Whitman, I would leave right now if I were you. I mean it. Right now! The words coming out of your mouth certainly aren't winning you any points. At least I have these puzzle books to occupy me, so maybe, just maybe, I'll forget this conversation ever happened."

"I can see that you want to play with your new toys. Don't worry, I'll be back real soon, and I'll come bearing more gifts." Jackson stood up and, to her utter amazement, bent down and kissed her.

Alyssa was dumbfounded. By the time she came up with a scathing reply, he was long gone. Next time she'd be more than ready for him.

"What in the world are you doing, Jackson?"

Jackson turned to find his brother Michael looking at him . . . and gaping. Busted looking at car seats and fairy wing thingies for infants! Jackson had to fight to suppress a raging blush.

"Um . . . can you just pretend you didn't see me here in the baby section?" Jackson asked hopefully. He was in no way ready to explain any of this to his family.

"Yeah, I can guarantee you there's no chance at all of that happening," Michael said as he took a stance and folded his arms. He wasn't going anywhere until Jackson spilled his guts.

"I really don't want to talk about it," Jackson told him firmly.

"Okay, I guess I can go home and tell Dad I saw you looking through baby items. It looks like he finally may get to be a grandfather," Michael said, and he turned as if about to leave.

"Stop!" Jackson yelled, winning a dirty look from a passing customer whose baby had just started to cry. "Sorry," he muttered, then chased after Michael.

"I'm heading to my car now," Michael said, and Jackson couldn't tell whether he was bluffing or not. The thing with his brothers, though, was that even if they were bluffing, they had no problem throwing each other under the bus. So if Jackson didn't give Michael something, his brother would indeed run home and tell his father where Jackson had been.

The two of them stepped out of the store in Billings and Jackson grabbed his arm. "Come with me to lunch and I'll tell you everything," Jackson said with a resigned sigh.

"I'll take a free meal," Michael said as he started following Jackson back to the parking lot. "Don't even think about not bringing me back here for my truck, though."

Jackson was seriously considering it. They jumped into his truck and he took them downtown to a bar he liked that served pretty damn good burgers and played great music.

After ordering a beer and their meal, Michael leaned back expectantly, waiting for Jackson to spill all. There was no way around it, and maybe it would help to talk to someone, 'cause he sure as hell didn't know what he was doing half the time.

"You know Alyssa Gerard, right?" he began.

"Yeah, the waitress at the Country Saloon. She's a great girl," he said before his eyes widened. "What in the hell have you done to her? You only met a few weeks ago."

"That's not true, actually. We met on New Year's Eve on a flight back from Paris. We had a delay, and well—" Jackson broke off, feeling guilty for saying anything. He would have to punch Michael if he thought anything bad about Alyssa.

"You met on New Year's and bedded her," Michael said with another glare.

"It wasn't like that," Jackson said, trying desperately to defend himself, but his brothers knew him well, and knew what he thought about women. They were for one purpose and one purpose only.

"Really? You suddenly had a change? You met her and talked all night? Didn't have sex?"

Squirming a bit beneath his brother's sarcastic questions, Jackson suddenly didn't know what to say. Yes, it had started out the way it always did. But there'd been something different with her.

"Well, we did have sex, but before you jump all over me, let me explain. We talked. I mean, we *really* talked, Michael, like I haven't talked to another woman. I found myself liking her. When I woke up the next day, she was gone, and I figured I'd never see her again, and then a few weeks ago, I walked in that bar and there she was," Jackson said.

"Damn, Jackson. It sounds like you really are into this woman," Michael said with wonder.

"Well, I wouldn't go that far. I mean, I do like her, and I want to be with her, but I'm not into *any* woman," Jackson said, immediately trying to backtrack.

"Okay, whatever. But still, none of that explains why you were in the baby section of a retail shop," Michael said, not buying Jackson's words even a little bit. Their waitress set down their food and then disappeared as Jackson tried to think of his next words.

"She's pregnant. About five months pregnant, and I know the fact that's she's pregnant should scare the shit out of me and have me running for the hills, but I can't get this woman from my head. It's just a baby—it's not like that changes things." *Stupid, stupid, stupid.*

Michael looked at him silently for several heartbeats before he began guffawing. "Did you honestly just say that? Really, Jackson? And people think *you're* the smart one . . ." he said in between fits of laughter that had Jackson clenching his teeth.

"What in the hell do you find so funny?" Jackson had lost all appetite, so he ignored the food in favor of chugging his beer.

"A baby changes everything, you dumb ass. They are messy and demanding, and the world revolves around them. Don't you remember?" Michael instantly stopped and his laughter died. No one ever talked about Jackson's daughter. It was just too painful to bring up.

"Yes, I remember," Jackson said, a deep sadness forever locked inside him. Instead of replying to what Michael had said, he went off on another tack. "But I think I'm moving on. Really moving on. I will never forget Olivia. She was my beautiful girl. I just realize that I have to let her go."

"I'm glad you're healing, Jackson. Truly, I am," Michael said as he reached out a hand and patted Jackson's shoulder before he leaned back. "But you can't play games with a pregnant woman. If you're not thinking about forever, you have no business being with her."

Jackson knew deep down that his brother was right, but if he said those words aloud, admitted the truth of that statement, that would mean he'd have to walk away from Alyssa, didn't it? Because he was in no way ready to admit to deeper feelings for the woman other than lust. To admit to that would mean he was weak, would mean that Alyssa had the power to hurt him.

He couldn't do that. Michael remained silent while Jackson spent several moments thinking about what he wanted to say next. He was grateful when the waitress came and handed each of them another beer, giving him an extra few seconds.

"I'm not trying to hurt her. She's fine," Jackson finally said, not knowing if he was trying to convince Michael or himself.

"I'm not going to rag on you, Jackson. We both know you've been through your share of hell. Just don't forget that she's a real person. She's not another one of your one-night stands. This woman is going to be a mother and she deserves more respect than some girl who knows the score."

"I'm not disrespecting her, Michael."

"If you're offering her anything less than marriage, that's exactly what you're doing."

"But I'm offering to take care of her."

"That's not enough, Jackson. I have a feeling that Alyssa isn't too keen to accept that offer. Am I right?"

"She's been less than accepting, but I know she's happy to see me when I visit."

Michael raised his brow as if calling Jackson on his crap. "Really?" That one word was filled with meaning.

"Okay, she may not thank me profusely, but a man can tell when a woman is into him or not. I can see that she wants me," Jackson insisted.

"There's a difference between wanting someone and wanting to be with them." Why in the hell did Michael have to point that out?

Jackson didn't feel any better after he and Michael talked. They turned the subject matter to more superficial topics, and by the time Jackson dropped Michael off at his truck, he still didn't know what he should do.

On the long drive back to Sterling, he had plenty of time to think, though. By the time he found himself pulling up in front of Alyssa's place, he still didn't know what he was going to say. So instead of going inside, he restarted his truck and drove home.

Maybe it was best if he just left her alone. But Jackson just wasn't sure if he was capable of doing that. He had a feeling he was already too involved to back out. It wasn't something he was ready to do. But absence made the heart grow fonder, right? Hell, he didn't know.

"You have another delivery," Teresa trilled as she entered the bedroom with a package.

"Can you open it, Mom?" Jackson hadn't been by in several days and she hated to admit, even to herself, how much she missed him, but she did. Getting a package from him wasn't the same thing as seeing him. Maybe he didn't want to see her anymore. She should be happy about that, but sadly, she wasn't.

"I'd love to." Her mother sat down at the foot of her bed and opened the box.

When her mom smiled and then paused before taking out the item, Alyssa wished that she'd just dealt with the box herself.

"Are you going to show me?" she finally asked.

"Oh, sorry, sweetie." With a chuckle, her mother brought out a beautiful mobile that was made up of sweet white bunnies and had a little music box attached. She wound it and it played lullabies. Attached was a note, which Teresa handed over. When Alyssa read yet it, she couldn't quite restrain her tears.

"What does it say, darling?" Teresa asked. Still

occupied with the darn gift box, she was now lifting out soft baby blankets and bedding.

"Nothing is as soothing as a song. The right one can spark a memory to last a lifetime. I miss you."

"Oh, that's very sweet," Teresa said.

"It's not sweet, Mother. He has to quit buying me stuff."

Teresa's smile disappeared. "He cares about you, darling, and I don't think he's overdone it."

"All we had was one night, Mom. We weren't supposed to see each other again. I was feeling vulnerable because my career had ended and I'd been dumped in the most brutal and unceremonious manner possible. Jackson was . . . I don't know what he was feeling. But now I'm so confused. He's not an easy man to ignore. And he's been so dang attentive since I've been on bed rest, well up until he disappeared." Alyssa slid her fingers over the soft white blanket that her mother had handed to her.

Teresa's "thinking look" took over her face. Alyssa had no idea what had sparked that look, but she was afraid she'd soon find out.

"You had one night together?"

"Yes. It was a while ago. He just can't seem to let it go," Alyssa huffed. Granted, she wasn't sure right now that she wanted him to let it go. Everything would be so much easier if she disliked him, if she weren't attracted to him, but he made that impossible. Even when he was being arrogant. Hell, to be honest, probably because of his arrogance.

"And how long ago was 'a while'?"

Oh, crap! Alyssa's cheeks flushed as she looked at her mom. She had no earthly idea how to answer that question. It seemed parents weren't as clueless as their kids believed.

"Jackson is the father, isn't he?"

Alyssa felt like she was caught in the scope of a high-powered rifle. There was no way she could lie to her mother outright, but she was so not ready for this conversation.

"I won't make you answer that right now. I can see it upsets you," Teresa said as she looked at her daughter with understanding and a little hurt.

"Mom . . ." Alyssa didn't know what to say.

"I guess the real question is this: Do you really *want* to ignore Jackson? Does he repel you, or disgust you? He seems to be trying, but would it make it better for you if he stopped."

"I did want to forget him . . ."

"And now?"

"Now I just don't know, Mom. He's made it more than clear that he tried marriage once and it was a disaster. I'm afraid that if I try to enter into *anything* with him, I'll just have my heart broken."

"Do you really have a choice?" Teresa asked her.

"I always have a choice," Alyssa stubbornly

stated. "I choose who I am with, and with Jackson, I'm afraid to risk it."

"Sometimes we have to risk everything before we can find true happiness."

"But what if I risk everything and end up with nothing?"

"Sweetheart, I don't have all the answers. I just know that when we find someone who wants to be with us, and we want to be with that someone, that's something special. Not everyone gets a happy ending, and not everyone is courageous enough to take hold of what's in front of them. Will you regret it if you don't give it a try?"

"I don't know, Mom. I really don't know. I haven't seen him in a few days and I still don't know. I am finding that I miss him, though." Alyssa let out a frustrated sigh.

"I think he's afraid to give you too much time to think," Teresa said. "I just know that, since he's pursuing you so steadily, there has to be more to it than basic attraction. A man doesn't do all he's doing just to get a woman into bed."

"Mom!" Alyssa was horrified her mother would even think such a thing, much less speak about it.

"I do have a child, Alyssa. I know what sex is," Teresa told her with a laugh.

Oh, this was getting worse and worse by the minute. Now Alyssa really was speechless.

When the phone rang next to her bed, Alyssa scrambled to pick it up. Talking about anything to anyone would be better than speaking about sex with her mother, who had left the room.

"Good evening, beautiful."

There was no use in even pretending she didn't know it was Jackson. The huskiness of his voice had her insides melting, and she knew beyond a doubt now that she was in real trouble, because three little words had picked up her heart rate in a second.

"Hello, Jackson."

"What are you wearing?"

"My pink jammies." She closed her mouth instantly after she said it. She should have said it was none of his business, not answered him.

"Mmm, the pink pajamas. I like those."

"Oh, well . . . I didn't know that." She actually did know that and had worn them just in case he showed up that day. That's how pathetic she was right now.

"I'll let you think I believe that.

"Want to play a game of truth or dare?" he asked with an obvious smile in his voice.

"There is no way I'm playing truth or dare with you, Jackson. I would surely lose."

"You can't win or lose truth or dare," he told her.

"Wanna bet? I have no doubt you'll have it so you get all you want out of it, and I'm left gasping for air."

"Ah, I can make you gasp for air a lot more pleasantly than by playing a game."

"See. Right there, Jackson Whitman. You are too smooth for me. I'm not playing any more games with you unless it's checkers."

"You're feeling feisty tonight. I really have missed you. I was traveling for work, but I'm back in town, so I think I should just come over."

"No. You're just fine right where you are," she said, not sure if it was panic or excitement filling her at the thought of him stopping by. And didn't they have phones on the road? She wanted to point that out, but then he would know that she'd missed their conversations and she couldn't tell him that.

"Alyssa, when are you going to quit fighting me?"

She replied without hesitation. "Never."

"Good. I like the fight in you. It makes my day to think about what you're going to do next."

"Jackson . . ." How and why did she keep resisting him? He seemed sure that he wasn't going away, and she was beginning to feel like she didn't want him to leave. But was he sticking around because of the excitement? If they ended up in a relationship, then their days would become routine, and at that point, wouldn't he run? It's what he did.

"Yes, Alyssa?"

"Do you really want to know me?"

He paused for so long she thought she'd lost him.

When he spoke, his voice was warm as honey on a hot summer day. "I already know you, Alyssa. I know you love pink, that you fiddle with your hair when you're nervous. I know that you have a heart as big as Texas and that you are loyal to your family and friends. I know that when we make love you are uninhibited and give everything of yourself . . ."

"That's just scratching the surface, Jackson."

"Then go on real dates with me. Accept my offer," he said, suddenly very serious.

"To be your mistress?" She wanted everything between them clear-cut and unambiguous.

"No. I want more than that," he said.

"But how much more, Jackson?" She held her breath and waited. Because whether she liked it or not, slowly and surely, though unwillingly, she was getting to know Jackson, and she was beginning to like him. Even more than that, she was afraid she was starting to fall in love with him.

And that was a problem, because he'd been more than clear that he would never love again. This, to him, was a game. And Jackson Whitman was very good at playing games—he played to win. She was heading down a dangerous road. But for the life of her she couldn't seem to drag herself away from the oncoming wreck.

"I don't know," he said, suddenly seeming nervous.

"And that's the problem, Jackson. You need to figure out what you want. I won't be someone who is used and discarded. I'm going to be a mother, but besides that, no woman deserves to be treated no better than a recycled bottle. If you can't even figure out what you want, then you have no business playing with me."

When Jackson was silent for several heartbeats, Alyssa knew it was a good time to end their visit. "Good night, Jackson."

He began to protest, but she simply disconnected the phone and then leaned back. She would have to see what tomorrow brought. Maybe this would be the end of their game. Maybe now he would realize that he couldn't play with fire without getting scorched. He was pushing for an affair, but if he wanted to be with her, really be with her, then she would push for forever.

When three more days passed with no call and no sight of Jackson, she was almost devastated. That's when she realized she was in too deep. It wasn't just a matter of her falling in love with him; it was a matter of how deeply in love with him she already was.

She had to make a decision, and the decision was clear. She had to back away from him or lose herself forever in a man who didn't know the meaning of retreat and who also didn't know the meaning of love.

026

Finally! Alyssa was officially off bed rest and ready to party until she dropped. Five margaritas and break dancing! Okay, not quite, but a woman could dream, couldn't she? Walking into the saloon, geared up for work, she was immediately greeted with a lovefest of questions and hugs by both staff and customers.

"We're so glad you're back, Alyssa," Cody said. "The place hasn't been the same without you." He pulled her in for a hug.

"I've missed you guys so much. It's been hell staying in bed for over two weeks straight."

Of course, Jackson had made that hell a whole lot easier to endure—until he'd disappeared! Now she was just happy to be out and about, able to get back to her normal life, and in a world that didn't revolve around Jackson Whitman.

It was good that he'd backed off, because Jackson was too sophisticated for her. The man could twist anything she said to fit what he wanted to hear. She was discovering that it was much easier if she ignored him.

Of course, the word *ignore* wasn't quite right, because she hadn't seen him in what felt like forever. Goodness, three days without him and she was mopey! What in the hell was wrong with her? Also, *easy* might not be an appropriate word, either, because Jackson was a man who didn't allow others to ignore him, not when he wanted his presence to be known. But he sure as heck could back off when she asked the tough questions. Hypocrite!

"Hello, beautiful." All of a sudden, Alyssa was being lifted into the air and her lips were covered in a scorching-hot kiss. "Glad to see you up and about again."

Her shock evaporated, and indignation took over. She hadn't heard a word from him in days, and then he just showed up as if nothing was wrong and kissed her in a room full of people? Not freaking acceptable.

"Put me down, Jackson. You're making me dizzy," she gasped.

He slid her slowly down his body before allowing her to step back. By this time, she was sporting a noticeable baby bump and she tugged self-consciously at her shirt, which was now clinging to her belly. If anyone in the bar hadn't already known that she was pregnant, they sure did now.

"All right, people, the show's over. Let's actually do some work," Alyssa said as she walked toward the back room to grab her apron.

She took several extra minutes in the bathroom, hoping that the glow in her cheeks had subsided. Yes, Jackson was clearly getting to her. What he'd done hadn't been just a kiss. It was a brand. He was letting them know, one and all, that she was his property. And she didn't appreciate that. She'd *never* agreed to be his. She was her own woman. After returning to the bar, she saw Jackson at his usual table, his laptop in front of him and a wide smile on his face.

"Have your tastes changed in my absence?" she asked, notepad at the ready.

"Nope. Once I like something, there's no going back," he said with too much innocence.

"Really? 'Cause you sure were running scared after our last conversation," she pointed out.

"I had to think. Plus, I figured you needed to do the same."

"So you disappeared for me?" She should retreat, but she didn't want to.

"I don't want to back off." The intensity in his eyes frightened her, and she decided she was the one backing down yet again.

"Cold soda and chips and salsa coming right out," she told him before turning away. Just for the hell of it, she put a little extra sway in her hips, using her catwalk tricks, and she glanced over her shoulder just before she entered the kitchen. She was perversely pleased at the sight of his eyes on her ass.

Maybe it was because she was feeling fat. Maybe it was because she'd been in bed for what seemed like forever, or maybe it was because her body was in a constant state of arousal. Whatever the reason, the look of lust in his eyes gave a boost to her ego.

The bar soon got busy, and Alyssa brought Jackson his food, refilled his drink, and scurried around serving her other customers. She had to admit *to herself* that she was more tired than usual. It might have been a better idea to take the easier early shift, but her stubborn pride had made her want the night shift.

The tips were much better on the dinner shift, and she still needed to save—more than ever, in fact, now that she'd been off work almost three weeks. Jackson had paid her wages, which she'd tried to refuse, but they were nothing compared to her tips.

Still, she was grateful to see her bank account going back up, if slowly. She'd have had a whole heck of a lot more if her business manager hadn't wiped her clean. No. She couldn't dwell on that. It was a time in her life that was over. Done.

Yes, Camden was working on her case, but it didn't look hopeful, not at all. It was impossible to get money out of someone who'd already spent it. Even if she managed to win the case, what good would it do?

The end of her shift was nearing when Camden walked through the doors.

"Alyssa, I was hoping to catch you," he said, and he dropped a kiss on her cheek.

"It's great to see you, Cam. Is something wrong?"

Maybe most clients didn't have such a personal relationship with their lawyers, but Cam had been the one she'd sobbed her story to. He'd also been the one to give her a hug when she needed it, and he'd been the one fighting to get her something back.

She liked him. She was just disappointed that she didn't *like him* like him. Even if she had, it would have been a lost cause. It was more than obvious that Cam wasn't interested in any of the women in Sterling. Some woman had broken his heart and someday she might get the story out of him.

"No, nothing is wrong, Alyssa, and it could have waited until tomorrow, but I was out and thought I'd save a trip to town for you."

"Well, I could definitely use a break," she said. "Samantha, can you cover my tables for ten minutes?" she asked as her coworker walked past.

"No prob, Alyssa." Samantha made a beeline to Jackson's table to check on him first.

Alyssa watched her flirt with Jackson, and she felt a twinge of jealousy. There was no way she was going to fret over that. Turning away, she walked to the opposite end of the saloon and found a private table for her and Camden.

"We are finally making headway with Carl Avone. I told you I didn't want to get your hopes up, that in most of these cases no money is ever found. But it appears that Mr. Avone has done this before. It also appears that he wasn't as smart at hiding the money as he thought he was."

"What does that mean?" Her heart was racing and she looked hopefully at Camden. If she could get even a piece of the money back, it would go a long way. If she got anything back, she swore she'd never be frivolous again. She'd earned a decent amount of money her last couple of years modeling. She'd spent a lot of it, too. But she'd had a good bit in savings when Carl stole it and ran.

"His bank accounts are frozen, and we are meeting next week with the other attorneys. There are several cases out against him. If things go well, you won't get it all back, but we're certainly looking at something," he said apologetically.

"Anything would be great. You can't imagine what a help it would be." She was so happy, she rose from the table and moved over to him. He stood up just in time to accept her hug as she wrapped her arms tightly around him.

"Is this a private moment?"

The frozen fury in Jackson's voice warned Alyssa that she'd better back off from his brother. The last thing she'd ever want to do was cause a fight between Jackson and Camden. At the same time, though, it was none of Jackson's business who her friends were, and it certainly was none of his business if she wanted to hug one of them.

"Hi, Jackson. I was just sharing some good news with my client. Do you have a problem with that?" Cam asked, letting go of Alyssa and sitting back down. The man looked completely relaxed.

"I have a problem with the way you were pawing my girl," Jackson said, his eyes slits.

"I am *not* your *girl*!" Alyssa interjected, incredulous that he'd be making a scene like this.

Jackson's eyes left Cam and focused on her. "Yes, you *are*; of course you are."

"Just because you say something is a fact doesn't make it law, Jackson Whitman. As a matter of fact, I asked you specifically what you wanted, and you froze up and sputtered. You don't even know what in the hell you want. I can tell you what you *need*, though—to learn some manners. That's been abundantly clear as long as I've known you." Alyssa then showed him her impeccable manners by kicking him hard in the shin.

Instead of feeling guilty, she took great pleasure in the way he flinched, and with a flip of her hair, she spun around and walked away from the over-bearing thug. She'd never consent to be his girl if he had that kind of attitude.

Alyssa ignored Jackson for the rest of her shift. She didn't listen in as he and Camden talked, tried not to glance over when she heard the two of them laughing, and refused to make eye contact when her shift ended and she walked past him to go to the back room.

The bully needed to think about his actions, and he really needed to think about how he was going to speak to her. Yes, he'd spoiled her for a few weeks, but she wouldn't be bought. She also wouldn't be with a man who was so insecure that his woman couldn't speak to other men.

Okay, so they weren't a couple, and maybe that made him unsure where he stood, but his alpha dog routine was a complete turnoff. He'd best learn it fast if he wanted even the smallest chance at having her go on a date with him. Money was important, of course, but it wasn't what would ever lead her to fall in love with anyone. If Jackson thought the gifts he'd bought were a way to her heart, he'd been wasting his cash.

Alyssa also ignored Jackson's new rule that fe-male employees were to be escorted outside to their cars at the end of night shifts, and she stomped out the back door while Cody was in the middle of flipping burgers. She was finished with all men—at least for now.

When she made it barely ten yards into the parking lot and somebody scooped her up into his arms, she didn't even have time to scream.

027

"Are you trying to sneak away?"

Alyssa's heart thudded as she turned her head to glare at Jackson. "You scared me to death."

"Sorry. Didn't mean to frighten you, but you shouldn't just run off. There was a message left for you, and you would have received it if you hadn't run out the back door." He strode toward his truck with Alyssa still in his arms.

"What message? Who would be calling me at work?"

"You would know if you hadn't tried so desperately to get away from me," he replied as he stopped by his passenger door.

"What are you doing now, Jackson? Do you honestly think I'm going to leave here with you?"

"Yep. That's exactly what I think."

How desperately she wanted to wipe that smug smile off his face. "Well, then, you're going to be sorely disappointed."

"It might be sort of difficult for you to take off on your own, since you have nowhere to go tonight."

"What are you talking about? I'm going home," she said, while at the same time realizing that he still held her securely in his arms. "Put me down!"

Slowly, so that every inch of her body rubbed along every inch of his, Jackson lowered her to the ground. She was light-headed for a moment and had to clutch at his arms to stay upright. It had to be because he'd swept her off her feet—literally. It couldn't possibly be because she had enjoyed the slow slide down his body.

"Your parents left a message."

She waited in vain for him to continue. "Jackson, you're being exasperating. Would you give me the message?"

She stepped away and placed her hands on her growing hips. Instead of being upset about her new curves, she was thrilled—well, most of time. Sometimes she did feel she was getting fat, but during her eight years of modeling, she'd had to stay way too skinny, and she was sick of that. Now if she wanted a slice of chocolate cake, she was damn well going to eat it.

This pregnancy business was giving her feminine contours she'd always dreamed of having. In her old line of business, though, the only models allowed to have anything approaching voluptuous curves worked for Victoria's Secret.

"If you ask nicely, I'll tell you."

"Are we suddenly five years old, Jackson? Give me my message." She began tapping her foot as she stood in front of him. She should have just walked over to her car, gotten in, and gone home. She could get the message from her parents in person—if they were still awake, at least.

"There was a fire—"

She cut in. "A fire? At my parents' house?" Her heart began pounding violently.

"Whoa, hold on. Don't get upset. They're both fine. Apparently there was a short in the wiring in the living room. A loose connection inside the outlet caused a spark, and it set the insulation smoldering. By the time your parents discovered it, the wall was in flames. The fire department got there fast, and the house was saved."

"What about my parents?" She didn't care about the damn house.

"They got out of the house in plenty of time. There's a gaping hole, but their neighbors came up and helped them seal it, and no one can stay there for at least a couple of weeks. Not until the smoke damage is cleaned up and the wall is replaced. Plus, they need to have the rest of the wiring inspected now so nothing like this happens again. The house they bought is a hundred years old, you know."

"Oh, my." Alyssa didn't know what to say.

"Everyone is fine, Alyssa," he reminded her.

"That's good. That's what's important," she muttered. But where was she supposed to go now? "I don't understand why we can't stay there if the wall is sealed up."

"The fire was smoldering for a while in the wall, and when it came through, the curtains ignited. It's unsafe to stay there right now—especially with you pregnant. Those fumes could be deadly."

It was difficult to process his words. Her head was still spinning over the fact that her parents' home had caught fire. At least they were safe. She had to keep telling herself that.

"They wanted you to call them as soon as you could. They're staying with the neighbors so your dad can keep an eye on the place."

"My mom was so excited to get a historical house," Alyssa told him. "She has visions of remodeling it, returning it to its former glory. I never even thought about something like wiring shorting out."

"Yeah, old houses are a lot of fun, but also a lot of work," Jackson said, "and they need regular inspections. Your mother will eventually have the place back on track to a new youth, but this will put a dent in their plans."

"If I know my mom, though, she'll already be using this as an excuse to redecorate. She went through a period where every spring she was painting the inside of the house a new color. She said it made the house feel new. Our home always did look superclean."

"Then she won't be too upset."

"Not a lot upsets my mom. She's one of the happiest people I know. I wish I could be more like her."

He now spoke in a lower voice. "You're more like her than you think."

"Wait! You said I couldn't go home, but if they're at the neighbors', I can stay there." Alyssa was afraid to hear what was going to come from his mouth next, because the gleam in his eyes told her he felt things were going his way.

"Unfortunately, there's not enough room there. The neighbors only have two bedrooms. Their daughter was kind enough to give your parents her room, and she's sleeping on the couch. They said they found an apartment for you that you can move into next week. They already put a deposit down, but they asked if anyone working here at the saloon had an extra room for you for this week, and I assured them that we'd find you a place to stay until everything was all sorted out."

Alyssa didn't need to ask him where the room was. His practically glowing eyes had already told her.

She couldn't stay with him. Her resolve wouldn't last a day, let alone a week. Her morning sickness was long gone, and in its place were raging hormones.

Sex!

She wanted sex, day and night. If she slept under Jackson's roof, she would go to bed with him, no matter how hard she fought it. Hell, the smallest touch from him, and she'd be ripping off his clothes.

"I can't stay with you, Jackson." There. She'd said it. She could find a cheap hotel, couldn't she? The problem was that Sterling didn't have any hotels. Crap! Maybe Cody had a spare bed.

No. She remembered him talking about how much he wanted to get out of his parents' house. His dad drank too much, and the more the man drank, the rowdier he became. That wasn't an option.

And staying with Samantha would be even worse than staying with Jackson. Alyssa didn't think either of the women would survive it if they attempted to room together. Alyssa did have a ton of customers, and she could possibly ask one of them about a spare room, but she really didn't want to look for someone to house her. That was asking too much of them. If she weren't living at her parents' now, she wouldn't be in this mess. She should have had her own place before the fire, dang it. It was mortifying that she'd had to return home with her head down, a failure. Oh, this was so bad.

"I have a few extra bedrooms, Alyssa. I won't do

anything you don't want me to do," he said as he held up his hand in a "Scout's honor" salute.

"Yeah, I'm *sure* you won't."

She noticed he'd said that he wouldn't do anything she didn't want to do. He could probably tell there was a hell of a lot she wanted to do. The never-ending ache in her body could be soothed only one way, and Jackson would certainly be able to give her more pleasure than she could handle.

"What's it going to be, Alyssa? My place . . . or your car?" he asked as he leaned against the side of his truck, just oozing confidence.

"My mom probably wouldn't approve of my staying with you . . ."

"For one thing, Alyssa, you're a grown woman who can stay with anyone you want to stay with." He had to laugh before continuing. "For another, your mother was the one I spoke to. She asked *me* if I had a spare room." He was triumphant while delivering that message.

All Alyssa could think—not for the first time!—was that her mother was a traitor. Teresa knew Jackson was the baby's father, even though Alyssa hadn't come right out and told her. Her mom was trying to be a matchmaker.

Still, she hated having to do this. Hated that Jackson was so damn pleased about the entire situation. This was working out real well for the guy.

"Fine, Jackson," she said through gritted teeth. "I'll come for tonight. But tomorrow I'll figure something else out." She brushed past him and began walking toward her car.

"Where are you going?"

"I'll follow you. I'm not leaving my car here."

"It's not a problem. I'll bring you in to work tomorrow night. I was planning on coming in anyway," he said, and he took her arm and steered her back toward his truck.

"I don't need to be coddled, Jackson," she told him, and she yanked her arm away from his.

"I'm not coddling you. But I live up in the hills, high enough that there are still some slick areas in the parts of the road that are always in the shade. You'll be much safer if we're in my truck."

He sounded so logical. So why did she feel that he was once again saying whatever he needed to in order to get his way?

"I'm tired, my feet hurt, and I'm starving," she said, feeling on the verge of tears. Shouldn't she try to fight this harder? Wouldn't it be better to sleep in her car? No. And she knew that. With a sigh, she began moving toward his truck. "You win for now. But I'm staying only one night!"

Jackson just grinned as he opened the passenger door of his truck and helped her up into the ridiculously tall vehicle. When he joined her inside the large cab, it didn't seem so big anymore. As he started the engine and country music blared from the speakers, Alyssa sagged back against the headrest.

What had she gotten herself into now?

028

Just one night? As she sat up in bed, Alyssa mulled over that particular failure of hers. Not only had she been in Jackson's home for three nights now, but she was also in terrible shape.

True to his word, he hadn't made a move on her, hadn't touched her—not once! And she was ticked off. She wanted him to drag her into his arms, kiss her, strip off her clothes, and relieve the burning ache taking over her body.

But no. All of a sudden he'd turned into Mr. Nice Guy. He was making her meals, smiling and whistling, and he'd even patted her on the head once. She wasn't his freaking dog!

Well, his other dog, anyway. He had the most beautiful yellow Lab she'd ever been around, and the two of them were becoming very close. Poppy was currently keeping Alyssa's feet warm. Her devastating brown eyes were barely open now, their lids drooping so sweetly, and then the pup would almost wake up again. Alyssa was head over heels in love with Poppy.

As she'd never been much of a dog person, she

was thoroughly surprised by this form of love at first sight, but she knew that when she had to settle in elsewhere, she would miss this golden beauty of a dog terribly.

"Maybe Jackson thinks I'm too fat now," she said to Poppy, who opened her eyes and looked at her as if she could understand every word.

"I mean, I like my curves. I personally think they're sexy, but when I saw myself in the mirror last night, my stomach was sticking out. I'm going to have to break down and buy maternity jeans. I *really* don't want to, but I can't keep leaving the ones I have unbuttoned. What if they start to slip while I'm carrying a tray?"

Poppy let out a low, sweet little whine, and Alyssa took that as agreement.

"I don't know why I haven't gotten a dog before. I don't know why I thought I wasn't a dog person. You keep my feet warm, you're the perfect companion at bedtime—especially since I can't seem to sleep—and you listen so much better than a man ever does."

Poppy's head tilted, and then her tongue came out and swiped the bottom of Alyssa's foot.

She giggled. "If it wasn't for you, I would have gone crazy by now. Should I just give in and climb into Jackson's bed?"

Poppy's head tilted again, and she let out a quiet bark.

"Yeah, you're right. That's too desperate. Have you had babies, Poppy? Seriously, the body goes crazy."

Poppy licked her foot one more time, then rested her head on her paws and stared at Alyssa.

"Okay, it's official. I've lost my sanity. I am actually holding a conversation with a dog." She ran a hand through her mussed-up hair.

"I think it's quite charming."

Alyssa froze as she looked up and found Jackson standing in the doorway. Oh, no! How long had he been there? Please, only fifteen seconds. Please! She rewound her conversation with Poppy in her head and felt her cheeks heat.

"I thought you were out with your brothers," she muttered, embarrassed beyond belief.

"Just got home and heard you talking."

From the gleam in his eyes, she wasn't sure what he'd overheard, but it had to be something good. Of course, she had Poppy with her right now. It wasn't like he was going to crawl into her bed.

"By the way, yes, Poppy did have a litter of puppies," Jackson said with a big grin. "They are spread out with various family members, and we make sure to give them reunions several times a year. I didn't actually want a dog in the first place, but Poppy was found near my dad's ranch, very pregnant, and my brother Spence brought her over. I fought him, but he left her sitting in my living room. I caved when she looked at me with those pathetic eyes."

Yeah, he'd heard it all. Dang. And how was she going to keep her distance when he said he was so against commitment, but then took in a beautiful lost dog? He might say one thing, but his actions said another. Alyssa was more confused than ever as she sat there not knowing what to say.

"Also, I have had many an erotic dream over your curves. You are unbelievably sexy and I would be more than happy if you climbed into my bed—completely naked. Anytime, night or day. You can wake me; you can call me back to the house. Hell, you just crook your little finger, and I will make you purr."

He was standing there, his breathing shallow, his eyes bright, and when she glanced down and saw the bulge in his pants, her forehead broke out in a sweat.

One word and she could be flying high. One word and this ache would go away. All it would take was one word. She tried to open her mouth, tried to lift her finger, tried to tell him that, yes, she wanted to make love. About a thousand times in a row. But no words came out. She just stared at him, taking a giant gulp when she realized she was too chicken or too stubborn to ask for what she really wanted.

"You're missing out, Alyssa," he said as he began unbuttoning his shirt.

No. No. No. She just wouldn't look. The last thing she needed to see was his glorious chest.

Though she told herself not to look, she found her head turning back just as the last button came undone, showing off an expanse of hard muscles and taut flesh that had her drooling. How in the heck did a business guy have such an incredible physique? Pretty hot and tempting, indeed.

"It's too bad," Jackson said as he turned away, giving her an unhindered view of his beautiful back. As far as she could tell, there wasn't a single piece of Jackson that wasn't tasty and delicious. Yes, the perfect word to describe Jackson was *yummy*.

And she was pretty damn hungry right now!

"I'm just across the hall if you want me," he said before turning back around and looking at her. "The door's open and I sleep . . . commando."

He disappeared into his room. She watched as the light flashed on, then she heard his steps on the hardwood floor. A few seconds later, his shower started, and she groaned. He was getting soapy and wet right now. She could slide against him so easily.

"How much am I supposed to take, Poppy? Really. He's so not playing fair. I know what he's doing, dammit. If I make the first move, he wins."

Poppy was losing interest in her ramblings.

Heck, she would lose interest, too, if she were the dog. She was sounding more and more irrational every day. But she had her reasons, and they were valid. They were! she insisted in her own head.

"It's just that this . . ." She paused, trying to think of the word. "It's not a lie," she said defensively, as if Poppy were judging her. "I just haven't told him. There's nothing wrong with that."

Alyssa could have sworn that Poppy rolled her eyes.

"A good night's rest. That's all this is about. I just can't sleep on this bed. It's terrible," she grumbled as she sank down so she was lying on her back.

In reality, it was the best mattress she'd ever slept on, and she'd slept in some fancy hotels during her better photo shoots. The pillows and blankets were soft and heavenly as well.

No, it wasn't the bedding that was causing her lack of sleep. When the shower shut off and the light across the hall soon went out, Alyssa had to force herself not to scream. He was climbing into his bed, naked, and now he was lying there. All she had to do was slip from her bed, go across the hall, slide beneath the covers, and he'd take over.

She closed her eyes, picturing him removing her pajamas, his hands sliding across her aching flesh, his mouth following his hands, those lips . . . ah, those lips could do magical things to her body.

Then, when she was wet, ready, he'd slip inside her, fill her body . . . A groan slipped past her throat as she flipped over to her other side, her core pulsing, her heart racing.

Flipping over again, she punched her pillow and Poppy looked up, her ears high as she tried to figure out what in the world was wrong with Alyssa.

"I'm sexually frustrated, okay?" she said.

Poppy closed her eyes and snuggled a little closer, the conversation done for the dog. Alyssa really needed to make up her mind sooner or later, because this indecision was causing her far too much stress.

029

The smell of fresh biscuits and hot chocolate drifted up the staircase and straight to Alyssa's nose. Her stomach rumbled loudly enough to wake her, and she found Poppy curled up in a ball at her side, better than any electric blanket.

"Do you smell that?" she mumbled.

Poppy's tail wagged, and Alyssa took that as a yes.

"Oh, this could be bad," she said as she reluctantly threw off the covers and got to her feet. Poppy whined and looked beseechingly at her from the bed.

"I know the bed is nice and warm, but I'm starving," she told the pitiful dog.

Taking the world's fastest shower, Alyssa dressed in comfortable clothes and made her way downstairs. It was her day off, and though she wasn't going to admit it to Jackson, she needed it. Coming back and working three days straight had been a lot when she was just getting off bed rest.

However, if Jackson got even an inkling of what the shifts were doing to her worn-out ankles, he'd move her to part-time or, worse yet, start her maternity leave now.

Nope. She'd just suck it up. Maybe take a relaxing stroll around the lake about half a mile from his house. Jackson was a lucky man. Although his house was only ten minutes from town, he still lived in seclusion in the foothills. He had his own stream, she didn't know how many acres of lush green lawns, and healthy, full trees. To her, it was paradise.

When she turned the corner into the kitchen, she and Jackson exchanged greetings, and she immediately honed in on what mattered.

"Something smells mouthwatering," she said. She walked right up to the stove and found crispy bacon sitting on a napkin-covered plate. When Jackson's back was turned, she swiped two pieces, gulped one down, and handed the other to Poppy, who was right on her heels.

"I saw that," Jackson said with a chuckle, though he hadn't turned away from the sink, where he was rinsing a bowl.

"What?" She did her best to inject innocence into her tone, but her mouth was full and she punctuated her question by licking her lips.

Jackson finally turned to face her. "Not only are you sneaking into breakfast early, but it also appears that you've stolen my dog."

"I have no idea what you're talking about." She sat down at the table, and Poppy stretched out at her feet. The shrewd dog knew Alyssa would sneak her more treats.

"Of course you don't," he said with a chuckle. "Are you hungry?"

Was she ever not hungry during this pregnancy? That was the real question. Unwilling to seem too eager, however, she waited a moment before replying.

"I could eat. Smells good." She was trying to sound bored, but since she was practically drooling, she suspected her act wasn't entirely convincing. "Do you need any help, Jackson?"

"Nope. It's all ready. Want me to dish you up a plate?"

"I'll get it," she said quickly. Though she didn't mind being coddled on occasion, what ended up on her plate was too serious a matter to leave to a mere man. "Why do you do so much cooking anyway, Jackson?"

He paused while he set the platters of food on the counter. "I don't know. I guess I just always enjoyed it. We had a cook at Dad's house, and I discovered early that if I wanted fresh-baked cookies and bread, the cook would give me whatever I wanted if I helped her out. I just sort of began loving to cook."

As Jackson spoke, Alyssa looked at the mounds

of food on the counter and said hello to five more pounds. He'd made bacon, eggs, French toast, and biscuits, and he was now placing fruit, butter, syrup, and jams on the table. Just looking at all that made her feel fatter.

What to do, what to do? Unable to decide, Alyssa took a little of everything and brought an overflowing plate back to the dining table. Even before her modeling days, with those constant breakfasts of a few berries and a skinny latte, she'd never begun the day with such decadence.

Waiting just about killed her, but she didn't touch a single bite until Jackson joined her and shifted a piece of bacon off the table and straight into Poppy's mouth. Only then did she pick up a piece of her own and begin nibbling on it.

"Good?" he asked.

"Fantastic. I wish I could cook as well as you. Maybe you can give me a few lessons."

"The best compliment to the cook is a hearty appetite," Jackson said. "And I think cooking lessons could be quite fun." The way he said it had her heart racing again. Then he put two over-easy eggs on top of his French toast and doused it all in syrup.

She looked at him in horror as he scooped up a big bite. "That's disgusting."

"What?" He looked genuinely confused.

"You're mixing egg yolk with syrup. Gah."

"Your scrambled eggs touch your syrup. What's the difference?" He went ahead and took another bite.

"There's a big difference. My eggs are cooked all the way through. And I don't *dip* them in the syrup. Or pour syrup over them. Some might just run off the French toast and hit the corner of my eggs, but that's incidental."

She did, however, love dipping her bacon in syrup. Yum.

"To each his own," he said, scarfing down two pieces of French toast in no time flat.

She threw him a dubious glance. "I guess so," she replied. But why quibble? It kept her from eating. The biscuits were buttery and flaky, just the way she liked them, and by the time she was finished, she knew she'd need that walk for sure.

"Do you have plans for today?" Jackson asked her as he sat back, his plate empty and a steaming cup of coffee in his hand.

She looked at it and sighed. She'd kill for a hot mocha right now, but she was doing her best to listen to her doctor and he'd said no caffeine.

When Alyssa didn't reply—she was clearly caught up in java lust—he continued. "I wanted to spend some time together, Alyssa."

"Doing what?"

"It's a family tradition, but trust me, you'll love it."

His eyes were glowing with excitement, and she found that she did trust him . . . well, as much as she trusted any man. Which wasn't a whole heck of a lot lately.

"I wanted to take a walk, Jackson." Going somewhere civilized with him seemed more pleasant than hiking through the foothills, but she needed to burn off her two-thousand-calorie breakfast.

"You'll get in plenty of walking where we're going," he assured her.

"I don't like surprises."

"Liar. I know you love them. I'm on good terms with your parents now, you know. They've filled me in."

"You shouldn't be speaking to my parents," she said, her eyes narrowing. "We aren't a couple, Jackson, just because I'm staying here. I know that sounds ungrateful, and I'm sorry, but I think talking to my parents about me crosses a line." What were they talking to him about? She hoped that her mother and father weren't giving Jackson any ammo to use against her. And she really hoped that her mother wasn't giving him clues about the parentage of the baby. She still hadn't made her decision about how to tell him.

"I think your parents are great. Besides, your dad is killing it as foreman at the oil fields," Jackson said. "Anyway, since this is a small town, we all act quite neighborly. I can most certainly be friends with your parents."

"I don't like it."

"Tough." That was the end for him on this subject.

Once again Jackson thought he could win the argument. Well, she'd find a time when he didn't win. But, as of now, she couldn't think of a more valid reason that he should keep his distance from her parents. Even thinking it in her own head made her see that she sounded unreasonable.

"I need to call and check in with my mom, then we can go. Does Poppy get to come?"

Poppy knew they were talking about her, because she scooted out from beneath the table, still licking her lips from the bacon grease, and looked up imploringly at Jackson.

"You are such a faker," Jackson said as he bent down and scratched the dog's head.

Alyssa's heart beat an extra few times when Poppy leaned her head into his hand, showing how very much she trusted him. If you really wanted to know a man's character, a good way to find out was by watching the way he treated animals. He obviously loved Poppy and Poppy loved him. Dang it. This was just one more thing that stacked the deck against her.

"Yes, Poppy can come. She usually goes everywhere with me," he said, not giving Alyssa any clues.

"All right, then, I'll come. Let me get my boots."

Alyssa took her time getting ready for the outing. He'd only told her they would be outdoors. So she dressed in layers—that way she could discard clothes depending on if this early summer day decided to be warm or cool.

On her way back down the stairs, Alyssa paused. Jackson and Poppy were waiting at the bottom, their eyes shining, both of them eager for their outing. When Jackson smiled, his whole face lighting up, she knew he wasn't the same man she'd met a little over five months earlier on that plane ride from Paris.

She also knew she no longer had a valid reason for keeping the pregnancy from him. What she didn't know was how she was going to tell him. Their truce would surely end, and she was finding that she enjoyed his friendship. What if telling him made him hate her?

She was in real trouble, because whether she wanted to believe in him or not, she now did, and she didn't want him to suddenly start looking at her like she was a liar. Pasting on a smile, she descended the stairs.

The words were on the tip of her tongue, but

when his arm easily moved behind her back, and his hand brushed her skin, she shuddered. She couldn't say anything now, or their day would be ruined.

Soon. She swore to herself she would tell him soon. Preferably once she was moved in nice and safe to her new apartment where she would be able to escape his wrath if he was furious with her.

030

"Um, Jackson . . ."

Alyssa felt like the classic impatient kid who kept asking, "Are we there yet?" And she didn't even know where "there" was. She'd already asked him at least three times now where they were headed, and he was remaining tight-lipped.

"Not much longer," he said with a grin.

She hoped not. They were bumping along a gravel road, and it wasn't her idea of fun.

"Seriously, I'm starting to get a little carsick," she said, not wanting to put a damper on anything, but this wasn't the best of roads.

"Here we are."

They turned a corner, and Alyssa looked straight ahead to find a giant cliff and about a dozen trucks all parked with people milling about. And a lot of them were toting guns.

"What is this?"

She wasn't worried he'd brought her here to shove her over the side, but even the most trusting soul would have felt a bit of paranoia when confronted with a scene like this.

"We're going to do some skeet shooting," he told her as he opened his door. Poppy was the first one out of the truck. She jumped down and ran gleefully toward the crowd of people.

"I didn't think you were going to make it."

Alyssa's door opened and Camden was standing there with a Cheshire cat grin on his face.

"I didn't know we were coming," she said as she accepted his hand and climbed down.

"What? Jackson didn't fill you in?"

"Nope." She was now walking between Camden and Jackson as they strolled over to a giant contraption that was set up on the bumper of one of the large blue trucks.

Michael appeared and told her, "You're just in time to give it a whirl," and a shotgun was thrust into her arms.

She was given a quick safety lesson, and she didn't have the heart to tell them she'd been shooting targets from the time she was a little girl. No real Texas woman was raised without knowing how to fire a weapon. But she now understood Jackson's secrecy about their destination. He probably thought she'd squeal, "Ewwww, guns!" and head for the hills—running like a girl, of course.

She was boiling over with excitement as a disk of clay was launched into the air. Taking aim, Alyssa shattered the disk, and she felt immense pride as a cheer went up. Another disk was launched and she knocked it from the sky, too. After a few more rounds, it was time to hand the gun over. Setting the safety, she then gave it to Camden.

"Hmm, another thing I didn't know about you," Jackson said with a laugh as he opened a can of Diet Coke and took a large swallow.

"You never asked," she pointed out.

"That was impressive. I wouldn't think a former model would know how to handle a gun."

Alyssa glared at him as she tapped her foot. "Jackson Whitman, just when I think you are growing as a person, you make an asinine statement like that."

"Okay, okay, I admit, I can be an ass," he said with a laugh. "But I have to say that I like a woman holding a gun."

"I like a man who knows it's not wise to approach a woman holding a gun, especially when he's being an ass."

"Ooh, I like her, Jackson. She's a keeper."

Alyssa turned to find Spence standing beside her. Of all Jackson's brothers, she was least familiar with Jackson's oldest sibling.

"Damn straight she is," Jackson said, and he flung his arm around her shoulders.

Alyssa was having too much fun to correct him or shrug off his hold. He'd brought her out here to be with his entire family. That meant he had to be changing, didn't it? She'd already concluded that he was a different man from the one she'd met on that plane, and now she was getting to know him more. Was it time she stopped fighting this? Did she give them a real chance?

There was the secret of their baby between them, but this wasn't news she could just blurt out. She had to figure out a way to tell him, and as she stood there with him, his face beaming, his family accepting her with no questions, she felt tremendous guilt for holding on to her secret.

"That was great shooting, Alyssa." Now Martin was talking as he walked up with Bethel, Maggie, and Eileen. "Your parents are right over there."

She turned to see another truck set up with a skeet shooter; her mom fired expertly at a small clay disk. "Excuse me," she said, beaming at Jackson, which made his smile falter for a moment in surprise. She didn't normally let her guard down enough to show him such pleasure. She knew he was wondering what was going on. Let him wonder.

Standing at a safe distance, she waited for her mother to finish with her disks.

"I was wondering when you were going to get here," Teresa said when she turned around and saw her daughter. "Martin assured us you were coming." She gave Alyssa a warm hug.

"Jackson didn't give me any warning; he just said we were going out. And why didn't you tell me when I spoke to you that you were going to be here?"

"Because I like to surprise you once in a while. Plus, Jackson was so sure he was about to teach you something new. I wanted to be here when he learned you're much better than him. Have you gotten to shoot yet?"

"Yeah, I knocked them out of the sky." Alyssa patted her stomach. "Even with the bump trying to throw me off."

"That's my girl," Teresa said. "Don't you *ever* let a man win just to feel like a man. Too many women do that. Drives me crazy."

"Come on, Mom. You taught me far better than that," Alyssa said.

"That I did, baby girl," she said before giving her daughter a hug. "You are glowing today. You must not be sick."

"No. The morning sickness has all but evaporated, and I feel better than I have in a long time."

"Good. Now, let's get away from all these trigger-happy people and take a walk," Teresa said as she wound an arm through her daughter's.

The two of them strolled along a path, and Alyssa said, "I haven't been out this far before. It's beautiful."

When someone rushed by them, the two stepped aside.

"Get it!"

"What in the heck are they after?" Teresa said as they picked up their pace.

A few younger kids were carrying BB guns and chasing what appeared to be a giant rat. "Is that a muskrat?" Alyssa had no idea. The vermin here were different from those in Texas.

"Not sure what that is," her mother said.

Before they could say anything more, Jackson dashed past them, making Alyssa really curious now. She and her mother quickly trailed behind him to where they found the group of kids and Jackson at the edge of a flowing stream.

"What are you chasing?" she asked as they stood back, a little worried, since they were getting farther from their group of people. Safety was always better when in numbers.

"The kids were hunting," Jackson said with a laugh. "But we couldn't let them get too far away."

"What are they hunting?"

"Rabbits, squirrels, birds," he answered casually.

"That's terrible, Jackson. Those creatures aren't doing anything to them," Alyssa said.

"Hey! I'm just assigned as this hour's babysitter." He held up his hand in self-defense.

"Well, then, watch them and make them head

back." Alyssa stamped her foot now and glared at him.

"Yes, ma'am," he said with a big grin before turning to find one of the boys balancing on some rocks at the edge of the creek.

"Jimmy, get down," Jackson yelled, but it was too late. The boy fell forward, soaking his clothes. The stream wasn't deep enough to be dangerous, but that water looked frigid.

Jackson ran down, and when he reached out a hand to help Jimmy back up, he slipped on a moss-covered rock and tumbled into the creek with him. With a pained and incredulous look on his face, Jackson tried to scramble to his feet, but he slipped again. This time, like a child throwing a tantrum, he slapped his hands down, spraying water everywhere around him. Which, of course, sparked a spontaneous water fight.

"It's time to retreat," Teresa said as a few droplets reached them.

"I couldn't agree with you more," Alyssa said, and they began backing away.

"Jackson is sure good with those kids," Teresa remarked.

"You know he's the father." It wasn't a question.

"Yes. When are you going to tell him?"

Alyssa let out a relieved breath. It felt so good to finally speak about it. Even if it wasn't to Jackson. Her mother had always been there for her. Why she'd waited so long she would never know.

"I'm going to, Mom. I promise. It's just that when I met him, he told me some things about his past, told me he would never be in a relationship again. And then Samantha spoke about the nasty custody battle he was in with his ex before she passed. It was just supposed to be one night. We were strangers passing. We weren't supposed to see each other again." Alyssa felt a smidgen of guilt when her mother flinched.

"I know you're an adult, but it still pangs a mother's heart to hear her daughter speak so casually about sex, darling."

"I don't take sex casually, Mom. Jackson was only the second man I've ever been with. I've told you about Carl and what a mistake that was. The thing is that this last month I've gotten to know Jackson a lot more. I did fear he would try to take my baby, try to replace the daughter he'd lost. I know now I was wrong to think that, but I didn't know him, only what he'd said and what others had said. Now I just don't know how to tell him." Alyssa prayed that her mother could impart some words of wisdom.

"The longer you wait, the harder it will be, Alyssa. It's like ripping off a bandage. You just have to do it and face the consequences."

"I was afraid that's what you were going to say," Alyssa said with a long sigh.

"This isn't something that goes away, and I have grown to know the Whitman family. They are good people. I think you should trust Jackson."

A silence fell as they continued walking back to the group, with Alyssa trying to process her thoughts. When they heard the kids' war cry behind them, the two women picked up their pace, and Alyssa did some power walking up the path, back to where it was safe and dry.

The afternoon passed quickly, and Alyssa was surprised by the good mood Jackson was in despite his soaked clothes and his less-than-manly control of a shotgun. Those clay pigeons just flew off unscathed, and Jackson endured the good-natured ribbing of the entire Whitman clan.

When the sun began setting, several of the vehicles pulled away, but instead of making Alyssa jump straight back into his truck, Jackson grabbed her hand and led her to a bench with a spectacular view of the valley.

"This has always been one of my favorite places, Alyssa."

"I can see why," she said as she snuggled into his arms.

"I've never brought a woman up here before, though. Up until today, I've been here only with family."

As he said those words, he pulled her more

closely against his side. "I don't know how, or when, but you're becoming a part of that family."

Closing her eyes, Alyssa melted against him. What was she supposed to say? Did she confess her growing feelings? Did she say that she wanted them all to be a family?

"There's so much I need to tell you," she finally said while his hand slowly drifted up and down her back.

"I hope you know that you can tell me anything, Alyssa."

It was on the tip of her tongue. This moment seemed perfect; they seemed perfect. But what if it caused a fight? She couldn't bear that right now.

"You were pretty adorable with those kids today" was all she could think of saying. Maybe it would help her figure out more of his thinking about having another child of his own.

"I love kids. Always have. The older we get, the more we feel a need to protect ourselves, having to be careful about what we say and when. Kids are pure; they're honest. If you just show them love, they will love you back. There are no games."

Alyssa was surprised by his words. "You love to play games, Jackson."

"I used to," he said with a sigh. "I think it's how I survived the last few years. Being with you has done something to me. I can't figure it out . . ."

"I understand how you feel. You know, Jackson, I really like being with you." It wasn't exactly a confession of love, but she was giving him something.

"That's a start," he said as he turned her so he could look into her eyes.

"We seem to have had quite a few starts," she said with a laugh, trying to lighten the intense moment.

"I'm not going to let you pull away, Alyssa," he said as he cupped her face.

"I don't want you to."

He bent down and kissed her, and it felt right. There was no hesitation on her part as her arms circled his neck and she got lost in his embrace. The moment, however, was too short—they were interrupted when some of the older kids started whistling at the two of them.

Jackson gave her an apologetic look before he jumped up to chase down the culprits. Alyssa sat on the bench and watched him. He seemed happier than she'd ever seen him before. Yes, it was time to tell him the entire truth. She just needed to marshal enough courage to do it.

031

Jackson took his time in front of the fireplace, moving logs around and thinking about what he wanted to say. Yes, it was warm out, but the whole idea of having a fire in June made him smile, and he felt drawn to the warmth and to the mindless activity required to get a good blaze going.

Alyssa was curled up on the sofa, her legs tucked beneath a purple knitted blanket. She looked so calm and content. If only he could feel that way. Thankfully, the tenants in her apartment had yet to vacate, and the delay was working to his benefit. He'd thank them personally if he didn't think it would get him into trouble. They'd had a good week since the skeet shooting, kissing often, holding each other, talking. But he wanted more. He needed more.

He wasn't normally one of those touchy-feely, let-it-all-hang-out kind of guys. He usually just buried emotions deep inside, thought about work instead. But he needed Alyssa beyond anything that was rational. The more she was showing in her pregnancy, the more desire he felt to protect her and her unborn child.

Did it make sense? No. But even knowing that, he still couldn't seem to stop himself. Everything in his life now seemed to point directly to Alyssa and her baby. How had one night shaped him so much? Why couldn't he let Alyssa go? How was it possible that meeting in the airport had changed both of their lives so irrevocably?

Damned questions.

Jackson now asked one aloud. "Are you comfortable?"

"Yes, thank you," Alyssa said as she sat on the couch. "I'm getting pretty tired, though. It's been a long day."

"Not yet," he said, then added, "please."

"Is something on your mind, Jackson?"

Yeah, making love to you, he wanted to say. Instead, he took a deep breath, then stood, moved over to his liquor cabinet, and poured himself a generous shot of scotch. After downing it in one gulp, he refilled his glass and moved over to the chair across from her. Alyssa waited, just sipping on her soda water.

"You trust me now, don't you, Alyssa?"

She paused, but he was pleased when she didn't look away. Instead she took another sip and used a little time to form her words.

"I believe I do," she said finally.

That answer pained him. "I wouldn't intentionally hurt you. I swear to that."

"I believe you, Jackson. I think both of us have changed since we met on New Year's Eve."

"I didn't think I wanted to change, but being around you has altered me, made me think in a whole new way."

"I'm not special, Jackson. And you should never change for another person. You should change because you want to be a better man."

"That's one of the reasons I care about you, Alyssa. You don't expect people to be who they aren't. You have so much love for your family, for your friends. Is there room in your life for me?"

Jackson was almost shocked when he said those words. By the look in her eyes, Alyssa was pretty shocked, too.

"I . . . uh . . . I do care about you, Jackson."

"That's not what I asked. I asked if there's room in your life for me." He didn't want to push this, but he needed to.

"I don't know how to answer that." She was clearly still guarding herself.

"It's really hard for me to trust people, Alyssa. I think it's because of the way I grew up. You know I was in foster care, that my dad adopted Spence, Camden, and me when we were teenagers. But you don't know the hell we went through before coming to live with our dad, Martin. There are a lot of cruel people in the world and it makes your skin grow a bit thicker when you live like that."

"I'm not trying to be cruel," she said quickly. "I'm sorry you went through so much."

"I wasn't implying that you were being cruel. And I certainly don't want your sympathy." He was growing frustrated—this wasn't where he wanted this conversation to go. His last few words had come out a little bit harsher than they should have and she'd flinched, making him feel like a heel. "I'm sorry."

"Don't apologize. It's how you feel," she said, but there was hurt in her tone.

"It's just that lots of people have sympathy—they're just full of it, you know? To me, that's meaningless. I don't like it when people say they are sorry but their actions don't prove it. I don't like it when someone puts on one face to the world and then becomes a monster behind closed doors. I don't like it when people lie to get their way."

She flinched again, and Jackson ran a hand through his hair, knowing he was messing this all up. He tried to calm himself so he could get back on track. He couldn't tell her he loved her, as he wasn't even sure he knew what romantic love was. But he could tell her that he cared—he knew that beyond any doubt—and that he didn't want to lose her.

"Sometimes not everything is black-and-white, Jackson. Sometimes people have a reason for keeping secrets."

"What does that mean? If someone has something to hide, then that's never good."

"Like I said, not everything is black-and-white." She was frowning at him.

"We are getting off track here, Alyssa. I don't even know what we're talking about anymore."

"What is it that you're trying to say, Jackson?"

"If you could go back and change certain aspects of your life, knowing what you know now, would you?"

Alyssa sat there for a moment, clearly giving the question serious thought.

"I might change some things, but I might not. I believe that every experience in our lives shapes us, teaches us where we went wrong, and there's some sort of lesson to be learned at the end."

"What about your being pregnant without the kid's father anywhere to be found? Would you do that all over again?" He watched as she flinched again and her eyes darted away. "What? Too close to home?"

"I just don't want to talk about that right now," she finally said, still refusing to look into his eyes.

"You are more than willing to listen to other people, but you don't like speaking about yourself, do you?"

"No. I don't."

"You've shared with me, though, Alyssa. I think we're good together." This was where he wanted the conversation to go.

"I think we're not bad together," she said with a hint of a smile.

"Then let me be there for you. Open up to me. Share with me."

"You're asking for a lot," she said, but she wasn't looking away.

"With you, I find that I want it all."

"What does that mean to you, Jackson?"

He stopped, not knowing the answer to that. But he wouldn't lie to her anymore. Enough secrets had been kept between them in their attempts to guard themselves. Honesty would probably get him a lot further than deception.

"I want to be with you, take care of you. I don't want to let you go."

He saw the internal battle raging within her and he waited. He'd opened up to her, told her he cared, showed her how much he cared this past month and a half, and confessed more than he had to any other person since his ex-wife's betrayal. The ball was now in her court.

When Alyssa didn't say anything, just shifted the blanket off her lap and stood up, Jackson's heart stopped. He didn't know if she was going to walk to him or away from him. He felt that if she walked away this time, it would be the end for them. He'd given her all he could at this point.

When she came toward him slowly, and then climbed into his lap, pure joy filled him. She reached up and cupped his face, looking directly into his eyes. "I need you, too, Jackson."

When she kissed him, there was no more question of what would happen . . .

032

Jackson took the sweet kiss that Alyssa offered and transformed it. He held her as if he would never let go, and the two of them sank to the floor, onto the soft rug that was spread out in front of the blazing fire.

As his mouth trailed down her neck, Alyssa felt excitement take the place of pain and sorrow, felt passion rise in place of fear. For tonight, she was in Jackson's hands, and skilled hands they were. He was a masterful lover, confident and sure of himself, able to take her so high that she feared she'd never touch back down again. This had been too long in coming. She needed him. And he needed her.

As he tugged her shirt from her body, she feared this would end too quickly, that being held in his arms for hours was a mere wish that couldn't come true. Once her shirt and bra fell away, his mouth moved downward, brushing across her breasts and then going lower. She shook as his hands roamed. So fast! Much too fast!

But as if he sensed her anxiety, his hands and

mouth slowed. He looked up, his eyes sparkling as his tongue lazily circled the quivering flesh of her stomach.

"You are so beautiful, Alyssa," he whispered reverently.

"So are you, Jackson."

He chuckled, then grasped her jeans and panties and drew them off in one fell swoop, leaving her bare to his view. She didn't have time to feel self-conscious about her gently swelling belly in the well-lit room. He didn't allow it. He lowered his head and began doing delicious things to the part of her that ached the most. Moaning in encouragement, Alyssa moved her body to the rhythm of his tongue as she sought fulfillment.

Time ceased having any meaning as his tongue and fingers lifted her higher and higher, as her body reached toward release. Why had she been fighting this? It was exactly what she'd needed for so long. And there was no one other than Jackson capable of bringing her body such pleasure.

When she reached her peak and came against his mouth, Alyssa thought she might stay suspended in the sky like a burst of stars. But when she opened her eyes and found Jackson poised above her, a satisfied smile on his face, his thick erection pressing against her thigh, she realized that this was only the beginning.

"Why have we wasted so much time? This is exactly where the two of us should always be," he said, his voice serious, his body throbbing against hers.

"I don't know," Alyssa sighed. Suddenly her reasons for trying to keep her distance seemed foolish, ridiculous, even. "I shouldn't have prevented something that feels so good." Why would she want to put distance between them when he so clearly wanted them to be together?

"I will treat you like royalty," he said, his words whispered in her ear before he began kissing the skin of her neck, making shivers race up and down her entire body.

"I've been so afraid this can't last forever. But isn't everyone unsure of that same thing? It doesn't matter, though, because for now this is exactly what I need and if we don't finish tonight, surely I'll melt away into nothingness."

"Alyssa, I guarantee you will finish many times over," he said before taking her nipple into his mouth and making her lose her ability to speak.

All that mattered right now was that this *felt* real. It felt better than real. When his mouth trailed a line of kisses back up her neck and then he was once again leaning over her, looking into her eyes with passion and . . . love, she knew she was his forever, or for as long as he would have her.

"Take me, Jackson," she panted, overcome with emotion as he slid against her.

His next kiss was soft, gentle, incredibly tender. He'd never kissed her that way before, and it brought a sheen of tears to her eyes. She closed them to hide her emotion. He was holding nothing back from her, and she was falling irrevocably in love.

When his knees pushed against the insides of her thighs, she didn't fight him. Opening willingly, she gave him her body—along with the rest of her heart. His tender kiss turned urgent as he pressed the tip of his arousal against her heat.

This was the man she knew; she knew the hunger rippling through him, impatience burning in every pore. He wanted her, and she wanted to be wanted this way. The fires within her ignited again when with one sure thrust he buried himself deep inside her aching core.

As her body tensed, as the fire built, Alyssa gripped his arms. She opened her eyes and looked up with greedy fascination at him, at the strength of his muscles flexing, at the pure hunger etched into his features.

He began to move, making her body sing. When his eyes opened, and their gazes connected, Alyssa was stunned to see so much raw power capturing her. When he shook and gave a groan of release, she held him tight and joined him in an awe-inspiring orgasm, wave upon wave of rapture.

When their passionate tremors finally ceased, he collapsed, half on her and half beside her, his breathing still heavy as he cradled her to him. How had she lived her whole life without this man? Without the pleasure he brought? Without the passion he ignited? And how would she ever be able to let him go?

"Jackson . . ."

She needed to tell him, had a burning need to share with him the fact that he was going to be a father again in just a few months.

"It's okay, Alyssa. I know it's overwhelming, but it will all be okay," he said, and then he kissed the corner of her mouth.

As he held her, touched her, began stirring the hormones in her needy body yet again, she lost her courage to speak. She fell under his spell and allowed herself to just feel.

Tomorrow. Tomorrow she would tell him . . .

033

For two days straight, Alyssa had been content to do almost nothing but lie in Jackson's arms. They made love, ate, showered, and made love again. Neither of them spoke of the future. Neither of them spoke of anything more than this moment, this time they'd carved out for themselves in what felt like paradise.

Late the night before, a thunderstorm had blown through, knocking out their power, but it hadn't slowed them down even a bit. Instead, Jackson had turned on an old battery-operated radio, lit some candles, and then pulled her into his arms as the two of them danced naked in his den.

She'd refused at first, horrified that someone might show up. But she was powerless against his pursuit, and soon she'd surrendered, needing the feel of his hands against her body. No one else would ever be able to pleasure her again, not after these uninterrupted days with Jackson.

"We should eventually climb from bed," she said while her hand lazily drew patterns on the hard contours of his chest.

The bedding was in shambles, only partially covering them now, but Alyssa didn't mind. She was still hot from the last time they'd made love.

"Why leave? I very much like this bed."

"There's work to do, and people who are probably worried about us. My parents are most likely ready to gather a search party."

"Nah. They love me."

What confidence! It was probably one of the things she loved most about him.

"Hmm. I don't know about that," she told him. Admit to him how much power he wielded in this relationship? No way. And she wasn't such a fool as to think they weren't in a relationship now.

Not after the last couple of days. For that matter, from the moment he'd set foot in the saloon, they'd been in a relationship. If she really wanted to get technical, she hadn't even thought of another man since their plane ride—since making love in New York.

Jackson had owned her heart and soul from that night on. And wasn't love exactly what he was showing her right now? Maybe he was incapable of saying the words, but weren't actions much more real, much more meaningful, than the words slipping from his mouth?

"I know for a fact that both of our families would be thrilled if we stopped fighting against this attraction we share. My brothers think the world of you.

I'm sure my father does as well, since every time I talk to him, he asks me how I'm treating you."

"But they know I'm pregnant."

There was a pause before he spoke. "Yes. That doesn't change how they feel."

"And how do they feel about that?"

She held her breath as she waited for him to speak. "You realize how I came to be with my family, right?"

"Yes," she answered, not understanding what this had to do with anything.

"If we are together, do you honestly think they would love your child any less just because it doesn't share my blood?"

"I haven't really thought about it," she said, squirming beside him as she always did when he brought up the parentage of her unborn child.

"My dad is my dad because he loved a child enough to give him a chance—loved three of us enough, actually. He wouldn't hesitate to claim your baby as his grandchild. It nearly destroyed him when Olivia was lost."

His voice tightened with his last words, and Alyssa melted against his side, not wanting him to feel that pain all over again.

"Tell me about your family, Jackson. I only know bits and pieces," she said, hoping to turn his thoughts from sorrow to a better time in his life.

"It's a long story," he warned her, but her words did the trick and he relaxed against her.

"I don't have anywhere to be, Jackson." She should check in with her parents, but she was too comfortable even to think about moving.

"I lived in the foster-care system from the time I was a baby. I never knew my mother or father. It was just how it was . . ."

"Did you ever look for them?"

He was silent for a little while as he thought either about her question or about whether he wanted to answer it or not.

"No. I thought about it when I was twenty-one, and then decided I really didn't care. I love my father and my brothers. Even if my birth parents are still alive, it doesn't interest me. I wouldn't know them. Even if I looked like them, even if there were brothers or sisters out there, they wouldn't be my family. My family is right here and they are the ones who have always been there for me."

"Did you tell your dad you were curious?" She worried that Martin might have been hurt.

"Yes. I've always been able to tell my dad anything. He didn't try to make me feel guilty; hell, he offered to search for them if I wanted. He told me not to make a snap decision and had me think about it. After a week, I realized that I really didn't want to find them, and I never brought it up again."

"Were the homes you were in bad?" Her voice was barely a whisper.

"Some of them were terrible. Some of the parents were abusive, and some were just pathetic. Not one of them made me feel wanted. Camden, Spence, and I were together in a foster home for a couple of years before we met Martin and his biological son, Michael. That day forever changed our lives," he said, a smile flitting across his mouth.

As the two of them lay in a perfect pocket of sun streaming in through the window—a sign that the storm was over and it was safe to come back into the real world—Alyssa realized she didn't want to be in that world.

She wanted to stay in this one, where Jackson held her tight, where he shared with her, where only good things happened, and where she felt alive and cared for. She didn't ever want to move again.

But instead of saying all this, she simply listened as Jackson told her about his first meeting with Martin and the day that changed his life.

034

A loud cry rent the air as Alyssa walked to the barn, hand in hand with Jackson. She froze and looked around frantically. Jackson walked another step, until he felt the pull of her hand against his.

"What?" he asked. "Are you feeling okay, Alyssa?"

She knew her eyes must be bugging out of her head. He had to have heard the cry. Why wasn't he more concerned? Why wasn't he rushing toward the barn to see whether he could help?

"What is wrong with you?" she finally gasped.

"Me? You're the one who stopped."

"Didn't you hear that?" Right as she said it, another shout spilled through the open doors of the barn. She wasn't sure whether she should rush forward or turn back and run for her life.

Of course she'd rush forward. Her parents had been invited to the party, too, so they'd most likely be in there, and she couldn't run away without helping them. She had to choose fight over flight. But she and Jackson were wasting valuable time just standing still.

When he began to laugh, her mind raced around in utter confusion. What was there to laugh about? It sounded as if assassins had descended upon his family and were picking them off one by one. When he doubled over and let go of her hand, she had the strong urge to kick him. Instead, she rushed toward the sound.

"Wait!" he yelled, but the lout was laughing so hard he couldn't catch up to her.

Trembling in fear—how on earth was she going to stop the mass murder?—she tore through the barn doors. And was shot right in the chest.

"Alyssa!"

Scanning the room with incredulous eyes, Alyssa lifted her hand and rubbed the spot where she'd felt the dart hit. The foam dart. It looked like World War III was going on, and she wasn't sure which side was winning.

The men were cowering behind a large bundle of hay, all holding Nerf guns of various sizes and firing shot after shot at the women rushing from station to station.

"Don't let them get the flag!" Camden yelled out to Michael.

Alyssa turned.

"I got it," Michael shouted back as his machine gun spit Nerf darts out at . . . her mother!

Alyssa gasped, but her mom rolled away in the

nick of time. Was that really her mom grabbing a large Nerf gun from some sort of side holster and aiming it straight at Camden's head? Yes, it was. And the woman was blessed with deadly accuracy.

Firing off several rapid shots, her mom pinged Camden; he dropped back behind the hay bales to reload as her mom ran off toward a blue flag flying high in the barn's loft. The deadly Nerf warriors all ran around with delighted grins on their faces as darts whizzed through the air.

"I'm so sorry for laughing," Jackson said as he appeared at Alyssa's side. "I should have warned you." And the jerk was still laughing.

"You think?" she snapped. Then she saw the humor in the situation, and a smile split her face.

"Um, Spence is really a giant-size kid who loves to instigate wars. He has an arsenal of Nerf guns, arrows, and water guns. The time of year determines which weapons he brings out."

"This isn't for a children's party?" Alyssa saw several small children taking part in the game, but she noticed the adults were careful with them. The kids giggled in delight when they got hit in their padded stomachs or on the shin guards they were wearing.

"Well, a lot of the neighbors bring their kids, but sadly, no. This is all about Spence," Jackson said, and then took off to join in the war.

Alyssa moved to a corner of the barn that looked relatively safe. Several tables were set up with food and drinks; the few adults who weren't participating in the battle were laughing and taking photos of the activity that whirled around them.

She sat down, reached for a cookie and soda, and watched as Jackson grabbed a weapon, then did an army crawl behind what appeared to be the men's barricade. Michael got hit near the side of one eye, and to Alyssa's amazement he cried out, inviting taunts from the women. Alyssa's jaw dropped when he stood up and blasted Bethel.

She had to be in her sixties, yet she was running around as vigorously as people half her age, and firing round after round of ammo from the two guns she was carrying. The battle continued for a good twenty minutes more before Bethel managed to grab hold of the blue flag and then did a victory dance.

The men groaned. They began putting down their weapons and then ambled over toward the food and drink, obviously breathing heavily. Water was guzzled greedily before anyone spoke.

When Jackson plopped down next to Alyssa, he had a sheen of sweat covering his forehead, and his shirt was damp. And just like that, she felt her stomach heat up. When his eyes met hers, his went from happy to excited in less than a second.

"I've had a good time. Want to leave?"

She was amazed he could even think about sex after the last few days. It seemed they had sex, then they both worked, then had more sex, and then caught maybe a few hours of sleep. She was exhausted. She'd have doubted that he could perform again so soon, but the look in his eyes and the bulge in his pants made it clear that he'd have no problem at all.

"We just got here, Jackson," she whispered, hoping no one was paying any attention to them.

"Alyssa! So glad you came." Camden appeared at her side, and before she knew it, he lifted her up and pulled her into his sweaty embrace.

"Good to see you, Cam," she said with a grimace. He released her and she tried to wipe away the sweat discreetly.

"Ahh, a bit of moisture won't hurt you," Jackson said with a laugh.

Wow! A lot had changed in a short time. The last time Camden had taken her in his arms, Alyssa had worried that Jackson might beat him to a bloody pulp. It seemed that a lot—a really, really lot—of sex calmed the man right down.

"I didn't think it would," she replied, hoping she hadn't offended Cam.

"Yeah, I always get a good workout at these parties," Cam said as he slung an arm around her shoulders.

"That's good to know," she said with a laugh. And they were both right. A bit of sweat would wash right off.

When she glanced toward the chocolate fountain, she noticed a woman dipping a strawberry in chocolate and looking over at their table. Her eyes were all for Cam, and for some reason there was a touch of sadness in them that made Alyssa want to jump up and go to her, to reassure her that everything would be okay.

"Who is that?" she asked, and Cam's eyes shot in the direction she was looking, but he said nothing, just seemed to tense.

"Ah, that's the very beautiful Grace Sinclair, my brother's one true love. She lives in New York now, but is here visiting her family . . . and Camden, of course."

"Shut up, Jackson," Cam said, shooting Jackson a look that could kill.

"Just speaking the truth," Jackson said, making Alyssa suddenly want to be anywhere but with the two brothers, who seemed to be about ready to start a duel.

Before she could pull away and go, Jackson took her from Cam's arms, lifted her up, and sat her on his lap. He turned her head toward him, gave her a short kiss, and whispered into her ear what his plans were when they got home. She was sure the blush that stole over her cheeks was bright enough to light up the entire darkening barn. She forgot all about the tense moment the brothers had just had.

"Who's ready for a nice fire?"

Alyssa looked up to find Martin standing at the barn doors, and that's when she noticed the glow outside.

"Want to go sit by the fire and listen to scary tales?" Jackson asked.

"You're joking, right?"

"Nope. Spence tells the best ones. He'll have all the kids screaming in no time at all. Then they'll rush inside and watch Disney flicks while the grown-ups have a few beers and visit."

"How many people are here, Jackson?" The crowd seemed to be growing.

"Ah, it seems like kind of a small gang, eh?"

"This is what you consider small?" As the two of them got up and made their way outside, Alyssa was sure that at least a hundred people were milling around.

"Yeah, normally we have half the town here," Jackson said. "Dad likes to throw a semiannual party for all the employees of the oil plant, and then for all our neighbors and friends as well. As you've noticed, Sterling isn't exactly a bustling town. We have to provide our own entertainment." He led her to a hay bale and sat down, wrapping his arm around her shoulders and pulling her in tightly against his side.

"This is pretty great, actually," she said as the sun dipped below the tree line and they were bathed in a soft glow from the roaring fire.

"I'm finding that anywhere I'm with you is pretty great," he replied, tipping her head back so he could give her another kiss—this one a little longer than the one she'd received inside the barn.

"All right, Jackson, quit smooching and let me say hello to Alyssa."

Alyssa turned to find Spence standing in front of them. The man was tall, maybe an inch taller than Jackson, and had shoulders like a linebacker. He had green eyes that were sure to star in more than a few women's fantasies, and a smile that surely set people at ease.

As Alyssa glanced in turn at all four brothers, she was amazed they weren't related by blood. Each one was stunning in his own right, had the same crooked smile, and boasted eyes whose sparkle was unmatched by anything she'd seen before.

She felt painfully shy all of a sudden. She'd seen Spence only a few times before, and she had to admit that he intimidated her just a bit.

"Yeah, Spence would love to steal you away, but I have game," Jackson said with a smile.

"I don't know. I'm pretty charming when I want

to be," Spence said with a wink that had Alyssa blushing. "When's the baby due?" he asked, and she looked down. Her stomach was really beginning to stick out.

She blushed again as she looked up. "In about three months," she said, praying the good doctor wouldn't ask about the father.

"Congrats, Alyssa. It's about time I got to be an uncle."

And that was the end of it. Whew!

Spence talked with Jackson for several more minutes, and Alyssa was awed by the way all of Jackson's family had accepted her immediately. They all knew she'd been in Sterling for four months without Jackson. They all knew she had to have been pregnant with someone else's child. It made more sense than that it was Jackson's.

They didn't know about her night with Jackson just under six months ago. She was actually a bit offended that he thought her so easy that she would sleep with him and another man within a couple of weeks of each other. Of course, he hadn't known her at all then. But he knew her now. Why hadn't he put the pieces together? Why hadn't he questioned her?

When Jackson went over to collect more food and drink for the two of them, Alyssa felt the last walls of resistance fall away when he first approached one of the neighbors, who was holding a newborn baby.

Jackson beamed as the woman handed over the infant, who was wrapped in a pink blanket, and then Alyssa watched as he admired the child. His strong arm looked so massive cradling the baby as he grinned at something the woman said.

When a man approached the two of them, Jackson held out his free hand and Alyssa could see that he was offering his congratulations. And when he handed the baby back, her heart melted because the look in his eyes reflected disappointment.

Jackson was made to be a father. If their child was a girl, she'd be his little princess. If it was a boy, he'd be his best friend. It was time that Alyssa told him the truth. She wouldn't make any more excuses.

035

He's had a bad day at work.

I'm not feeling well and need to sleep.

I've worked a double and my feet are killing me.

The lovemaking is perfect and I'm warm in his arms. I don't want to ruin the moment.

Excuses! Alyssa had sworn she wouldn't make them. She had failed both herself and Jackson. A week passed and the right opportunity never presented itself. It seemed her resolve at the bonfire had quickly been forgotten. Yes, Alyssa knew she was betraying a lack of spine by not telling Jackson the truth, but it wasn't as if she could just blurt the words out.

She dreaded his reaction. How would he feel about her once he knew? Would he consider her the worst of liars? Would he be so angry that he wanted nothing more to do with her? So she made up excuses, telling herself that she was waiting for just the right moment, though she knew there had been plenty of good moments. And she'd chickened out each time.

Tonight. She would do it tonight. Just as soon

as her shift was over, she would tell him that they needed to sit down and talk. It was the right thing to do, after all. It was easy to spout off to others about courage. Facing problems in one's own life wasn't at all simple. Alyssa knew that only too well. No matter how much fear she had of telling him, she was going to do it.

As the sultry July night came to a close, she was surprised that Jackson hadn't shown up at the door. Something must have come up, because he usually was there at work to make sure she got home safely. Her apartment was now ready. She should move into it, but when she'd told Jackson, he'd said they would get her moved soon, and then he'd changed the topic the next couple of times she'd spoken of it. The truth was, she didn't want to leave yet.

When the bell on the saloon door chimed and Cam walked in, she gave him a smile and went over to greet him. "You're here late, Cam. Is everything okay?"

"Can we talk, Alyssa?" The frown marring his normally cheerful face had her instantly worried.

"Of course. Let me grab my purse and you can walk me out." She turned and walked to the back room, overtaken by a sudden impulse to stall. She didn't know if she wanted to hear whatever Camden was about to say. The man surely was a bust at poker, because right now his face told her that she was about to hear something unpleasant.

With hormones sending her emotions all over the place, she wasn't up for bad news. The courage thing again. She'd rather keep her head in the sand than face real-world demons. But she couldn't hide forever. She grabbed her purse, plastered a false smile onto her face, and walked back out front, where she found Camden leaning against the bar.

"What's wrong, Cam?"

She was now determined to face whatever news he was bringing, and if it was bad, she'd decided she'd rather just hear it and get it over with.

"This really should wait until the morning, Alyssa, but we've never been too formal with our attorney-client relationship . . ."

Her stomach tightened. She hadn't wanted to get her hopes up, but she had. Not that long ago, he'd told her things were looking as if they were moving in her favor. From his expression, however, it appeared he'd been wrong.

"Just tell me, Cam. I don't want to drag it out," she said, straightening her shoulders and preparing herself for the blow.

"The money is gone, Alyssa. I'm so sorry. Your ex-manager was found yesterday in his prison cell . . . dead, and the funds that were frozen have been confiscated by the government. It seems he was much more of a crook than we knew, and the big guys are taking their money first. The man was too weak to face his accusers, too weak to spend his time behind bars. He decided to end it before a judgment could be brought against him."

Even though this was what Alyssa had expected him to say, hearing the words made her knees go to jelly and she had to fight to stay on her feet.

She'd known she wasn't going to get the full amount back, but she'd been hoping for something, just enough to get by while the baby was little. Yes, she knew that Jackson was wealthy—beyond wealthy, actually. But that was his money. That the two of them had shared a night together that had left her pregnant didn't mean he should now be responsible of taking care of her and a baby. Well, technically it did, but still . . .

She was enrolled to start community college in the fall, finally finding a passion in life. She was going to be a music teacher. Playing piano gave her joy beyond any other pastime, and they had a hard time finding music teachers in Sterling, so she already had an internship at the middle school while she was finishing her degree.

Looking at Cam, she felt terrible. This was Jackson's brother, and he was so good to her, as was Jackson and the rest of his family. She should have already told Jackson that he was going to be a father.

Now that the case was lost, would he think she was telling him because she wanted his money? Oh, the web of lies was finally ensnaring her and she was terrified of the consequences.

"Thanks for not making me wait, Cam. I appreciate it," Alyssa said. She was surprised by how strong her tone was, by how well she was managing to remain standing.

"I really am sorry, Alyssa. I'll keep checking into things over the next few months, but at this point, I'd have to say the odds of any of the women he's ripped off getting even a dime back are slim. This man . . . if he can even be called that . . . was a real piece of work."

Cam was shaking his head as he spoke to her, trying to catch her eye. Alyssa wouldn't look at him. She was too afraid she'd fall apart if he was too sympathetic, and she absolutely didn't want that to happen.

"Does Jackson know?"

"Of course not. Although he's my brother, you're my client, Alyssa. I certainly wouldn't speak to him about your business," he replied, sounding offended that she even needed to ask.

"I wasn't implying that," she said. But what else could she have been saying?

"Sorry. I know that. It was just one of those questions," Cam said, and patted her on the shoulder.

Just that little bit of movement nearly undid her. She had to get away.

"Thanks again for not making me wait to find out. I really should get back to Jackson's house now, though," she said, trying to act nonchalant. She hoped she was pulling it off.

"I almost forgot to tell you—Jackson asked me to stop by. He got called away to an emergency business meeting in Alaska. He may be gone for a few days," Cam told her as he walked her to her car. "That's why I came here in the first place."

"Oh, thanks," she said as she opened her car door. What else was there to say? She'd just received devastating news, and now she was heading back to Jackson's house, where she'd be all alone.

"I'll follow you home," Camden told her, and the way he said it let her know it wasn't an offer. She could refuse him, but he was going to do it no matter what.

"Thanks. You know I've been there a few times already, right?" she tried to joke, but her tone made it fall flat.

"Yeah. Still, I'll feel better if I follow you."

"If you want to waste your time . . ." She let her words fall away as she pulled her car door shut, then started the engine.

The car took several minutes to warm up, and it took every encouraging thing she could think of not to break into tears. This wasn't the end of the world. It was just one more minor setback in a long list of setbacks. She'd get through it, and one day she'd look back and wonder why she'd let it affect her so much.

As she put her car into drive and began the journey down the long, winding road to Jackson's house, the first tear blurred her vision. She never saw the deer leap out in front of her small car.

036

"Alyssa!" Cam jumped out of his truck and slid down the steep embankment into the ditch, screaming Alyssa's name while rushing to her car. It was resting upside down, one wheel spinning eerily and making a screeching sound.

When she didn't answer, he pulled out his phone in a panic, kicking himself for waiting even thirty seconds before calling the ambulance. The call made, he wrenched open her door. "Alyssa! Are you okay?"

Still no answer. His car lights were beaming down into the ditch, shining in through her broken back window, and they gave him a clear view of her hanging upside down in her seat. Reaching inside the car, he touched her shoulder, trying to be careful not to shift her in case there was any injury to her neck.

"Alyssa, I need you to wake up!" He spoke loudly, willing her to open her eyes.

If she was lost . . . Oh, hell, his brother. Camden feared Jackson would never heal. The poor guy was finally allowing himself to live again, to care for another person. He couldn't lose Alyssa like this. Camden wouldn't allow it.

"Alyssa, please wake up!"

Camden nearly cried in relief when he heard a moan and saw her body twitch. He continued calling her name as he listened for sirens. He wanted to get her out of the car, but he knew better than to move her without first checking for back and neck injuries.

"Jackson?" Alyssa's voice, sounding weak and pained, finally drifted to Cam's ears.

"No, Alyssa, it's me, Camden," he replied, touching her arm gently, trying to reassure her.

"What happened?" she asked hoarsely as she began to stir.

"Try to stay still, Alyssa. You've been in a car accident, and I don't want you to move."

The blessed sound of sirens wailed in the distance.

"Oh, Cam!" she cried as full consciousness returned. "It hurts!"

"I know, Alyssa. I know. They're almost here. Please just hold on. They will be here any second. They'll get your neck secured and then move you," he promised her as the sirens grew louder.

Cam didn't dare turn toward the sound of the approaching ambulance and fire engine, but instead kept his hand placed reassuringly against her arm and continued speaking so she wouldn't succumb to the panic he was sure she was battling.

"My head feels like it's going to explode," she cried, and then her body was racked with sobs.

"I know, Alyssa, but they're here now. They're coming," he promised.

And sure enough, the passenger door of her car was wrenched open and a paramedic climbed in. The man asked a few questions and then quickly secured her neck against a backboard. Another paramedic joined him, and Cam moved out of their way as they pulled her carefully and efficiently from the car.

When he saw blood staining her slacks, Cam felt his gut stir again, and as they loaded her into the back of the ambulance, he couldn't help but let go of the contents of his stomach on the side of the road. If she was losing the baby . . . No! He couldn't think that way.

"You can follow," the first paramedic called out to Cam before jumping into the ambulance and turning on the siren as they sped away.

Cam's stomach heaved again. That they were traveling as fast as they were with siren and lights meant her condition couldn't be good. How was he going to tell his brother? Before he could get into his car, Hawk Winchester and the sheriff stopped him to ask questions for their reports.

"What happened?"

"A deer jumped out. There was no way for her to avoid it, but she must have jerked her wheel at the last minute. She lost control . . ." He had to stop. He knew this was his fault. Why in the world had he told her about the case before she had to drive?

Cam felt lower than low. Alyssa had tried desperately to hide her devastation over his news, but she hadn't fooled him for even a minute, which is why he'd followed her. The poor woman had been barely holding it together. What should he have done, though? Lie?

No. Professional ethics and the law had tied his hands. He wished he could have just reached into his pockets and given her the money that she'd lost, but he knew better than to offer it to her. Not only would she most likely have slugged him for insulting her that way, but she'd have probably refused to speak to him ever again.

Cases like hers really upset him. She was clearly a victim, and there was nothing the law could do about it. Like so many others, she'd just been unlucky in the person she'd chosen to trust. Hell, *unlucky* didn't cover it.

She was pregnant, and living with his brother. It was more than obvious that his brother was head over heels in love with Alyssa. What smart man wouldn't fall for the woman? She was beautiful, talented, witty, and charming. She was a keeper. If Camden had felt even half a spark of passion for Alyssa, he would have chased after her—okay, he would have if she hadn't already belonged to his brother.

Cam was pulled from his thoughts by the sound of Hawk's voice asking him if he was okay.

"I'm sorry, Hawk. I can't think right now. I really need to get to the hospital."

"Then go," Hawk said.

"Thanks." Cam turned to leave.

"You were thinking on your feet, Cam. Both Alyssa and the baby have a real chance," Hawk said before Cam had taken more than a few steps.

"Thanks. I'll try to remember that when I call Jackson." Cam rushed to his truck and started it, his window down.

"She'll make it," Hawk said. "There's no way fate can be so cruel to Jackson again."

"I agree, Hawk. Jackson has been through enough." Cam took off, already too far behind, afraid something bad had happened. He knew the hospital wouldn't give him information, but as he made his way there, he picked up his phone, first calling Alyssa's parents and letting them know where they could find their daughter, then . . . then calling his brother.

"Jackson, I have bad news . . ."

037

Her eyes now open, Alyssa tried to process the sounds around her as she was wheeled directly into an emergency room. She heard phrases such as *early labor, uncontrollable bleeding, baby trauma*.

No! It was way too early. The baby couldn't come yet. They had to do something, had to stop whatever was happening.

"Alyssa, don't panic. We're going to do everything we can to save your baby," someone assured her.

"It's too early," she cried, her voice gurgling.

"There's blood in her mouth."

"No . . ."

Alyssa felt the mask slip over her face, felt the lights begin to dim. *It's too early. It's too early.* Those were her last thoughts before she went under.

JACKSON RAN FROM the jet to his brother's truck. "How is she?"

"She's still in surgery," Michael said. "I'm sorry, Jackson. We don't have any answers yet." He threw the truck into drive and peeled off down the road.

"Are her parents there?"

"Yes. The doctors have come out a few times to keep them informed, but so far her condition is the same. She's still alive. The baby's still alive. The last time the doctors came out, they were looking grim, though."

"It's been four hours. How freaking long can surgery last?" Jackson shouted, knowing it wasn't in any way Michael's fault, but feeling the need to take his outrage out on someone—anyone. He should have been home.

"It's not your fault," Michael said as if reading his mind.

"I shouldn't have taken off."

"Jackson, women are pregnant every day and they go about their lives. She was driving home. She hit a deer. There was nothing you could have done to stop it."

Michael had always been the most sensible of all of them. That didn't make Jackson any happier.

"If she would just drive the damn truck I bought her, she wouldn't be in this mess," Jackson thundered.

Last week he'd shown up at the house with a brand-new one-ton Ford pickup. It had good safety ratings, could easily handle any weather, and would have taken a hit from the deer without flying off into a ditch.

Had she been happy about the truck? Hardly.

She'd ranted at him for an hour about his wasting money on ridiculously expensive gifts for her, and about how she wasn't going to be bought by a spoiled billionaire.

He'd come back at her, telling her that she needed to learn how to say *thank you* and accept things when he gave them to her because he cared. The conversation had gone back and forth several more times before she'd stormed off. By the end of the "conversation," he'd felt as if a few layers of his skin had been taken off. The makeup sex had been well worth the lecture, though.

Afterward, he'd thought the matter had been solved, but she'd stubbornly refused to drive the truck. He'd been close to driving her other car off a cliff so she'd have no choice, but he'd been trying not to be so controlling. Look where easing off her had gotten them now.

The doctors had warned her family that there was a chance neither she nor the baby would make it through the surgery. They had said not to give up hope, told them that Alyssa was fighting for her life, but there was internal bleeding.

Jackson wasn't a praying man, but his head had been bent in prayer the entire flight home. There was no way he could lose this woman. Love wasn't something he'd ever thought he'd find again, but he was smart enough to realize how he felt about her was bordering on love. He knew beyond a shadow of a doubt that he needed her, and he missed her when she wasn't there.

When Michael pulled up to the ER, Jackson sprang from the truck and dashed inside. It wasn't hard to find Alyssa's parents; they were surrounded by members of his own family.

"You made it home quickly, son," Martin said as he rushed up and threw his arm around Jackson's shoulders.

"Is there any further news?"

Jackson didn't want to sit and chat, didn't want to hear sympathetic noises from anyone. He wanted just the facts, wanted to know what was happening in surgery.

"No one from the medical team has been out for about an hour. We're still waiting. Your brother just got here."

"Spence?"

"Yes."

"Why? Why do they need a heart surgeon?" Jackson's chest clenched at the news. His brother was one of the leading cardiothoracic surgeons in the country, quite a feat for a man so young. If he was here, something was definitely wrong.

"They're trying to keep the baby inside her womb. It's far too early for delivery. But even if they manage to stop the labor today, she will deliver before the baby's ready. It appears there's a problem with the baby's heart."

"Oh, my . . ." Jackson slumped into the seat behind him. Alyssa would be devastated if she lost her baby.

Jackson realized that he'd be devastated, too. Though the child wasn't his, it was a part of Alyssa and she was now a part of his life. He couldn't lose either of them.

"Mr. and Mrs. Gerard?"

Jackson turned as Spence walked out in his scrubs.

"Yes," they said in unison as Spence approached.

"They've stabilized Alyssa," he said, and her parents sagged against each other. Tears flowed down Teresa's cheeks.

"But . . ." her father said, seeing the distress on Spence's face.

"But we had to deliver the baby. It's a girl," he said, and he took a breath.

"Is . . . is she alive?" Teresa asked, a shudder racking her body.

"She's in critical condition. She was born three months early so her heart's not fully developed, and that places her at risk for a lot of complications. Alyssa won't be awake for some time, and I need to go in immediately and try to stabilize the baby's heart. I'll need to have permission to do this."

"Can't it wait for Alyssa to wake up? I don't want to make a wrong decision," Teresa said, shaking in her husband's arms.

"I'm afraid that if we wait, the baby won't live long enough for her mother to meet her." Spence spoke with confidence, clearly laying out the situation.

"What are the risks?" Donald asked.

"The risks are that the infant won't make it off the table. She only weighs two pounds three ounces right now. She's tiny and she isn't fully formed, but she *is* fighting, just like her mother. If we can stabilize her heart, keep her in the NICU, I think she stands a real chance."

Spence waited for Alyssa's parents to process what he'd just told them.

"Do whatever you can," Donald finally said. He moved to a chair and pulled his wife into his arms as she collapsed against him.

"I'll have the nurse bring you the papers to sign."

Without saying another word, Spence made eye contact with Jackson. Jackson could see clearly what his brother was telling him. Spence would fight with all he had to keep this child alive. Jackson nodded his thanks, struggling against the pressure building up in his chest. The waiting room was deathly silent.

The next few hours were going to decide the rest of their lives.

038

Pain radiated from just about every imaginable spot on Alyssa's body. She was afraid to open her eyes—what if it made the pain get worse? And anyway, if she opened her eyes, she would have to face whatever news the doctors had for her.

Someone was speaking to her. Someone knew she was awake. She could hear the monitors buzzing, and she could hear voices whispering in her dark world. No. She would just refuse to look. If she managed not to look, this was nothing more than a bad dream.

But her fingers twitched. She wanted desperately to lift her hands and feel her stomach, to assure herself that her baby was still safe inside her body. But without lifting them, without feeling the bump that was supposed to be on her body, she knew beyond any doubt that the baby wasn't there. She couldn't feel the infant, couldn't feel movement, couldn't feel his or her heart beating inside her.

Tears leaked from her eyes.

No. She wouldn't open her eyes. She wouldn't face this day. If they told her that her child had died, she would give up the fight altogether—she wouldn't care about her own life anymore. She just couldn't lose a baby she'd grown so fond of, couldn't let her child go before she'd even had a chance to hold it close to her heart. What cruel world would allow her to live while taking an innocent child?

"Alyssa, baby. Are you awake?"

That was her mother, and her tone bespoke so much anguish. That only confirmed to Alyssa that she couldn't wake up and face whatever they wanted to tell her.

"Alyssa, please wake up. Please open your eyes."

She wanted so much to assure her mother that she was okay. But she wasn't okay, so how could she look into her mother's eyes and lie to her?

"Alyssa. Come on. Wake up so we can tell you about your daughter."

This time Jackson spoke. What was he doing here? Wasn't he supposed to be in Alaska? It must be worse than she thought if he'd flown all the way back so soon. Or maybe she'd been in a coma. Maybe months had passed. A ray of hope shot through her. Maybe she'd delivered a healthy baby. But why would she hurt so much if that much time had passed?

But they said they wanted to tell her about her daughter. Jackson's words finally registered. Jackson wouldn't be so cruel as to say something like that if her baby wasn't still alive.

A girl. She had a baby girl!

Slowly, Alyssa's eyes opened, and she was grateful that the lighting in her room was dim. She turned her head and focused on her mother, who was sitting right beside her and holding her hand.

"Mama?" she croaked, her voice weak.

"Hi, baby girl," Teresa said through her tears. "You don't know how good it is to see your eyes open." She rested her cheek against Alyssa's for a brief moment.

"My baby?" That was all she cared about.

"You have a strong, beautiful daughter, Alyssa. She's tiny, but she's alive," Teresa said, her lips forming a smile.

"Really?" Alyssa didn't know whether she could believe her mom. Wouldn't a mother say anything to get her daughter to fight for her own life?

"She's alive, Alyssa," Jackson said. "Spence performed surgery yesterday. He's the best in his field. She came through the surgery beautifully, and she's a fighter." He wore a proud smile.

"Surgery? Why would a baby need surgery?" she asked, fear a constant inside her.

"There was a problem with her heart, but he fixed her, and her vitals are good," he said.

"Have you seen her?

"Yes! She is so beautiful, just like her mother."

Alyssa finally allowed herself to believe them, to hope that everything would be okay. She knew there was a long road ahead of them, but she felt a stirring of hope.

"Can I see her?" That's all she wanted.

"Oh, baby. I know you want to see her," Teresa said. "But you have to stay in bed right now, and she can't leave the neonatal ICU. I have pictures because I knew you'd want to look at her." She pulled up her phone and held it close for Alyssa to see.

Alyssa's tears fell in rivers; why did her first view of her child have to be on a piece of glass? She needed to hold her, care for her. "She's so small," she gasped, running her finger across the screen.

"She is, but she's strong, Alyssa. Don't let her size fool you," Donald told his daughter.

"You're a grandpa," Alyssa said. Her poor parents; they must be so worried, too.

"I sure am. I already passed out a whole box of cigars."

"A baby girl." Teresa sighed with wonder.

"Is someone with her?" Alyssa asked. "I don't want her to be alone." As her panic rose, her heart monitor began beeping.

"There's someone with her at all times," Teresa said, patting Alyssa's hand, trying to calm her daughter back down.

"No, Mama. Not strangers. She needs her family so she knows she's loved. So she knows she needs to fight."

"I just came from there, Alyssa. I'll go back right now," Jackson said as he moved to her side and leaned down. "I'll take care of her." It didn't occur to him to think he wasn't family.

Alyssa looked into his eyes and wanted desperately to tell him not to let their daughter die. She needed to tell him this was his child he had to protect. But he leaned down, gently caressed her lips with his, then walked out of the room.

The moment was gone.

Exhaustion pulled her back into a restless sleep as her body fought to be strong again. Fought to heal so she could be the mother she needed to be.

039

Two weeks had passed, and each day Alyssa grew stronger. The physical therapy was hell, but she was doing it. Whatever they asked of her, she accomplished it, even when tears poured down her cheeks. There was nothing she wouldn't do to be able to be with her daughter.

Because of the flu she'd picked up on top of her injuries, she hadn't been able to visit the NICU yet. It killed her a little bit more each day.

Her daughter was now almost three pounds, and though she was unbearably tiny, the doctors assured Alyssa that she was doing exceptionally well. Once the baby reached four and a half pounds, if she was healthy and eating, her mother would be able to take her home.

Alyssa wasn't sure whether she was ready for that. What if something went wrong? At least here she knew there was a competent staff to care for her child. At home, it would just be her. That was more frightening than she cared to admit.

Dr. Jarvis, her neonatologist, walked into the room. "Good morning, Alyssa."

"Morning," she mumbled back.

"I know this has been a rough haul for you, but you have every reason to smile today, because we are releasing you."

It took a few seconds for his words to sink in, and then Alyssa went from melancholy to hopeful in a heartbeat.

"Does that mean I get to see my daughter?" That was all she wanted.

"Yes, it does. Your flu is gone, your injuries are healing nicely, and your strength is back up. I want you to take it easy over the next couple of weeks, with no work for at least another month, but other than that you are free to go home. By the time your daughter is released, you should be in nearly perfect condition, so it will be no problem to care for her."

"I just want to be with her." Alyssa moved impatiently on her bed.

"I know. You've been more than patient. I'll have the nurse come in and unhook these monitors, and then, after you're dressed, we can have someone wheel you to your daughter. You can call whoever is picking you up to come and get you when your visit is over."

Alyssa hadn't thought about that. She didn't want to leave her daughter. Yes, she wanted out of this bed, and wanted these wires to be yanked from her arm, but she couldn't leave her baby behind. All her excitement at the prospect of finally seeing her daughter was tainted by the trauma of having to leave her.

"Thank you," she said, trying not to show her depression.

After the doctor left the room, it didn't take long for a nurse to come in, give Alyssa papers to sign, and lay out her clothes. Alyssa's parents weren't there, and she didn't want to call them yet, so she dressed slowly, amazed by how much energy it took just to put on a pair of sweats and a shirt. This recovery might take a little longer than she wanted it to.

"Are you ready to meet your little princess?"

Alyssa gave the nurse a genuine smile.

"I'm way past ready."

She was wheeled from her room for the final time, and not at all bummed to see the last of it. The room was beautiful, and the bed comfortable, but when someone was constantly coming in and drawing blood, or administering drugs, or checking your vital signs, it was impossible to get any decent sleep. She wished she could be home. Not that she really knew where home was anymore.

It wasn't with Jackson. That had been only a temporary solution. Her apartment was ready, but it was empty, and to be alone was not what she wanted at all right now. She needed people around her to keep her spirits up.

"Here's baby Gerard," the nurse said when they arrived at the neonatal ICU, and Alyssa's eyes filled with tears as she got her first look at her daughter. The infant lay in a tiny incubator, which kept her safe and helped ensure that she continued to live.

"Oh, she's even smaller than I pictured," Alyssa exclaimed. She reached into the small side vent and touched the tiny fingers of her beautiful baby girl.

One of her fingers completely covered her daughter's hand, making it disappear. How could Alyssa even hold her? She would surely break the precious child in two. How was it possible that her daughter could be so small and still be okay?

A little mask covered the baby's eyes, and the tubes sticking from her small body looked so out of place. Something so beautiful, so perfect, shouldn't have to struggle to live. It was heartbreaking.

"Now you can give her a name."

Alyssa smiled at the nurse before the woman left her alone to bond with her daughter. She had decided not to name the baby until she saw her. She said she wouldn't know her name until she looked into her tiny face.

"Angel. Your name is Angel," she whispered without hesitation.

"That's because she's a miracle."

Alyssa turned to find Jackson standing behind her, gazing down at their daughter with such a look of pure love in his eyes that Alyssa knew she couldn't keep the truth from him any longer.

He'd been at the hospital every single day, had visited with their daughter and filled Alyssa in on every milestone, no matter how small. He'd actually been the first person besides the medical staff who'd held Angel. The words had been on the tip of her tongue a hundred times—thousands of times, even—and yet she hadn't told him yet that Angel was his little girl.

As she faced the incubator holding Angel—keeping her warm, guarding her, and helping her grow—more tears welled up in her eyes. She wanted to be selfish, wanted to keep her daughter all to herself, but she knew that wasn't right. She knew that Jackson deserved to be a part of her life. He'd given so much of himself, loved his daughter without even knowing she was his.

He deserved to be told the truth, and that should have happened long ago. Despite the fear that nearly suffocated her, she took a breath and prepared to tell him. It was most likely far safer for her to tell him in public, where he wouldn't scream and yell, where he wouldn't tell her what a monster she was for not telling him sooner.

Would he hate her forever? She was about to find out.

"Jackson . . ." She paused as he rested his hand on her shoulder and smiled down at her.

"I know. It's overwhelming, Alyssa." He leaned down and brushed his lips across her cheek.

"No, it's not that. I mean, yes, it is overwhelming. But that's not what I'm having a difficult time telling you." Again she paused.

Jackson kneeled down and took her hands. "You can tell me anything," he said.

She believed him. Yes, she *could* tell him anything. Of course, he had no clue what he was about to be hit with.

"Jackson. She's your daughter."

The expression on his face lasted several heartbeats before it fell away and a stone mask appeared in its place.

"Excuse me?"

She couldn't tell from his tone what he was feeling.

"I know I should have told you before now. I know it was wrong of me, but I was scared. I didn't want you to take her from me. I didn't want to lose her. I didn't know . . ." What else could she really say?

She'd been living in his home, making love to him, lying in his arms night after night. And then he'd stayed by her side while she got better, taken care of their daughter as much as he was allowed, and barely left the hospital. And to repay him for all his kindness, she'd lied to him, kept him from knowing that the infant he was caring for was his child, and she'd betrayed him. How could he ever speak to her again?

"That's impossible. We used protection," he said, his face still a mask.

"It failed. I wasn't with anyone else, Jackson. She *is* your daughter." Saying it this time, her voice was stronger, but fear was eating her alive. What would he do now?

"She's my daughter?" The words were spoken quietly, a question, but at the same time not. He knew; it was just taking time to process.

"Yes, she's yours. I really didn't think I would see you again, and then when I did, I was in shock. And then . . ." She trailed off as she watched his eyes narrow.

"What, Alyssa?" he asked coldly. "There wasn't an opportunity?"

"I tried telling myself that. At first I was afraid. I was afraid you would try to take her from me, and then I was afraid because I'd waited so long. I didn't know how to tell you." No, her words weren't good enough, but she didn't know what else to say.

"You seem to be afraid quite often. Haven't I shown you that I'm trying? Haven't I given you all that I can of myself?"

"Yes, Jackson. This isn't about you. I know you will make an excellent father. You are a good man, and have been more than fair to me. I just didn't want to lose you," she blurted out, the last words coming out on a sob.

"You may have just done exactly that."

He walked from the room without another word.

Alyssa shook uncontrollably. She would have much preferred it if he'd yelled at her, or cried, or done anything other than skewer her with such a cold expression before he walked away. Had she just destroyed any chance whatsoever that they'd be friends? She was almost certain she'd killed their relationship. Lies never ended well.

What if he hated her with a burning passion, and the next eighteen years were filled with painfully uncomfortable meetings when they passed their daughter back and forth between them? She'd been a fool. Everything would have been so much easier if she'd simply told him the truth sooner. Now she would have to wait and wait . . . Hanging her head, Alyssa put her hand back inside the incubator and touched her daughter's delicate fingers again.

"It will be okay, Angel. It will all be okay."

Was she telling this to herself or her daughter? Alyssa really didn't know.

040

Before he was smart enough to stop himself, Jackson slammed his fist into the tailgate of his truck. Sharp pain exploded through his knuckles and up his arm. He couldn't regret it, though. The pain helped divert him from the ache that was consuming his chest.

How could she have lied to him for so long? Was he completely and utterly wrong about her? He'd thought he was getting to know the woman so well. Apparently not.

He grabbed a bottle of smoked-salmon vodka that he'd bought in Alaska as a gag gift for Camden. Since it was the only liquor available to him, he'd choke the awful stuff down. Opening his tailgate, he jumped up and made himself comfortable. He didn't know how long he'd sit there and think. Let them try to tell him he couldn't sit in the parking lot and take a medicinal shot of booze in the back of his own freaking truck. It was a hell of a day already, and it wasn't yet noon.

Then a wider reality started to sink in. He was a father.

That thought went around and around in his mind. He'd vowed that he would never have another child again, not after losing his daughter, Olivia. It had been too painful for him. But that was before Alyssa appeared in his life.

He'd felt safer taking care of her and her child. It wasn't his baby. He wasn't responsible for her. How stupid. Although he had thought she wasn't his, he had accepted that responsibility. He never had used a get-out-of-jail-free card and walked away from Alyssa and her baby—no, *their* baby.

Why hadn't he run like hell? Why had he set himself up for failure again? He could easily lose this daughter as well. She was strong, fighting and growing every day, but Spence had told him she wasn't out of the woods yet. There was just so much that could go wrong with a preemie, especially one with heart trouble. What if he allowed himself to love her and then he lost her? He wouldn't be able to survive the loss of a second baby.

Jackson hung his head as he threw back some of the disgusting vodka—*gag* gift indeed—then dropped the bottle in the bed of his truck. He didn't think he could keep on drinking the stuff. Besides, he didn't want to get drunk. He just wanted some of the pain to vanish.

Who was he fooling, wondering what would happen *if* he *allowed* himself to love the child? Whether that little girl was his or not, her loss would devastate him. He'd been with her every day since she'd been born, held her in his arms, sat by her side as she struggled to survive.

He was already invested in her life, and whether she carried his blood or not, her loss wouldn't be something he could get through easily. Yes, he loved his little Angel. So what did he do now?

Was he going to demand that Alyssa give him parental rights? Of course he was. The girl was his child, too. He deserved to be a part of her life. Was there any possibility that Alyssa was now lying to him? As Jackson thought about that, he knew with certainty that Angel was his daughter. Maybe he had known all along. Maybe he'd been just as afraid of voicing the question as she had been of telling him. Why hadn't he asked? Why hadn't he pushed her to tell him who Angel's father was? The longer he sat there and thought about that, the more his heart thudded.

Angel was his daughter.

"What are you doing out here, Jackson?"

He looked up to find Spence walking toward him. His brother hadn't yet changed into his scrubs, and he was wearing a pair of old jeans and a worn sweatshirt and carrying a can of soda in his hand. Looking at him as he jumped up onto the tailgate of the truck and sat next to Jackson, no one would ever realize he was a wealthy surgeon.

"I don't know," Jackson answered.

"You look upset. I know baby Gerard is fine."

"I really appreciate your sticking around and taking care of her," Jackson said.

"She's important to me. I want to ensure she makes it."

That's the kind of man Spence was. He truly cared about his patients, big or small. Yes, Spence could be an ass at times, but he was one of the best men Jackson knew. Jackson felt blessed to have him for a brother.

"I'm a father again, Spence." Just like that, he blurted out the words. Saying them aloud made it all so much more real. "I'm a dad." His voice held awe as he spoke it again.

Spence was quiet as he swigged his soda, taking his time before he spoke. He didn't ask who the baby was. It was more than obvious Jackson was speaking of Alyssa's baby.

"So, you asked Alyssa to marry you?" Spence asked.

"Not yet. I just found out I'm a dad," Jackson said, as if the reality was still sinking in.

"Wait. I don't think I quite understand. You feel like a father because you love this woman and baby and plan on being her father?"

Of course his brother was looking confused. Yes, Jackson had made it clear that he'd met Alyssa before, but he'd only told Spence a couple of months ago, on that night he'd met Alyssa again at the bar. He hadn't said when; he hadn't explained they'd slept together.

"No. I mean that Alyssa and I met on New Year's, had spectacular sex, and then she walked away from me, and I found her again very much pregnant."

Spence's mouth dropped, but he recovered quickly. He couldn't speak for a few moments. Jackson waited, wondering whether his brother would call him on being such an idiot. He should have known better.

"Congratulations. I will make sure your daughter has a long, healthy life."

Yes, Jackson had told the right person first.

"What do I say to Dad?" Jackson asked.

He suddenly felt as if he were five years old and had done something wrong. He'd gotten a woman pregnant without being married to her. Hell, a woman he'd met in an airport. But his worries fled quickly. He knew that his father wouldn't be upset over having a granddaughter. He'd be ecstatic. Martin had doted on Jackson's first daughter during her brief life and had been just as devastated as Jackson when her life had been taken.

"You say *congrats*," Spence replied as he finished his can of soda and crushed it, then tossed it into the bed of the truck.

"Yeah, I guess that's a start," Jackson said, and he flashed his first smile since finding out about his daughter.

"What are you going to do?"

Jackson wasn't a fool. He knew his brother was asking whether he was going to marry Alyssa. They had a child together. Jackson knew there was no other option other than to marry her. What surprised him was that he felt no panic. Yes, there was anger, and he knew there would be anger for a while longer, but there was no fear, no panic, and no feeling that he needed to run as far away as he could get.

"I will marry her."

"Hey. Why so blue? You and Alyssa were made for each other. She's a good woman."

"She lied to me, Spence." That was the short of it.

"Did she actually lie to you? Did she ever say to you, *This isn't your child*?"

Jackson thought about it, thought about their conversations. No. No, she hadn't lied outright, but she also hadn't volunteered the information when he'd asked her.

"I made an assumption that it was someone else's. She could have set me straight."

"Maybe she should have told you the truth," Spence began saying when Jackson gave him a solid glare. "Okay, okay, I'd be ticked about that, too. But you have a couple choices here, brother. You can hold a grudge against her, hold this over her head forever, and make both of your lives hell, or you can accept that she had her reasons. If your little girl was walking around and you'd missed out on years of her life, I'd be furious, but Alyssa did tell you now, when the child is only two weeks old. It's not as if you've missed out on anything but four months of morning sickness, if you think about it— you were around for the rest. So talk to her. Find out exactly why she didn't tell you."

"She told me she was afraid I would take the child away, and then when she knew I wouldn't do that, she told me she was afraid I'd be mad because she hadn't told me," Jackson said.

"Well, how did you act the day you created the baby?"

Jackson knew that Spence could probably take a pretty accurate guess as to how Jackson had acted that night. He'd only had one use for women during that time, had no desire for a commitment. He couldn't remember all he'd said to Alyssa back then, but he knew he would have told her their night together had no chance of turning permanent. Maybe she did have a valid reason in the beginning to keep her secret. But after two months of being together, her reasoning was no longer valid. Jackson had changed.

"This one isn't on me, Spence. She's known since we met up again that she was carrying my child. She knew when the baby was born, and she knew when I was by our daughter's side day and night. She'd been living with me for weeks before the wreck. She could have told me at any time."

"But she did tell you today."

"I know, Spence. But it should have been sooner." It didn't matter how many times he said it, he couldn't change that she hadn't told him before today. What he had to figure out was if he'd be able to forgive her.

"I know. I don't mean to give you a hard time, Jackson. I just don't want you to dwell on what could have been said, or what could have happened. I want you to focus on your daughter, on her getting well. Alyssa has been released from the hospital today. She needs someone to watch over her. Not only does she have a while before she is fully recovered from her injuries, but she has the added stress of having a premature infant who will require a lot of care. Don't be too hard on her."

Spence didn't give Jackson time to respond. He just hopped down from the truck and walked toward the hospital doors. Jackson still had a lot to think about. As he lay back in his truck and closed his eyes, he tried to decide what he would do next. He was so angry with Alyssa right now that he knew it would be best not to speak to her. What would yelling accomplish? What would accusations help?

They would marry. There was no doubt in his mind. His child would be raised by him, not by some man she might meet in the future. That meant that he needed either to yell a lot and get over his anger, or to decide to accept some of the responsibility.

Yes, she should have told him. Especially once they were staying in the same house. She'd had plenty of opportunities to give him the truth and she'd chosen not to. Again, though, wasn't she going through enough pain right now?

He still had no answers when he felt his muscles relax from the warm liquor he'd drunk, and he lay there lazily as his mind continued to spin. Life hadn't ever been easy for him, to be damn sure. Why should it change now?

041

Displaying a calm that he didn't feel, Jackson finally made his way back into the hospital. Anger still ate at his insides, but he and Alyssa were adults, and the two of them needed to speak as grown-ups, not as hurt children. Easier said than done.

Jackson found Alyssa right where he'd left her, sitting in her wheelchair with her hand inside the incubator, caressing their tiny daughter. She was exhausted, and he had no trouble seeing that she needed to get some rest. It wouldn't be fair to either of them if he barreled ahead and forced her into an immediate discussion about what came next.

"Alyssa, let's get you home."

When she turned her head, he saw the raw pain in her eyes and the dark circles beneath them. He felt like a monster.

"I'm confused right now, Alyssa, okay? Just give me some time. I'm not going to lay into you, make accusations, or make you feel any worse than you do right now. We both need time to think. But you aren't going to be any good to our daughter when she's finally released if you don't get some rest."

His tone was gentle, and he saw her shocked expression. Was he so frightening that she expected him to kick her while she was down? If so, he really needed to change her opinion of him.

"I don't want to leave her all alone. What if something happens and we're not here?" Such sadness haunted her voice.

"My brother is on shift. He will call us immediately if anything goes wrong."

"I will."

They both turned to find Spence standing there behind them in his scrubs. "I'll take good care of Angel," he told them.

Alyssa's shoulders slumped and Jackson knew she'd now allow him to take her away from the hospital.

"Thanks, Spence." With that, he helped her place her feet on the footrests, then wheeled her to the front of the hospital and out to his truck. She didn't fight him as he helped her climb inside.

Neither of them said a word as he drove the miles to his house. She moved lethargically, almost like a sleepwalker, when he arrived and helped her inside.

TREMBLING WITH ANXIETY, Alyssa waited, wondering if and when he would unload on her. But as she tried to prepare herself for the attack, a bit of anger built up within her. This wasn't all her fault. He had made love to her; in fact, he had come after her the way a tornado chases an old barn.

He hadn't taken no for an answer back on New Year's and she'd carried their child. Yes, it was wrong that she hadn't said anything to him, but was he really so dense that he couldn't do basic math? Any normal man would have had some suspicions. She waited, not willing to be the first person to speak.

When he approached, his dark eyes still kind, but with something else in his expression that made her shiver, she strengthened her resolve. She had to stay strong, for her own health and for her sick baby.

"I need to really understand why you didn't tell me sooner. You have grown to know me. The fear you spoke of earlier just doesn't make sense."

"I thought you weren't going to pressure me, Jackson."

"I just want some answers. I'm not yelling, and I'm not angry. But I think I deserve something from you, Alyssa."

He waited, his eyes boring dangerously into hers. From the first moment she'd encountered those eyes, she'd known she was in trouble. What this man could get her to confess with simply a look was terrifying to her.

"I was . . . scared. I'm still scared. That day on the plane you told me you would never love anyone again after your failed relationship. Then I thought I wouldn't see you again. And when I did see you, I was frightened all over again because I was told that you were ruthless, would do whatever it took to keep a child to yourself that was yours." She paused to take a breath. "Once I got to know you, the lie hung over us and I knew you wouldn't take her, but I didn't want you to hate me for keeping the truth from you. I can't give you anything more than that. It was foolish of me, but I can't change it."

She was terrified he would leave, but also petrified that he'd stay only because of their daughter, not ever able to love her. Waiting for a reply, Alyssa tried to turn away from Jackson's intense gaze, but he had her captured, and there was no escape.

She had never believed in fate, but it seemed that she and Jackson had somehow been destined to meet, destined to create a child, and finally, destined to stand in his house and face the choices they'd made. Fighting off the twinges of guilt that threatened her composure, she waited. It was his turn to speak.

"Since we found each other again," Jackson said, "you have pushed me away, acted as if I'm your enemy. Why? Yes, we had a one-night stand, but I wasn't the one to walk away. I wasn't the one who snuck out before the morning light. Can I positively say that I would have behaved any differently if I had woken up to find you asleep in the bed? I honestly don't know. What I do know, though, is that I had feelings for you then." Those words made her throat tighten. "And I still have feelings for you now. I don't understand why you fight me so much. I've never lied to you, never tried to deceive you about my past, about what I expect of my future. I've always been honest."

"Yes, you've been honest in telling me you will never love again," she pointed out.

"I may be wrong about that . . ."

Alyssa felt her heart thump hard in her chest. "What does that mean?" She wanted him to be very clear. There couldn't be any more questions about where they stood with each other.

"I . . . I . . . dammit!" Jackson turned away from her, and her heart broke into a million pieces.

What was he trying to say? She couldn't read him, couldn't figure any of this out. When he moved to the door wordlessly, opened it, and stepped through, the first tear fell down her face. When the door shut with a final click behind him, several more followed.

She had lost him. He couldn't accept her in his life, and he couldn't accept responsibility for Angel. She had never in all her life imagined feeling so much pain. Who in the hell thought that falling in love was a good idea? From all she'd discovered, it was nothing but immense agony and unfulfilled yearning. She'd rather go through a thousand more accidents than deal with the way her heart was breaking at this moment.

042

As he walked from the house, Jackson knew he should turn around, knew he'd promised not to yell, not to pressure her this first night away from the hospital, and then he'd done just that. His anger wasn't as under control as he'd thought it was.

He phoned her mom, told her where Alyssa was and that he didn't think it was a good idea for her to be alone, and then he climbed in his truck and waited. It didn't take her mother long to get there, and as soon as he knew Alyssa would have someone with her, he drove off.

He clearly wasn't ready for this conversation with her—he had to get his own head straight first. Yes, he'd told his brother he was going to marry her, and he hadn't changed his mind on that score, but was it only because of the baby?

That's what he needed to figure out. Driving to his dad's place without even realizing what he was doing, Jackson parked the truck before he found his heartbeat slowing. From the first moment he'd come into this house when he was twelve years old, he'd found comfort. It was only natural that during one of the most confusing moments of his life, he would find himself back here.

After climbing slowly from the truck, he went through the front door and straight to his dad's den, but the man wasn't there. However, Jackson knew all of Martin's favorite hangouts, so it didn't take long for him to find the old man in the horse barn, leaning up against the fence talking to a worker.

"Hey," he called out, and Martin turned with a grin.

"Wow, didn't think I'd ever see you come home again, not since baby Gerard was born," Martin said with a welcoming smile.

"Her name is Angel," Jackson said, wondering how he was going to tell his father the entire story.

"Ah, very fitting," Martin said.

"I thought so, too. She's been a blessing from the moment she entered this world, and a lot of people are touched by her life already."

"There's nothing more precious than a baby, son."

"I have to tell you something," Jackson said, shifting on his feet as he stood next to his father.

"Well, then, spit it out. You're acting like a teenager who just got caught smoking in the locker room."

"Angel is mine." He was quieter than he'd ever been before.

Martin said nothing for several moments; he just looked at his son with measuring eyes. Then a smile broke out on his face and he grasped Jackson's hand.

"Congratulations, boy! That means I'm a grandpa again," he said, his smile only growing brighter.

"Yeah, that's what it means." All of Jackson's anxiety vanished at the open acceptance from his father. Most people would have thrown out a million questions at this point, but his dad just accepted those few short words, and was happy about it, no less.

"When's the wedding?"

"A lot of water has passed under the bridge. Alyssa and I really need to work through it all. I got angry with her for not telling me sooner, and sort of stormed from the hospital, then went back, took her home, and we fought again, and I left the house." At the instant disapproval on his father's face, he felt even worse than he had earlier.

"Did you give her a chance to explain, Jackson?"

"Yes. She told me she didn't think we'd see each other again, and then when she did see me she was afraid I'd take the baby, and then she was afraid because she'd waited so long." Jackson grabbed a bag of oats and fed his favorite horse, Thunder.

"Well, as you stormed away, I guess she had a valid reason to be afraid," Martin said.

"It's not that simple. Had she told me sooner, I wouldn't be so upset. But Angel has been fighting for her life for the past couple of weeks. I've been by her side the entire time, been falling head over heels in love with my daughter, and I didn't even know she was mine. That's not fair," Jackson said, his voice rising.

"I agree she should have come to you sooner, but I also know how much pain you have gone through these past five and a half years. You shut yourself off from the world for a long time. Hell, Jackson, you tried to push your brothers and me away, too. She had valid reasons to be concerned," Martin pointed out. "I'm not saying you didn't have good reasons yourself to protect your heart any way you deemed you should, but I'm saying if I were her, I'd be protective of myself and of my child as well."

"But these last two months, I've proved myself over and over again. Doesn't that count for anything?"

"Of course it does, boy. But have you ever told Alyssa that you love her? Have you ever told her you don't want to let her go?"

"I didn't know I was in love with her," he said, and then stopped before looking up at his father through slightly blurred eyes.

Since she'd told him about his daughter, all he'd been thinking about was the fact that she hadn't told him, but he was in love with Alyssa. He was in love with her smile, with her laughter, with the way she couldn't seem to get close enough to him while she was sound asleep, with how kind she was to strangers, and how loyal she was to her family, with how accepting she was of him, faults and all. He loved her more than he thought he was capable of loving a woman.

"I really do love her, Dad. The kind of love that means I never want to let her go."

"Well, of course you do, boy. You don't chase after a woman as hard as you've chased after Alyssa just to mess up some bedsheets. You chase after her because the thought of being without her is incomprehensible."

"I guess we've both kept secrets from one another," Jackson said.

"Yeah. We all tend to do that. It's never wise to keep secrets and it's never good to lie, but we are all human, and we make mistakes. Don't let stupid pride keep you from living a life of happiness with a wonderful woman. She's worth letting the past go, and she's worth believing in. I couldn't be happier for you."

Then his father did something he didn't do nearly as often as he had when Jackson was younger. He walked up and gave him a solid hug, patting him on the back before stepping back, but with his hands firmly on Jackson's shoulders.

"Don't let her get away, and don't make her suffer too long. She's been through enough."

Jackson stood there for a moment without saying a word, and then he felt the remainder of his anger drain away.

"You're right, Dad. Life is too short. I've wasted enough time with issues that don't matter, and I've spent enough years punishing myself for not being able to save Olivia. I'm ready to give my heart to Alyssa and our daughter, and I think they will hold it just fine."

"Go get the girl, Jackson."

Jackson turned around and ran back to his truck. It was time to tell Alyssa exactly how he felt about her. It was time for both of them to let go of old hurts and to move forward so they could enjoy the rest of their lives and raise their daughter well— plus, he very much hoped, a few more kids.

It was time to free himself from too many years of pain and sorrow.

043

Opening the door to his house, Jackson looked around for Teresa, but didn't see her. He walked to the back, where Alyssa was sitting on the couch, her face awash with tears, her cheeks red, and the light vanquished from her beautiful blue eyes.

He found a note from Teresa on the end table, telling him that she'd left because his father had called and said he was on his way back to talk to Alyssa. Jackson almost smiled when he read her last sentence:

Get it together and both of you quit denying your love.
Love,
Your future mother-in-law, Teresa

Without saying a word, he kneeled before Alyssa, hating her look of utter defeat. *He* had done this to her. He only hoped he could make it right again. He only hoped that his love would show through and they could indeed both forgive each other.

"I'm sorry, Alyssa."

She didn't speak and he worried that he'd pushed her too far, that he'd somehow taken her remaining strength. Standing up, he moved to the bathroom and ran a bath. She always seemed to relax when she took them at home.

Her injuries had been extensive and maybe this would help. When he came back out, the vacant look in her eyes made him feel like a monster. Taking her hand, he pulled her to her feet. "Let's get you in the tub. I'm sure that will help after your two weeks in the hospital."

She said nothing as he led her to the bathroom. But her eyes filled with tears when the scent of jasmine hit her. It was her favorite and he'd stocked up for when she was able to come back home. It was those small things he knew about her that should have clued him in so much earlier about how much he cared.

He knew that when it rained she would get a big smile on her face and rush outside to feel it soak her face. She'd said that was because she'd lived in Texas for so long, and rain was a real treat. He'd see whether the rain in Montana still made her smile after a particularly wet spring. He also knew she liked to make smiley faces on her pancakes with the syrup, and she always sang in the shower.

These were only a few things he knew about her, and he would enjoy spending the rest of his life learning so much more. And he planned to open up his entire life to her, because there was no use in keeping anything from her because he loved her— he wanted her to know him inside and out.

"We'll talk more, but for now, let's have a bath and relax. I'm not going to hurt you anymore. I promise," he whispered. He moved his hands gently down her sides and found the hem of her shirt.

She lifted her arms, and he pulled the shirt over her head and felt a stirring inside, but he quickly stopped it. This wasn't the time. Tonight was for healing, not seduction. He'd soon stripped her bare and then he held her hand as she stepped over the side of the tub and sank into the scented water.

Jackson thought about leaving for all of two seconds, and then he undressed and slid in behind her, needing to hold her, to assure her they were fine, that they were more than fine because they were together. He leaned against the back of the tub, then pulled her back against his chest.

She tensed for only an instant before her body melted against his and she let a small sigh escape from her lips. Slowly, carefully, with a gentleness he didn't know he possessed, Jackson ran his soapy hands over her body, being gentle where she was still healing. The feel of her skin beneath his fingers was torture and yet comforting at the same time.

"In New York, I made some assumptions," he

started, not knowing how to say this. She was quiet as she waited for him to continue. "I assumed that we were simply two strangers passing in the night. I assumed that we could have sex and walk away. I assumed that, as a model, you probably did that sort of thing often," he admitted, feeling horrible when she flinched. "I now know that I was so very wrong."

How had he been so blind? How could he have ignored his feelings for her? Yes, he'd wanted her, but it was so much more, even then. Though he'd promised himself it would never happen again, though he'd done everything in his power not to fall in love, it had snuck up on him.

Alyssa Gerard had found a way through the barriers guarding his heart, and now what once was broken was whole again. He caressed her body, but though he felt desire, he also felt peace. There wasn't a burning need to possess her now, because he knew that he already did possess her in the most important way a man could possess a woman.

He loved her. And he had no doubt that she loved him, too. He could easily spend the rest of his life with this woman and never grow tired of her. Never lose his passion for her, never lose his interest in her. That was what true love was.

Yes, a couple needed to work at a marriage, at a relationship. But what the two of them had was something that wasn't easily defined, wasn't easily placed into a nice box with a ribbon on top. What the two of them had would be a crime to throw away.

"I can't ever let you go, Alyssa," he whispered into her ear. Even with this knowledge harbored deep in his heart, he found himself struggling to express his innermost feelings.

"What if I'm not yours to hold on to?" she asked. From the tone of her voice, he couldn't tell what she was thinking or feeling. Was it animosity, or was she simply trying to make a point?

Jackson had his own point to make. "You want to be held," he said, and to prove that, he slid his hands gently up her stomach, and then he cupped her beautiful, lush breasts and used his thumbs to graze the perfect red nipples as they hardened for him. She gasped, and her head fell against his neck as she sighed at the sensations he was sending through her healing body.

"Just because you can turn me on doesn't mean I'm yours to keep," she said huskily. But she scooted closer, and her exquisite derrière rubbed against his growing arousal.

"Tell me this, my lovely Alyssa: Have you ever wanted to lie in a tub full of scented water with another man while he caressed your body?"

She sighed again as he continued lavishing attention on her breasts. He waited for her answer.

"No," she finally said.

He would keep this about feelings and emotion. He wouldn't turn this into sex—he couldn't. Her body was in no way ready for that. But he suspected that he'd have to remind himself of that several times. With great reluctance, he moved his hands away from her breasts and ran them again down her stomach.

"Don't touch me there," she said, squirming.

"Where?"

"My stomach. I'm . . . it's . . . the baby flab . . ." She stopped and he saw color suffuse her cheeks.

His hands stopped on her stomach as he sat there in shock.

"You're even more beautiful now than the first time I met you, Alyssa."

"I'm not, Jackson. I just had a baby. I've been in bed for two weeks. My body . . ."

Jackson carefully stood and moved in front of her, then sat so she was facing him. With deliberate motions, he lifted both of her legs over his own, then pulled her onto his lap, thankful that his body was behaving, though he doubted it would be long before it acted up again. He gazed steadily into her eyes as he took time to touch every part of her.

"You need to hear what I'm saying now, Alyssa. You are even more beautiful than the first night I met you. The shape of your hips, the curve of your stomach, the fullness of your breasts, the sparkle in your eyes. All of that shows me that you carried my child, that you delivered her. I can't see a single thing wrong with your body, and it's taking every ounce of willpower that I possess not to sink deep inside you right this second. The only reason I'm holding back is because you need to heal. It might kill me, but I'll wait until your body is ready for me."

He gave her a smile as he rubbed against her, his erection back and fully ready. A small smile tilted her lips upward.

"Jackson, I lied to you by not telling you the truth. I . . . I've held back. Why are you being so good to me?"

"Because I love you."

He didn't need to make a speech, didn't need to go the hearts-and-flowers route, done up with ribbons and bows and greeting-card sentiments. He loved her. It was simple and it was powerful.

Tears filled her eyes and spilled over as she sat against him, as his hands smoothed up and down her body, as they said so much with nothing but a look between them.

"I love you, too, Jackson."

Finally. No more barriers stood between them. Nothing would stand in the way of their making a life together. They would wait until their daughter was ready to leave the hospital, and then they would bring her back and turn his house into a real home. They would stay together forever.

He leaned forward and captured her lips, his kiss tender, his touch showing her how much he loved her. It was the kind of love that was meant to last a lifetime and beyond.

"How did I get so lucky as to meet you in Paris, to find you on the very day that my life was falling apart?" she said when he released her lips and allowed them both to come up for air.

"No, Alyssa. I'm the one who got lucky that day. I met a beautiful, stubborn, brilliant woman, and I get to spend the rest of my life with her."

And then he kissed her again. And then his noble intentions were washed away, because Alyssa brought her arms up around his neck and pulled him even closer.

"Show me, Jackson. I need you to show me," she pleaded.

Jackson lifted her from the tub, carried her to their bed, and gently kissed every surface of her body, telling her exactly what she meant to him. Somehow he managed to only touch her, but it would cost him much pain for the next few weeks. When she fell asleep in his arms hours later, he knew that they were only just beginning and he knew he would go through any amount of pain for this woman he would love for time and all eternity.

EPILOGUE

"We sure have done well."

Martin stood at the back of the yard as he watched his son dancing with his new bride, both their faces glowing as Jackson dipped Alyssa and kissed her in a way that left no doubt in Martin's mind that this time his son would have real happiness that he truly deserved.

"Yes, we did, my friend. Yes, we did," Joseph said, and he clapped Martin on the back.

"What did you both do? Certainly not very much. Those two almost didn't make it," Bethel grumbled. She was standing beside Eileen and Maggie while also looking out at the dance floor.

Sage was home, and Bethel was thrilled to see her, but her granddaughter didn't seem the least bit interested in finding her own lifelong dance partner. Bethel had asked Sage whether she was going to settle down, and her granddaughter had actually had the nerve to laugh. Bethel found herself just a bit disgruntled.

"We did plenty. I bought the saloon," Martin said in his defense, sending a severe look Bethel's way.

"Anyone can buy a bar," Eileen replied with a chuckle.

"Well, it wasn't just anyone who did it. It was *me*." Martin was unwilling to lose the credit he felt he richly deserved.

"That's all it takes, my friend. That's all it takes," Joseph said. At least Joseph knew that Martin had done well.

"Pshaw," Bethel said. "Let's see if you can do it again, or if this was just a lucky coincidence. After all, those two kids met months before you decided they'd make the perfect couple."

As Martin cradled his beautiful granddaughter in his arms, he tuned out his friends, tuned out his troubles, tuned out everything but Angel. This was right where he needed to be—among friends and family, holding his four-month-old granddaughter.

"You've been hogging the baby all night. It's my turn," Joseph told him, and he held out his arms. Martin reluctantly handed her over and Joseph beamed at the little marvel of a girl.

"Well, I know you want to focus on your boys, Martin, but Taylor is stubborn as sin and she scares me witless with all her stunts on those dirt bikes. I would love nothing more than to see her happily married and settled down," Maggie said, obviously missing her daughter.

"Oooh, I like your thinking, Maggie," Bethel said.

"I have watched Taylor grow up through the years. What a beautiful, strong daughter you have. I think it would be quite fun to see what we could arrange for her."

"Don't you worry, ladies. I have a few more tricks up my sleeve. I'm sure we could come up with a plan," Martin said.

"These kids just have no idea how much effort we put into their future happiness," Joseph said. His hearty laugh made a number of heads turn in his direction.

"No, they sure don't," Martin said.

Then the five friends leaned in tight as they began making plans. Taylor Winchester might be up for more than she could handle in a very short time.

Don't want to leave the Winchester family just yet?
Keep reading for a sneak peek at

WHO I AM WITH YOU,

the next installment in *New York Times* bestselling
author Melody Anne's Unexpected Heroes series!

Coming spring 2015 from Pocket Star Books!

PROLOGUE

Was this a dream? It had to be, because time had suddenly stopped. Taylor Winchester found herself flying through the air, her bike released from her hands, and the ground coming up fast. She knew there was nothing she could do, knew in reality she was hurtling through space, but still, it seemed like a dream.

She was in a race for a semifinal slot on the motocross circuit. She was winning. Or she *had* been winning. Until she'd gone over the jump, and—while she was seventy feet in the air, feeling the wind whip across her face—something had gone wrong.

Instead of landing gracefully back on the ground and zipping farther into the lead, she was falling . . . falling in slow motion.

The dream turned quickly into a nightmare as her body slammed into the dirt track. When her bike landed on top of her, everything went black. Her last thought was that darkness was good, it was pure, it was relief, because her entire body was radiating pain, and the blackness took that pain away . . .

001

A sigh escaped her lips as she rested her head on the steering wheel of her father's oversized truck. "Come on, Taylor. If you haven't been broken yet, you're certainly not going to let this be your demise."

New determination firming her shoulders, she lifted her head as her words echoed through the cab of the pickup. After shutting off the engine, she sat there a moment longer before opening the door.

She refused to allow the terrors of the pitch-black night to creep up and choke her. Besides, she was home, or near enough to it. There was nothing frightening about home, she told herself. Still, a tremor ran down her spine. Frustration mounted inside her. Before her near-fatal injury, Taylor had never had to deal with fear.

Many people had commented on her daringness; they'd told her she was too brave for her own good. These days, though, even the smallest of noises seemed to terrify her. It frustrated her, but the doctor had told her that was normal after a head injury, and that it shouldn't last forever. The sooner she was back to normal, the better.

"There is nothing to be afraid of," she said aloud. "Well, except for maybe the coyotes waiting on the other side of the tree line, looking forward to their next meal," she murmured as her eyes strained to see ahead.

The overcast sky of this early June night didn't even allow the light of the moon to peek through. Leaving her headlights on, she walked to the back of the truck to find her father's heavy-duty Maglite. It had always rolled noisily around in the bed of his many trucks, and she'd wanted to take it out each time she'd borrowed the vehicles, but her father wouldn't let her. Its ever-annoying clanging sound served as a constant reminder that it was there if needed. For the first time, she was thankful for the miserable flashlight. She gripped it tightly in her hand. If a coyote attacked, she could strike it with the flashlight-slash-weapon.

Not that doing so would do a hell of a lot of good against all those teeth and claws coming straight at her. And didn't coyotes travel in packs, flush out their victim, and strike when the prey was at its weakest? Of course they did, but it wasn't going to happen to her, she assured herself. She still trembled.

She shined the light onto the back of the truck and wanted to scream. Yep, the tire was trashed. Whatever she'd run over had shredded it and there was no way she could get out of changing the darn thing. If she even attempted to drive the five miles home, the rim of her dad's truck would be ruined beyond repair. Not that she'd make it anyway—the sparks caused by driving on metal would start a forest fire in this dry county.

Changing a tire would normally be no big deal. Taylor knew basic mechanics. As a champion motocross racer, how could she not? But even three months after her accident, she was still fighting to move around, and lifting anything heavy would be super tough.

But there was no help for it—or for her. So, resigned to her fate, she pulled out the jack and lug wrench. After prying off the hubcap, she let out only a small groan as she got onto her back to find a solid jacking point. When she'd positioned the jack, she turned back to face the tire.

Taylor determinedly rose to her feet, lug wrench in hand. It took three times as long as it should have, but she finally managed to get the bolts off the tire. Then she stood there, already exhausted, her healing ribs screaming as she contemplated the jack she now had to pump up, and the tire she'd have to remove.

Getting into a crouch in front of the jack, sweat beading on her forehead, she began pumping the handle to lift the truck. Completely out of breath and more than a little frustrated, Taylor had to sit on the ground when she finally got the truck high enough in the air to remove the tire. Tears filled her eyes at such weakness.

"I am *not* this girl," she cried out, her voice reverberating off the trees nearby.

Taylor couldn't stand simpering females who needed a man to do every little task. She was strong and independent, and had been on her own for the past six years. Well, to be fair, she'd been on her own as much as her two older brothers had allowed.

She wasn't a fool. She knew they haunted her races obsessively, ready to catch her if she fell. She loved Hawk and Bryson more than any other men alive, but her brothers were overprotective, ridiculously so.

She'd only ever wanted to prove she was just as capable as they were. She hadn't wanted to be dolled up in a pretty pink dress with a bejeweled tiara on her head. When her mother had once come home with a Cinderella dress and a smile, Taylor, age six, had cried. She hadn't wanted to be a princess for Halloween. She'd wanted to be a pirate like Hawk had been the year before.

To her mother's credit, she'd taken Taylor to the Halloween store the next day and let her pick out her costume. Her mom had always been supportive of her daughter's choices. Though Taylor knew that the career she'd chosen stressed her parents out, they never tried to talk her out of it.

"Enough!" she snapped, done with her pity party.

Her doctor would be furious, but Taylor refused to call her brothers or her father. For the past three months she'd been cooped up in her parents' house while she recovered from the wreck that could have easily taken her life. She'd had to give up her apartment in California that she'd been so proud of, and she was going stir crazy being looked after.

She was through with being coddled, dammit.

A coyote howled in the trees behind her, far enough away that she knew it wasn't watching, but the sound still sent a chill down her spine. She'd grown up in the wild lands of Montana, and knew she was safe right here—coyote attacks on humans were rare, and she'd never heard of one in Montana—but her head was still slightly fuzzy from the concussion she'd suffered three months earlier, and she wasn't as rational and confident as she normally would be.

"You're fine," she told herself as she set the flashlight on the ground, facing the enemy tire before her. "Easy-peasy."

She gripped the tire and began to work it free, her efforts making her shake. But the satisfaction she felt when the freaking thing popped off and landed on the ground at her feet was priceless.

Her body would pay in the morning, but Taylor didn't care. She was proving to herself that she was still quite capable. She didn't need to lean on anyone and . . . *damn.* Her euphoria died a quick but painful death when she realized the next step would be to take the spare that was hooked beneath the truck and lift it onto the wheel studs.

Pulling the old tire off had nearly wiped her out. How in the world was she going to lift another one up and then put this one onto the bed of the truck? "Slow and sure," she said, not allowing anything to beat her tonight. This was a challenge, and though she knew it was ridiculous, she felt that if she couldn't manage something as simple as changing a tire, she'd never get back on a dirt bike again.

Unacceptable. She'd devoted too many years to training, put too much time and love into her career. Though her doctor had sounded pessimistic when she'd asked about returning to racing, she *would* prove the man wrong.

It was absolutely absurd that she needed a release from the doctor before the powers that be would allow her to race again. Wasn't it up to her what she could or couldn't do? Apparently not. Well, the first step was changing a tire. The next was getting back on her bike.

It again took too long to get the spare tire down from the bottom of the truck, and she felt close to passing out, but with a few good swear words and a lot of expended energy, she finally managed to get the tire free from where it had been sitting since her dad had bought the truck last year.

Rolling the stupid thing toward the back of the truck, she attempted to lift it up, but the agony in her sides was too much. She collapsed to the ground with pain shooting through her body, and dragged huge gulps of air into her lungs as she fought desperately not to cave in to the blackness that was offering her blessed relief.

This couldn't be happening. She'd almost rather sit there on the cold asphalt of this quiet Montana road than call for help. But ten minutes later, when she made her second attempt to lift the tire, she knew it wasn't happening.

Her body was still too beat up to do something so simple as to lift a tire onto the bolts that were sticking out and waiting for it. The last thing she wanted was to call her brothers, but she didn't seem to have any other choice.

Still, she did nothing but pull out her cell phone and look at the face of it, not wanting to dial a number, not wanting to admit she was too weak to finish the task she had begun.

When a few minutes later headlights appeared down the road, Taylor didn't know whether she was relieved or upset that someone would find her like this. She knew without a doubt that whoever was heading toward her would stop.

That's just the kind of place she'd grown up in. A place where a neighbor would never pass by a vehicle stuck on the side of the road. When the oncoming truck slowed and then pulled in front of hers, blinding her with its bright lights and breaking the quiet of night with the soft purr of its diesel engine, Taylor held up a hand to shield her eyes from the beams and squinted to see who it was. Without a worry in the world that she'd be face-to-face with a stranger—there were no strangers in Sterling, Montana—she stood up, though slowly, not wanting to be seen sitting in defeat on the ground.

The door to the truck opened and a shadow emerged. With the headlights in her eyes she couldn't identify the driver, but it was a man's silhouette walking slowly toward her. And then the figure spoke.

"Looks like you're having some difficulty."

Taylor froze as everything in her tried to deny that voice, deny who was approaching her. She stiffened her spine and spoke as if she'd never met the man before. "I'm fine. You can be on your way." Her tone was acid, sure to dissolve him.

Or not. To her distinct displeasure, the man continued walking forward until he was in the light with her and she could see his face all too clearly.

"Doesn't look like you're fine, Taylor. Don't I get a hello hug? It's been a few years."

"And as far as I'm concerned, it can be a hell of a lot more years, Travis Montclave!"

"Aw, hell, Taylor. What's with the attitude?"

"Oh, let's see. Probably because you left me high and dry after you were finished getting your rocks off and leaving me with a less-than-memorable experience of having sex for the first time."

Travis was now standing only inches from her, looking even more suave than he had six years earlier, the night he'd taken her virginity. His dark hair was cut short, military style, and she was sure his bright blue eyes were sparkling, as everything was always amusing to him. That was a trait she'd once found charming about the man. The dimple in his cheek was just one more thing that added to his charm, but Taylor wouldn't ever be charmed by him again.

"I don't think so, Taylor. It seems you've gotten that all mixed up. I wasn't the one sober, and I certainly wasn't the one who chased after you."

"Go to hell, Travis, or wherever it is you run away to."

"Nah. I'm back. And I've decided I don't want to leave this time."

His words were a clear challenge, and though she hated this man with a passion, the thundering of her heart had nothing to do with her struggles to change the tire and everything to do with the giant of a man standing before her.